Published by Alex Stone
Kindle Amazon Edition

Copyright 2018 Alex Stone
Kindle Amazon Edition, License Notes

No part of this publication may be reproduced, or transmitted in any form or by any means, electronic or otherwise, without written permission from the author, except in the case of brief quotations embodied in critical reviews and certain other noncommercial uses permitted by copyright law. Thank you for respecting the creative work of this author.

* * * * * *

Contents

Author's Note
Chapter 1: Tian-tai Esoterism
Chapter 2: Call of Zen
Chapter 3: A Monk Making
Chapter 4: A Man Making
Chapter 5: Tigress's Roar
Chapter 6: The Real World
Chapter 7: The Bedchamber Art
Chapter 8: Alchemy of Love
Chapter 9: Marketplace
Chapter 10: The Middle Path
Chapter 11: Predestination
Chapter 12: Dreams
Chapter 13: Magic Healing
Chapter 14: Preaching
About the Author
Endnote

Author's Note

Since ancient times, the writings on the art of relations between men and women have been circulated all over the world. Cervantes wrote, and so did Boccaccio, out of the sheer delight of creation. We find there many prescriptions that are correct and useful for the human body and spirit manifested in the realm of sexual life.

The rules and methods of the so-called 'Oriental Erotica' are a part of the world's cultural heritage, and so I thought to make my own modest contribution to this critical side of human life.

In Daoism and Zen Buddhism, for example, as in some other eastern religions, such as Tantrism, we find a very different attitude to sexual life. Many Chinese novels, like the tales of Boccaccio, have accused the monks and nuns of immorality. This is based on the universal human delight taken in exposing all forms of hypocrisy. It is natural and comfortable therefore to make Casanovas of Chinese monks, provided with witchcraft and secret aphrodisiacs. There are actual cases, in certain parts of the coastal provinces of China, for example, where a nunnery is but a brothel, but on the whole, the charge is unfair, and most monks are good, retiring, polite, and well-behaved people who perceive the Daoist bedchamber art very seriously, at the level of secret alchemy. So, any Don Juan exploits are limited to transgressing individuals and are grossly exaggerated in novels for a juicy but shallow effect. Besides, this misjudgment is because of the failure to see the connection between sex and religion in the Far-eastern region. For the Daoist and Zen Buddhist monks sex is the herald of that inscrutable, always only full of original properties of being, to which all their efforts to nurture life are well directed. They recognize sexuality as the natural part of human character, to renounce it is utterly unreasonable and even harmful. On the other part, however, it is just as foolish and fatal as to be a blind slave to one's passions. The bodily solaces are genuinely accessible to a mature and wise soul only. As the Swiss psychologist, Carl Jung states, "Man is equally used to live with his inherent instincts and overcome them." Hence, we can conclude that the inherent relaxation does not deny self-control, but, actually, only thanks to it, this intrinsic relaxation becomes possible. Daoism and Zen teach us, first of all, to accept the feeling like a genuinely integral element of life; and, like life itself, the sense, in the eyes of them, justifies itself and finds in itself the strength and power for any further creative growth. A sagely minded man, according to the ancient thinker Zhuang-zi (4th century BCE), does not see with his eyes, and does not listen to with his ears, and does not rely on his mind, but entrusts himself to his spiritual desire. Identification in oneself this genuine desire, which is like life itself, has neither beginning nor ending, and free from any burden of attachment to any object, remaining to be crystal-clear, like the Great Emptiness or the Dao itself, is the ultimate goal of the Daoist and Zen asceticism. Cultivation of senses imposed by the conventions of civilization is replaced by the Daoists with their concept of awareness through cultivating the real feeling. And love that is made between a man and a woman is the best remedy for that.

Coming across with the Daoist sexual practice, we readily understand the fact that it is indeed being spoken about a kind of art, not merely entertainment. The unknown authors who wrote about this subject did it in a businesslike and genuinely chaste tone, taking care only to teach the practitioners of the bedchamber art to derive the more significant benefit and happiness out of love affairs. Money had nothing to do with this. Even in modern times, where there are royalties and copyright protection, no amount of money can make an uncreative mind tell a good story. A secure living made the writing by our creative minds possible, but a safe life never created anything. A very sensible approach it is. As a proof of this purely technical function, a desire not to amaze or entertain, but merely to teach the art, is inherent to all without exception erotic drawings created in old China. We would never see on them the images of a woman depicted as an object of aesthetic contemplation that is separated from the flow of real life, attractive and inaccessible. We only see the pictures of sexual intercourse, which serve as a precept to action required an intimate union with a female as the element of creative renewal of being.

In a broad sense, for the Daoists and Zen Buddhists, the intercourse of a man and a woman turns out to be the best prototype of the universe, in which, as we already know, there are no separate bodies, but only the proportion of forces and functional relationship.

There all things dissolve and lose themselves in the vast net of Heaven, in the midst of constant chaos, which is, formless, losing itself and, thereby, makes possible the existence of all variety of things. The love game is rooted in this chaos, this unchanging in itself variability, where there's neither being nor carrier, neither presence nor absence, but everything replaces something else, everything is a miraculous encountering of some incompatible things. Besides, the sexual arousal can be considered as an analogy to the great Dao, as a life that is lived intensively, full-blooded, with the full presence of consciousness, that sort of inner and sublime experience, in which and through which the everlasting continuity of spirit is realized by all devoted lovers.

The Tian-tai Buddhist sect represents an interesting variation on this theme. For the fusion of white lead and vermilion mercury, the technique practitioners of this alchemy employ are rigorous and unremitting, though highly disciplined, sexual intercourse. The male permanently defers ejaculation to prevent the loss of vital Yang fluids, which, unlike the Yin, is limited and irreplaceable. By this means -- by unconsummated sex -- the inner reservoir of this precious, life-prolonging essence, drop by drop, is filled up. Well-known as the White Tiger and Green Dragon Yoga, the Tian-tai sect was abhorrent even to many orthodox Daoists and has supposedly died out due to suppression by the authorities. And yet, who knows, . . is it so impossible to think that in a ruined temple somewhere in a remote corner of the great Central Kingdom (another old name of China) a pair of ancient adepts with toothless and withered faces but bright and youthful eyes, are going at it, religiously, in hope of saving their immortal souls?

The Tiger--Dragon Yoga was apparently designed by males for their own use. Since their store of the Yang fluids was small and easily depleted, they needed to supplement it with the Yin fluids which women possess in inexhaustible quantities. The women, generally speaking, have little to gain from the practice (except perhaps some pleasurable sexual activity in a charitable cause), but willingly subordinate themselves in the act of 'sexual noblesse oblige.' On the other part, there was a subtle and insidious variation on the theme of the sexual yoga practice (represented in the literature mostly by the characters of fox spirits) in which the female set out to subvert the male's intention. Attempting to excite him to that pitch of passion where self-control became impossible, she made him spill his load in her Jade Gates, garnering his Yang fluids to enhance her own longevity. It was by this means that Xi-wang Mu, the Royal Mother of the Western Heavens, attained her immortality in the process using up thousands of young men's lives. The male's exhaustion or his enrichment by getting the Yin energy from her sexual organs for his own benefit. . . Who will conquer in this eternal battle of opposites?!

When properly managed, the primordial power of sex and its creative compounds, such as the substance, essence, and spirit that initiate all earthly existence can be used to achieve anything you want. In the spring of this vital power also lie the sources of good health, practical wisdom, and utterly pleasurable satisfaction throughout one's lifetime. At the same time, sex can be the source of degeneration if not to keep within limits. The proper decision is in maintaining equilibrium between the two ends. This Oriental novel tells you how. This actually cognizant book is intended for adults, especially couples, who desire to enlarge their enjoyment, as well as their knowledge of the mysteries of sex well-known from of old and, therefore, time-proved but mostly forgotten, deriving superior benefits from proper engagement in that profound act of conjugal love. It aims to stimulate the reader to seek a more profound understanding of the secrets, not just of sex, but of real satisfaction itself.

This book purpose is to add some additional details, fill in the gaps and make it a favorite reference for those who seek to achieve the fullest satisfaction in their sexual life. Yes, it is so powerful and so dangerous transformation; and this book is a good pattern of merging the sexual practice with the Daoist tradition of internal alchemy -- a striking example of the Oriental culture maturity.

-- A.S.

Written on the fifteenth day of the sixth lunar month of the cyclical year Wu-Xu

"The whole world is but one long sleep;
Hence, it's the best to sleep with your lover. . .
Now put this book down and go to sleep with your dearest!"

-- Alex Stone

Chapter 1: Tian-tai Esoterism

Well-known from time immemorial, the Tian-tai Mountains, or the Heavenly Terraces, the name which applies to a range of mountains, seventy miles southeast of Hangzhou Bay along the Eastern coast of the Central Kingdom, Great China. Our journey up to the Tian-tai peaks and gorges begins by understanding the classic symbols of longevity and bringers of life, mountains inspired religious awe as 'the parents of all things.' According to myths, Tian-tai Mountains used to be carried by a giant turtle named Ao swum in the South China Sea. When during the time of formation of the world progenitress the goddess Nuwa had to cut off the turtle's legs to use them to support the falling sky, she moved the mountains to the dry land so that it would not settle in the ocean.

Starting from the mid-Tang-period (8th century CE), it became one of the biggest Buddhist and Daoist centers in all under heaven, the homeland of Tian-tai sect of Zen Buddhism and Nan-zong (Southern) School of Daoism. That was a wonderland of spirits and legends. Starting out with the dualistic notion of Yin (feminine) and Yang (masculine) principles, already current in the period of the Warring States (5th - 3rd centuries BCE), Daoism soon added to its territory the fairies of the ancient barbarians. They all dreamed of a fairyland out on the deep blue seas, to which place the first emperor of Qin (221 BCE) actually started out with five hundred boys and virgins to seek his immortality. The hold on the imagination then became irresistible, and from that time Daoism widened the sphere of man's nature, including under its arts medicine, or secret knowledge of the herbs, physiology, and cosmogony symbolically explained by the Yin and Yang principles and the Five Phase elements. Magic, witchcraft, aphrodisiacs, incantations, astrology, a whole hierarchy of gods and deities, some beautiful legends, a priesthood and a monkhood -- all those paraphernalia that go to make up a solid philosophy and popular religion. It took care, too, of Chinese martial arts, by specializing in boxing, and the combination of boxing and witchcraft produced by frequent rebellions starting from the end of the Han dynasty (206 BCE - 220 CE). Last, of all, it offered a formula for bodily hygiene, chiefly by deep-breathing, leading up to immortality by ascent to Heaven on the back of a white crane. Its most useful word was 'qi-energy' which, being invisible, was most susceptible to mystic handling. The application of this sort of essence was practically universal, from the rays of a comet to martial arts, deep-breathing, and sexual union, which was sedulously practiced as an art in the cause of prolongation of life. Daoism was, in short, the Chinese attempt of the ancients to discover the mysteries of human nature and its environment.

A good many Buddhist monks and Daoist priests who came from many far away provinces and countries, including Japan, Thailand, and Korea, and who wandered from temple to temple, were also called 'brothers of clouds and rivers.' It always was the place of mists and cliffs piled up near the sky. Legends grew dramatically in those gripping lands where rocks beetled over abysses so deep that a poor traveler could fall, they said, for almost a quarter of an hour straight without hitting bottom. Till nowadays, ranging to left and right beneath the seven stars of the Dipper, wanderers, and pilgrims hold their breath treading on a path called Stone Bridge, which is like a dashing wave hanging in the mountains as aura configuration of the Great Void (also known as 'Heaven and Earth's breath'). It melts to form the valley streams and brooks, congeals to form plenty of summits and slopes. A stone beam spans two steep cliffs known as Shi-liang Waterfall, the path of Stone Bridge, ranges from seven inches wide at the narrowest and to about nineteen inches at the widest point. The waterfall plummets a whole one hundred feet into a deep pool with a thundering roar. The site is magnificent, but much composure and surefootedness are required to walk across the beam. This path is not several tens of paces long associated with the name of Xue Feng who, at the critical crossing of Stone Bridge, took off from individual paths and soared into the hyperspace of intellectual transcendence of Zen Buddhism. Straddling heaven-vaulting suspended stone-stair and overlooking the myriad-fathom cut-off dark-abyss -- every step is extremely slippery, while below it looks down on the fathomless and rocky Tian-lao Gorge. We are here to trace Xue Feng's free-spirited roving through the Great Void, ultimately merging with the hidden attributes of Dao, the core of Daoism, to find some enlightenment before we turn over the last page. It is the dark outgrowth on steep shelves, the spirit-giving herb in the thickets, the purple fungus fluorescent light in the secluded caves, the whitish jade high on their peaks, sliced cliffs studded throughout with gems. Lofty pine trees wriggle like mythical green-blue dragons sent down by Heaven, and imaginary flame-red phoenixes brought up in the bowels of mountains. Lines of tigers' footprints seal their slopes; gods and spirits stand at their sides; sages and deities guard their vast realms. At night they sit in state accepting the homage of the other beasts and strange critters which come to drink there in the gorge devoutly pillowing their heads to lap up the cold and transparent water of the mountain sources gushed out from the Yellow Spring hidden in the deep mountains, blinking their fluorescent eyes.

There are mountain ranges rising and falling, plains crisscrossing, rivers flowing long distance and boulders scattering all over valleys like stars and constellations on the Milky Way. Among them Cinnabar Mound, the ancient site of immortals located thirty miles south of Ninghai County, on which an adherent of the Dao, searching for immortality's delightful halls, can meet the feathered and winged figures. The group of Five Peaks (Wuding) and Flourishing Peak (Huading) and the site of Xiang-lin temple, which stands about fifteen miles southwest of the Flourishing Peak, and which stands in such a remote and out-of-the-way place that the roads there are still so long and hard to trace. The Red Fort Summit (Chichengshan), a rocky cliff rising perpendicularly several hundred feet, locates just a few miles south of Tian-tai County and is known as one of the 'Two Wonders' (the other is Shiliang Waterfall that thunders in the south-western part of the range, drifting in flight marks out of its path). The Red Fort Summit is marked with horizontal strata, eroded in some cases into deep caves, giving from a distance the appearance of the layered cliff.

Thousands of pilgrims, old and young, men and women, might be seen on the trail carrying sticks and yellow bags, traveling nights and days to the sacred temples. Among them, the spirit of jollity prevailed as it did in olden times, and tales were told on the way like those old recorded. It provided them with a chance to enjoy mountain scenery, for most Buddhist temples were situated on high summits at scenic spots. It was the one little pleasure the pilgrims and officials in retreat allowed themselves in their usual humdrum everyday life. They arrived and put up in what seemed to be hostel rooms, and had tea and gossiped with the monks. The monks were polite conversationalists; they offered good vegetarian dinners and reaped an enormous sum in their coffers. The pilgrims then went home with freshened spirits and renewed energy for their rigorous daily routine.

To enter the Tian-tai Mountains proper, most pass through its southern portal, with Red Fort on their left. Right away it hits you what a red mountain this seems. You have just come through dusty Chichengshan town, lanes of red clay where they have not yet paved, and at least two cuts through red sandstone hills. Then you behold the Fort's dull-red face, with red-walled cloisters and caves layered like Mawangdui's cells. Geologically, Mount Red Fort differs from any other Tian-tai peaks; only when you proceed north do you hit good solid granite. But all throughout Tian-tai, you will observe more or less reddish dirt, more ochre, where the local habitants have cultivated mountain terraces, brighter red swatches from the iron oxides in eroded and exposed patches. To stay at Red Fort meant to remain on this side of the transcendental world, in two senses. Firstly, the physical peak, the southern boundary of the Tian-tai range, lay well south of the Stone Bridge that, to the founders and patriarchs of Tian-tai sect and their heirs, symbolized a passage to transcendence. Secondly, symbolically, from of old Red Fort was always surrounded with the Daoist Arbiter of Destiny's Rampart, so, in that sense, living at Red Fort meant remaining just on the border of Celestial Enceinte.

In a way, Tian-tai reads as a very 'red place,' from its peach-blossoms to its Red Fort, from the rose clouds on its misty peaks to the red-capped cranes conveying its immortal denizens from Heaven's Grotto to Celestial Palace. And though on a pilgrim's visit one can see more pink azaleas and lavender wisterias than peach-blossoms -- and the white-reddish rhododendrons on the Flourishing Peak lie in bud, just waiting for a few more warm days to burst open -- everyone will concur with commonly red sign of the place -- the color of overwhelming desire and lust.

And the Tian-tai sect represented an interesting variation on this theme. Some believed in repression of the passions, and others felt in naturalistic abandon, but Tian-tai philosophy counseled moderation in all things. Take the question of sexual desire in particular. There were two opposite views of sexual ethics, one represented by orthodox Buddhism, which regarded sex as the culmination of sin, the natural consequence of which is asceticism. The other extreme was naturalism which glorified virility, of which many inhabitants of monasteries and nunneries were secret followers. The conflict between these points of view gave them their restlessness of spirit.

For the fusion of feminine power represented by lead and the masculine, by mercury, on the chemistry of the human body, also known as making love internal breathing techniques, the practitioners of this alchemy employ were rigorous and unremitting, though highly disciplined in mastering the art of sexual intercourse. The male permanently deferred ejaculation to prevent the loss of vital Yang fluids, which, unlike the feminine's (Yin), was limited and irreplaceable. Employing this unconsummated sex the inner reservoir of the precious, life-prolonging essence, drop by drop, was filled up. Called 'White Tiger and Green Dragon Yoga,' this school was abhorrent even to some orthodox Daoists and has died out as a result of suppression by the authorities, on the one hand, and too much secrecy and clandestinity, on the other. For there were dangers associated with its practice, poisoning primarily. Attempting to transform the corruptible parts of their natures, some monks resorted to the direct ingestion of lead and mercury, small quantities at first, but gradually building up the dosage as the body's tolerance increased -- an alchemical mithridatism. As the reader imagines, this had a disastrous effect on the liver and, in fact, generally proved fatal. Nevertheless, its adherents (survivors) pointed with a certain satisfaction to the undeniable success of their technique in preserving the body in the grave. And yet, who knows, is it so impossible to think that in a ruined temple somewhere in a remote corner of the kingdom a pair of ancient adepts with toothless and withered faces, but bright and youthful eyes, are going at it, religiously and diligently cultivating their 'bedchamber art,' in the hope of saving their immortal souls? In this sense, Zen was an unconscious gesture of a man in his battle with life, a form of revenge somewhat similar in psychology to suicide, when life proved too cruelly superior. Many beautiful and talented girls at the end of the Tang Dynasty took the monastic vow through disappointment in love caused by those catastrophic changes, and the first emperor of the Manchurian Dynasty became a monk for the same reason.

It is good to mention here that Daoist priests and sagely minded Zen monks in practice were among the most prolific writers on the sexual part of human life. They explained this by stating that if the act of joining the opposed Yin (feminine) and Yang (masculine) is a beautiful moment when they go beyond the wretched and miserable earthly existence, enjoying the merger with the universe, it is undoubtedly a spiritual phenomenon that must be researched and developed. For this reason, many ordinary people have accused the monks and nuns of immorality. This is based on the universal human delight taken in exposing all forms of hypocrisy. It is natural and comfortable therefore to make Casanovas of Zen monks, provided with witchcraft and secret aphrodisiacs. There were actually cases, in certain parts of Tian-tai where a nunnery was but a house of prostitution. But on the whole, the charge was unfair, and most monks were good, retiring, polite and well-behaved people who cultivated the bedchamber art with sole responsibility in full secrecy; and any Don Juan exploits were limited to transgressing individuals, and were grossly exaggerated in novels for the outer effect. What's more, this misjudgment was due to the failure to see the connection between sex and religion. The monks have a higher chance to see beautifully dressed women than any other class of people. The practice of their faith, whether in private homes or in their temples, brought them in daily contact with women who were otherwise shut away from the public. Thanks to the Confucian seclusion of women, the only unimpeachable pretext for women to appear publicly was to go to the temples and burn incense. On the first and fifteenth of every month, and on every festive occasion, the Buddhist temple was the rendezvous of all the local beauties, married or otherwise, dressed in their best. If any monk ate pork on the sly, he might also be expected to indulge in occasional irregularities. Add to this the fact that many monasteries were exceptionally well endowed, and many monks had plenty of money to spend, which was the cause of mischief in many cases that had come to light in the afterward. They also invented many of the great names and terms used to denote sexual intercourse, genital organs, and other related things. For example, Clouds and Rain, Clouds and Winds, Fog and Rain, Rapture of the Lodge for sexual intercourse; Male Stem, Jade Stalk, Turtle's Head for penis; the Jade Gate, Jade Pavilion, Secret Womanhood, Magic Field for female genital organs; Pearl at the Jade Stupa, Precious Terrace for clitoris; Examination Hall for vagina, and so forth. Such names clearly illustrate the role of poetic imagination in their no-nonsense approach.

The mountains, rivers, lakes, forests, groves, and flowers compose beautiful sceneries which are magnificent and extraordinarily precipitous now quite like a young virgin and now moved like a dragon, now higher than the seventh sky and then deeper than the sea-pit, or like mountains and rivers in a painting hang-scroll, or like ten thousand wild horses galloping all together. These extraordinary mountains and rivers have fostered generations of outstanding figures and always attracted guests from all sides and corners of the world, leaving historical and religious sites all over Tian-tai. Till today we may follow this sacred mountain trails by tracing the poems and works of many whose appreciation of the majestic Tian-tai sceneries is definite. This is how one of the hermits, tarrying once in the deep mountains, depicted the Tian-tai Range in his poem:

"Cinnabar Mound is high and afar,
Standing equal with the solemn clouds;
There are in mid-air the tops of Five Peaks—
Seen from afar they seem lower than they are.
The Wild Goose Pagoda towers up,
Exceeding the green and shield-like peak;
The Buddhist temple with its age-old walls—
All merging with the colors
Of the rainbow spectrum. Wind shakes up
The twigs on the knotted pine trees—
The Red Fort is awesomely elegant;
Fog spews out at mid-cliff—the pathway
To the grove of immortals is indistinct and stray.
Green-jade sky falls on a thousand peaks—
Each ten thousand feet high,
While creeping wisteria vines intertwine,
Chaining down all valleys, one by one."

This upland has always supplied the whole the world if not with outstanding thinkers and poets (from of old there was no distinction between these two categories of men), then certainly with exquisite dreamers, or both poets and dreamers, supplied them and been their refuge when the entire world turned the face of displeasure and even hatred. Here, in far away and secluded scenes, if you are very still and listen in the proper spirit, you may hear the weird solo of a hermitical flute played by some recluse. His skin is as ice and snow and whose loveliness is like that of a maiden, and who eats not some sort of the five grains but lives only on air moisture and dew; mounted on a flying dragon he rides above the clouds and wanders beyond the four seas. His spirit is such that by concentrating its power he can stay the natural process of decay and ensure abundant harvests. As is said,

"He who knows well how to live,
For a time of traveling the countryside,
Comes across no tigers or rhinoceroses on his way;
Upon entering a battle, he remains untouched by arms of war."

The dragon in the east is a benevolent mythical creature which is subdivided into three kinds: the flying dragon, the water, and terrestrial ones, but the clouds are considered to be the cradle for all of them. In fact, most variety of dragons in the eastern pantheon of mythology provides them with the massive benevolent features so long as, in most cases, their positive (Yang) assistance is highly appreciated as an auspicious sign -- dragons move in spiral motion whereas evil spirits can move only in straight lines.

From olden times of the regional development, the recluses who busied themselves in the Tian-tai Mountains with these things were all interested in the problem of discovering a remedy, which could release vital energy in such a way as to make men immune against sickness and death. They lived there on dewdrops and pinecones; they fed on the wind and vapor, and their minds were as bright and still as a surface of the mountain lake. They were open and very friendly. It seemed there was no fear, no anger, no tension, and no dissatisfaction between them; no one was superior or inferior to anyone else. Everything was bountiful, and everyone enjoyed the providence predefined by an interaction of the high heavens and low-lying vales. The sun and the moon sent gentle light, the seasons were never harsh, the soil in the valleys and on the terraces was, and the inhabitants were genuinely kind. The deities blessed the land, and the hungry ghosts and evil spirits never went near it. From time out of mind, this was the land the legendary Yellow Emperor once visited in his dream. Hundreds of poets of Tang-period and other dynasties left their traces and inscriptions in Tian-tai, famous for fathomless scenic spots, picturesque landscapes, and misty views sprung up from the breath of heaven and earth. This desire to learn the secrets of Nature and to use them for enjoying Yin-Yang relationship as much as possible is an excellent example of how the moral principles and strict rules of Buddhism were combined with Daoist paganism. After learning in full the practical aspects of the matter, they could, as much as possible, indulge in the satisfaction of natural desires. This understanding of the opposite sides of human nature and the need to reconcile them with each other has become an integral part of the Tian-tai Buddhist sect.

These men wandered around beyond the material things. They considered themselves as companions of the Creator and walked around within the One Spirit of the universe. They looked upon life as a large excrescence and upon death as the breaking of a tumor. How could such people be concerned about the coming of life and death or their sequence? They borrowed their forms from the different elements, and took temporary abode in the conventional ways, unconscious of their internal organs and oblivious of their senses of hearing and vision. They went through life backward and forwards as in a circle without beginning or end, strolling forgetfully beyond the dust and dirt of mortality, and wandering around with the affairs of precise acting, and leaving aside any repentance or further ado. How should such men bustle about the conventionalities of this world for ordinary people to look at? Living as hermits on the peaks and in the secluded groves, they were brought into close contact with nature, obtaining an intimate knowledge of plants and minerals. Their thinking and view of life were colored creatively by impressions of beauty gained from nature at the sight of its mighty waterfalls, fast-flowing streams, pure fountains and spring waters, fleeting rosy racks and white clouds, variegated birds and striped beasts, thin air and changing the scenery. None had a more intimate knowledge of the properties of various herbs, plants, and fruits, and none was more proficient in distinguishing nutritious and healing plants from poisonous ones. Some of the most venerable and celebrated masters lived entirely on herbs and vegetable food. As for plants, you might suspect the rare Udumbara (Ficus racemosa) blossom, a symbol of Buddhist enlightenment; monks built an Udumbara Terraces near Stone Bridge; or, perhaps, the prized Lohan Tribute tea. But far and away the most prominent plant in Tian-tai lore was the peach blossom, a symbol of Daoist transcendence. With a variety of ginseng called 'golden essence' they could taste 'golden rice,' the sweetness of monkish cuisine, made with 'golden essence'; fresh 'yellow root,' also known as the earth-spirit root, tasted like sweet ginger, which used to be found and collected in the beautiful valleys of Tian-tai, and which the hermits served in place of tea, as it was a very effective tonic. There also were 'lingzhi,' or spirit-giving herb, and the 'he-sou' herb, which shape was strikingly reminiscent of the human body and, therefore, was called 'manlike madder.' The well-known 'dufulin' (Smilax Chinensis) was there too, which grew from two to three feet beneath the earth; and, of course, two or three sorts of fern and pteridophyte plants cropped there up as well. As is famously known from traditional Chinese medicine, if the sour taste prevails over all the others, the number of childbearing juices decreases; the predominance of sweet taste oppresses the mind and reduces its receptivity to pleasure. When the bitter taste prevails, the stomach hardens and the spleen, the central organ, dries up. When the bitter taste prevails over all others, the face becomes distorted, and the smell of feminine secretion increases significantly. Therefore, it is essential to support regularly the harmony of all the five tastes.

What's more, the itinerant monks and hermits did not confine themselves to the study of herbs, fruits, and plants. From of old, they had also included the mineral kingdom in their investigations. They claimed to have found that the decoction of certain minerals' combination was especially effective as pills, or as an elixir of immortality. To live on a vegetarian diet, on 'pills of immortality' was considered as a proper fast and those who observed it was given great honor and dignity. It could even be noticed how those lean and ethereal-looking men gradually faded away. The recipe for such a concoction was undoubtedly very startling, and it wasn't surprising that history mentioned several men who succumbed soon after they had tried the cure. As an instance, these were the following ingredients: cinnabar, arsenic, alum, copper oxide, pulverized porcelain, and some others. Great care and strict sequence had to be taken in the preparation: the pot had to be of unique shape and size; the mixture had to be continuously stirred for nine months, and must be given nine different types of boiling.

Still, another method of longevity or, instead, immortality was the astrological one. According to the Daoist teachings, every person has access to and capacity for intimate relationship with the divine worthies to whom Heaven has entrusted the responsibility of being patrons for the human beings living on earth. These worthies control the five-phase elements, which are to constitute parts of every living being and depict symbolically by the images of Wood, Metal, Fire, Water, and Earth. Their exalted excellent features to run differently with various energies are thought to have a residence on the planets, but they may also be projected down to the respective places and individuals on earth who belong to their particular domain. They also represent the five primary colors, seasons, tastes, senses, sounds, smells, and the four directions of the compass, plus the ultimate center. The west conventionally harbors a white tiger, while azure dragon belongs to the east; the north houses a black tortoise entwined with a snake, but a heraldic animal of the south is a red bird. While our account singled out one symbolic animal per site, in truth, we simplified by selecting what seemed the most distinctive critter. Zen monk Xue Feng usually gets painted leaning fondly on a sleepy tigress; Zhi Yi, the founder of the Tian-tai sect with its main temples and monasteries, Guo-qing and Xiang-lin, also got credited with taming a tiger, and you can still find a 'Tame-tiger Ridge' west of Mount Tian-tai. But for Tian-tai's most appropriate zoological emblem you would have to choose the image of a crane, or, more broadly, the range of cranes, wild geese, storks, and swans, which serves as a flying steed for a wandering transcendent. We have already seen many examples. Tian-tai still boasts a "White Crane Town" northwest of Tong-bai town, the main street of which bears the name of 'the Soaring Crane.' Besides, one can see signs for the Soaring Crane paintings on the way up to Xiang-lin temple.

By now the reader may excuse me for such a tedious demonstration. However, he or she will want to keep in mind the unique complex of plants, animals, and cultural features that have helped each site to create its own unique numinous magic.

But let's assume you have got this far. You have now found out a way to Tian-tai mountains; you arrive later in the day, proving tactically astute if you don't know whether you can expect a welcome in one of their numerous monasteries and temples. In fact, it's always harder to turn away a supplicant when the sun's sinking low. So, try to find a sympathetic-looking Buddhist monk or a Daoist priest, introduce yourself as a Buddhist or Daoist lay believer, and ask if you might spend a couple of nights. Lucky beggar you are if you find a cell, hopefully, get a pot of boiled water, and next day acquaint yourself with the temple as diligently as you can. Besides, again, if lucky, you can become a whole attentive audience, absorbing many local legends and stories that are spewed forth by some talkative monks (especially by some novices) as though from the horn of plenty.

Chapter 2: Call of Zen

When Xue Feng was a child, he was quite slow-witted. In fact, he didn't begin to talk until he was about five years old. Subsequently, when the boy left home to become a novice, he had great difficulty in reading sutras. He couldn't memorize anything. His first master told him, "You really are too clumsy and stupid." He also said that his karmic obstructions were substantial and that only by prostrating five hundred times a day to Guanyin Bodhisattva (whose name means Bodhisattva Who Hears the Sounds of the World or, more straightforward, Great Compassion Bodhisattva) could he succeed in removing them. Xue Feng did as his master said for seven or eight months until one day his head felt calm and serene. It seemed to have opened up, and everything that had weighed him down for so long had been lifted. From that time on he had no trouble memorizing and reciting verses from sutras. His master said that this was the bodhisattva's responding to him. What was more critical, Xue Feng strongly believed himself that this was the case and, therefore, this function was purely mental in that the bodhisattva had intervened and helped him.

The county where Xue Feng lived south of the Yellow River was once prosperous, but it underwent a slow decline at the end of the Southern Chen dynasty. By the time he was born, the region was impoverished. He was born at night of the full moon in the seventh lunar month when the late summer was in its final blaze. The window of his mother's room had been thrown open to catch that fresh breath of coming fall. The old midwife grumbled at this, but the healer who had been brought from the neighboring village said it could do no harm. It was a relatively uncomplicated delivery. Toward the end though something peculiar happened. As the woman in childbirth lay in bed, propped up pillows struggling to breathe, in the midst of a forceful contraction she called her husband's name. As she did, the light blinked and a fluttering shadow crossed the bed -- a considerable bat which had flown in through the open window was circling silently throughout the room. The sight sent a chill through her whole body. In an instant, a rare fragrance filled the room. A white beam from the sky linked with the earth, and the trees in the nearest forest turned the white tint. The birds chirped out noisily in joy.

Xue Feng was the youngest of four children. His mother was already thirty-three years old when he was born. She had no milk to nurse him with, and domestic animals' milk was rare there. Even female dogs were unable to produce milk to feed their young. Animals were all emaciated. People also were malnourished. It was not until Xue Feng was three that he learned to walk, and it was not until he was five that he could speak with any facility. Growing up, he then started to help his grandfather with his land work. A few years later a local abbot was looking for two novices to live at the temple. He was in some quandary as to how to find his young monks. He prayed to the Buddha for guidance, and it was indicated to him that he should look in a village south of his temple. The monastery was north of the Yellow River, so the abbot crossed to the side where Xue Feng's family lived. Once passing through the village, he saw the boy and asked his mother if she was willing to let her son leave home.

She answered, "If he wants to become a monk, it is up to him. Our family is impoverished. I'm afraid that if he stays with us, he won't have enough money to find himself a wife."

The abbot turned to the boy and asked, "How would you like to become a monk, good boy?"

The kid didn't have the foggiest idea what a monk was or what a monk did. But somehow the idea appealed to him, and he said, "Yes, I would like that."

The abbot wrote the name and birthday in his book and soon left.

About three months later one layman appeared and said to the woman, "I am going to take your son now. I will take him north of the river to become a novice."

During those last months, the abbot on the north side of the river had taken the date of Xue Feng's birth and put it before Guanyin Bodhisattva, entreating the image to reveal whether the boy would be suitable for monkhood or not. He asked three times, and all three times the answer was affirmative. When the layman came to take Xue Feng to the temple, the boy had no quite positive feeling about going. At last, he was ready to go. This took his mother by surprise: "I thought you were kidding about becoming a monk," she said. But the next day he left with the layman for the monastery.

As it has been mentioned previously, from the very beginning Xue Feng (actually, this was his monastic name, meaning 'Snow Peak') had a problem with the recitation of sutras, especially mantras; so, he did five hundred prostrations to Guanyin Bodhisattva each day. At first, he found this practice exhausting, but after a short while, he realized that he could even do six hundred prostrations in a few hours. In a few months, he also found that his ability to memorize sutras, as well as his ability to learn in general, had vastly improved. Soon he felt that reciting was not enough. He wanted to understand more in-depth the meanings contained in the scriptures.

Many of the names of Zen patriarchs reflect the cold environment of the places where they practiced. Very rarely do we find them associated with summertime. Winter and cold symbolized by falling snow represent the spirit of Zen, whereas the essence of summer is entirely different. In hot weather, it is effortless to feel sleepy and dull-minded, while cold weather, especially in the mountains, is perfect for those who are already advanced in retreat practice. To give a few examples, one master's name was Snow Cavern; then there was Snow Ravine, Snow Cliff, Snow Slope, and the like. These Zen masters sought out places where there was a lot of snow. An old verse sounds like this:

"In the deep mountains—why it is so cold?!
From ancient times it's so—not just this season.
The piled up peaks are clotted continuously with snow;
Secluded forest every day spews out thick mist.
All grasses start to grow here after the solar period
Of 'Bearded Grain,' in the fifth month, but leaves

Come down even before the Beginning of Fall.
Up here is a rover who has hopelessly lost his way
And who is staring into the distance but can't see
The clearness and cloudlessness of the azure sky."

By unexpected good fortune, he was soon able to hear one wandering sutra-exponent quoted from the Mahaparinirvana Sutra, which assimilated to the principle teachings of the Lotus Sutra. That quotation illuminated Xue Feng's mind and set his soul afire. Asking where he could learn more, he was referred to Tian-tai Buddhist Sect, six hundred miles southeast of his monastery. As he could find out some time later, that Xiang-lin temple was located nearby Tian-tai County seat (the central area of present-day Zhejiang Province that faces the East Sea on the east and borders Wenzhou County in the south) on the south side of the southern peak of Tian-tai mountain range, one hundred and twenty miles south of Hangzhou. The novice-monk also found out that the temple offered preaches on the sutras, and he requested his master's permission to attend. That other monastery required a kind of entrance examination for those who wished to participate in the sutra lectures. His master helped him write a petition -- that was what he thought they wanted. As it turned out, a request was not what they wanted at all -- an entirely different topic was required, but they liked his short essay, and they thought that his literary skills were quite excellent, so they accepted him anyway.

As the reader can imagine, on both counts Xiang-lin (Fragrant Forest) temple was well named. It was hidden in a rocky nest of cliffs carved out of Tian-tai by the flows of several streams, which raced down from the fathomless source high somewhere up in the heavenly roof and for long ages past the mountain. It was a retreat for those priests and monks who came there leaving behind their attachments in the mundane world to embark on the course of the arduous route back to the Dao or Dharma -- a journey which traditionally is called 'Return to the Yellow Spring.'

Tian-tai Buddhists and Daoists displayed a notably syncretic spirit, even for sectarians. Tian-tai itself, from the very beginning syncretic teaching, had particularly close ties to the Pure Land salvationist devotion. When Xue Feng arrived at the temple, the abbot by the name of Zhao Zhou came to greet him, saying, "How can you, an uneducated novice, possibly hope to attain Buddhahood?" He mocked.

Xue Feng answered him this way: "Though people are distinguished as wise and silly, there is neither wisdom nor stupidity in Buddha-nature. In physical appearance humble novices and celebrated abbots may look different, but what difference is there in their Buddha-nature?"

By way of response, the abbot sent him off to the granary, where he was put to work hulling rice grains and chopping up firewood. In fact, Xue Feng's diligence let him grind the grains alone instead of several monks who had arranged this hardest job in the monastery with more than a hundred of its inhabitants.

From the time when Xue Feng left home to become a monk, insensibly, the Wonderful Dharma brought him more awakening and understanding, and he grew to extinguish most of his outflows. In a couple of years he was in charge of the monastery rice supply and grinding, but at night he used to lock himself in his cell. No one had any clue of what was happening inside, but some novices could hear his strangely vibrated sounds and rhythms he uttered in a manner of spell or incantation.

Xue Feng was well-known all over the area for his devotion and frankness. Making a mass of good friends among senior monks and young novices, he had the talent to be himself. But one young novice from Guo-qing monastery was particularly close to him. His nickname was Foundling and when he heard his name pronounced by some of his senior brothers his eyes flamed with anger -- so much fire had been amassed in his young heart. Therefore, all tried to call him merely 'brother.' However, this feature of his peculiar oddity revealed itself as volatile temper and tendency to brawl should have been named among the brethren 'a wild-spirit,' the term which in their innate monkish cant suggested willfulness, the frenzy of imagination, disobedience and restless, fiery heart. Even Xue Feng, his elder friend, and protector indulged in occasional jibes though, and it was true, with more tenderness and humor than the rest. As he reproached the boy for his transgressions, the monk often emphasized this last quality particularly -- 'hot temper.' Had not the oracle with tremendous prevision pegged this as an attribute of his character? This was the reading the oracle returned when the monks consulted it on the boy's behalf for the first time: the third undivided line of the Sun hexagram (no. 57) showed its subject as him who pretended to be an obedient man by violent and repeated efforts. "There thus will be an occasion for blame and regret that arise from the false obedience," was the verdict. Therefore, bowing to superior force, the novice always took the perceived insults with the blows (his hexagram Sun consisted of double trigram Wind); then stole away to console himself with silent weeping. In the aftermath, Xue Feng, who was sentimental and big-hearted, became unchangingly stricken with remorse. He would come to comfort the boy, offering a couple of rice cakes in his rough hands. Then the monk always said that he was too tender-hearted, too gentle and vulnerable. The monk had a rather massive beard, which he was obliged to shave every few days at most, except for a tuft in the cavity between his bottom lip and chin, which he retained out of vanity. As a result, his lower jaw was overcast continuously by a dusky blue shadow, like the floor of an evergreen forest. Whenever the boy succeeded in irritating him to the point of requital, Xue Feng would bend close to him, as though to impart some secret, then nibbed these bristles against his smooth head like a vindictive hedgehog. This was harsh punishment indeed, but richly rightful. For the monk was always fair; and his earthiness was the perfect antidote to the unworldly realm of the other monks who, unlike him, generally came from the upper stratum of society.

Following the general comprehension, during quite a brief lifespan a man is tormented by hardships and tribulations, oppressed by his duties he pursues the need to work. As for other living beings, all this is not a condition of their lives, and they are quite happy that Mother Nature takes care of all the worries. In the world of animals, everything happens by itself. As for the humans, a substantial share of private life, however, is brightened up with those brief moments when he or she can pleasantly enjoy themselves the moments of a sexual act. Those who do not want to recognize this truth just let them compare the life of monks with that of eunuchs. Regarding longevity, a monk is no different from a layman because, though he is deprived of healthy family life, he finds some satisfaction among the novices and nuns. He can spend most of his days in the cell, but there usually is enough room for two. A eunuch, on the other hand, is not capable of penetrating into the Jade Gate of a female. When some claim that total abstinence allows a person to live to the ancient age, think of the eunuchs who live without male genitals. If the whole point is about abstinence, they should have lived a hundred years, or so. However, the facts are that their faces are covered with wrinkles by thirty, their hair turns gray, and their backs are stooped when they are still relatively young. Do you, while passing through a cemetery, ever see a tombstone on the grave of a eunuch who lived a hundred year or so? Just never happens.

It is well-known that intimate relationship and sex, the carnal root of the human beings, yet holds the key to their regeneration. This is because sexual desire is not only inborn, it is also the strongest desire of the human beings. Even the baby male child of a few months old sprouts an erection while suckling her mother's breasts, albeit unconsciously. As the great thinker Lao-zi, the founder of Daoism, says:

"He who has accumulated a considerable amount of inner resources
Can be compared to a newborn child:
Poisonous serpents and wasps do not sting him;
Fierce beasts do not pounce on him; birds of prey never attack him.
The infant's bones are soft and his muscles weak,
But yet his grip is undoubtedly firm. He knows not yet sexual intercourse,
And again his penis arousal is caused by the perfection of his substance.
Screaming all day long, he doesn't get hoarse,
And this is caused by the harmony of his original vitality, his essence."

There was a peculiar earnestness and warmth over the whole presentation when venerable masters discussed original questions. In the 'dao-yin,' breathing yoga, for instance, chastity was the way to accumulate spiritual energy. Consummation of the sexual act was usually perceived by the male as vital depredation -- the loss of semen, the vital essence entailed a loss of energy. From this viewpoint, sex was not only a hindrance, but it could also make one lose the benefits of a long ascetic practice. The loss of energy caused by the sexual act, so-called 'small death,' was obviously a major concern for ascetic virgins. For the ordinary priests and monks, however, the karmic consequences of desire seemed to have been more important. Time and again it was said that it was in this thing that men found their heaven or their hell. The language was highly poetic and figurative, dignified and serious, without any perverse suggestions. Sexual instinct in the female was referred to under the figure of the White Tiger, and that in the male under the figure of the Green or Yellow (Golden) Dragon. Abdominal part of the body was called the Dragon-n-Tiger Cave, another title for the Golden Elixir Pill, which is to be ultimately accumulated in this middle (therefore central) elixir field, well known as 'dan-tian.' In fact, chastity was the rule of the order -- an unwritten rule but strictly obeyed. At least, as far as the monk knew it, to his knowledge of the rites was at second and third hand. Alchemy of the Dragon and Tiger transmutation of the body (the lead and mercury chemical combination) was practiced only by the mature adepts. It always occurred under the watchful eye of the abbot who, as they said, had tasted the sweet peace of Dharma and learned to live contentedly with coarse rice to eat, cold water from the well, the crook of a bent elbow for a pillow, and who was said to have already distilled the liquor of spiritual and corporal immortality.

As it has been mentioned earlier, Dragon and Tiger symbolized the love between the sexes. This formula was designed for widespread consumption. Initially, their intercourse alluded to esoteric rituals, which only superficially resembled romantic, erotic love embodied in the White Tiger and Green Dragon yoga. The adepts of the Tian-tai Sect must have had some exposure to the mysteries of 'dual cultivation,' even if only through conversation. What they knew about the White Tiger and Green Dragon technique they learned from masters who were knowledgeable about all the esoteric schools, ancient and modern, and their secret practices. This yoga was related to alchemy and attempted the compounding of the Golden Elixir Pill, the fusion of Yin and Yang into the chaos of One, the feminine and masculine forces implemented through a regimen of rigorous and highly formalized sexual intercourse undertaken at certain times and seasons following astrological configurations and oracle's advice. The object of such intercourse was for the male, while maintaining strict seminal continence (by artificial means if necessary: a tight-fitting jade ring placed at the base of the penis, strangulating the ejaculation, inducing the 'backward flow'), to excite his partner to repeated climax, absorbing the Yin fluids she expended with each orgasm for his own benefit. These Yin fluids mixed with his semen were drawn back into the body and heated as in a kiln, the breath acting as a kind of bellows. At last, it began to rise through two channels parallel to the spine to the upper elixir center (dan-tian) located on top of the head and named Niwan or Clay Pill (actually, a stable crystal set at the center of brains). This was a distillation process in which all impurities were removed. Out of the residue, which was allowed to condense and dripped back down, the Golden Elixir Pill was compounded by descending the energy to the middle elixir field (dan-tian) in the lower part of the belly. The technique was apparently designed by males for their own use. Since their store of the Yang fluids was supposedly small and easily depleted, they needed to supplement it with the Yin fluids. And that was the whole notion while the secret, the trick of the trade, still remained to be open: How to do it in practice. The nature of these experiences was described figuratively and the used figures, of course, were not to be pressed too far. Morality was generally preserved, at least in sexual matters, even in the case of some Zen eccentricity. However, here is the character which, nevertheless, was quite eccentric and rose up against this morality, first of all, on the grounds of the superior freedom of Zen achieved merely through continued practice of meditating.

Yes, the young novice nicknamed Foundling was of some vague barbarian extraction; though he lacked his sturdy health, his hardihood was always with him. He was of slight build, even frail. His health was partly ruined by a severe bout of fever as a child, scarlet fever probably, for he carried the terrible signature in the pockmarks on his face, a disfigurement that only enhanced his beauty, like the chance scars time inflicted in antique porcelain. Some of the monks suggested another interpretation of his delicacy, physical and otherwise. It was whispered that the novice was fond of, or had been a sexual fun. From the time he was very young, with the same dark, illicit craving, with which an ordinary boy fantasizes about sex, he looked forward to the day when the abbot would initiate him into those forbidden rites. It was perhaps the source of his keenest regret that he had still not begun his training. Time after time the abbot put him off, telling him that he wasn't ready. Xue Feng said that the abbot would never teach him until he learned to control his own spirit that it was his 'wilderness,' which made the master hesitate over and over again. Perhaps he was right, though the boy certainly didn't think so at the time. He had then a tendency to dismiss his master's counsel out of hand, especially in this matter, since he had never been initiated into the mysteries.

Xue Feng tried, in his turn, to explain to him that during the first three years of practices this was particularly important, for during this period the Yin and Yang forces became violently active. A genuine life and death struggle would take place, the White Tiger and Golden Dragon continuing violent assaults. However, as it goes, 'When the commandment came, sin revived.' Though sexual desire might be the most fundamental form of desires, sex was, as usual, the essential object of continence in Buddhism. Since they met the vital needs of the practitioner, other types of avidity might be controlled, but they couldn't be entirely suppressed. They reached their limits more efficiently, however, whereas sexual desire, based in significant part on imagination, could lead an adherent to his decease. This was a severe test to pass. In his earlier poetry, the novice alluded to masturbation as a remedy for his sexual regulation. That was the thing he had experienced rambling closer to the cliffs of Stone Bridge where he found some unusual rock formations. Wandering in the deep mountains, he could see along the cliffs the most ridiculously priapic stones. It was just got to be man-made, yet the glans alone might weigh no less than ten thousand massive pounds. Presumably, its upper tip rested on softer sediments that got eroded, leaving only the granite shaft beneath -- somewhat an amusing landmark for Buddhist reclusion. He then adventurously confessed:

"Behind the bolted door I sin in private, pretending
My try to elude distress and confusion. I grasp it --
The evil part of my body is swollen up;
I lift it up as if I report to Yama, the King of Hell.
If I not be placed in boiling caldron
Of the Underworld, I'll definitely be lying
On the iron prickly couch, under torture.
Letting nobody else be involved in this my sin,
I serve myself, suffering alone thru my own flesh."

The reason of suffering is hidden not in the social life or out of it, but in personal delusions and ambitions, which produce 'karma' or the causal effect. Delusions include greed, avidity, and stupidity while 'karma' consists of body, mouth, and false thoughts; both produce cause while effect correlates with life and death. Depending on one's right or wrongdoing, one can increase and decrease the karmic wheel. To get out of the 'wheel of suffering,' one should study 'Tripitaka' (Collection of Buddhist sutras), exercise one's body and observe moral rules to get out of the wheel of life and death and reach the higher state of Nirvana, translated as 'release.' Zen Buddhism, with its vision of wise and brave adepts, states: "If not me entering the hell, who does?" Bodhisattva states that the hell is not empty; he who swears never becomes a buddha. Buddha is he who has reached Nirvana and who is out of the circle of rebirth. Bodhisattva is he who seeks to become a buddha on high and save all those who are in the lower regions. This is a kind of education of all living beings through love and compassion. Enlightenment can be reached by one who is destined to enlightenment. 'If you have reached enlightenment, I'll take you to paradise.' It doesn't matter which way you go, the ultimate goal is attaining enlightenment. A Zen monk in practice is he who does it himself; he doesn't care for others, reaching his understanding independently. As an old song runs:

"We view the deep, so somber and dangerous,
The vale where the dragon is softly humming its song;
The gloomy ravine where the tiger patiently
Waits for its prey with roaring and growling.
Behold, here's at once man's most precious possession,
And passion's flower-bed, a lair for the beasts.
Just here is the place where life's primordial forces --
The Yin and Yang, unfold themselves in a love battlefield.
Here is the place where the chief of the Underworld,
Almighty Yama, King of Hell, inhabits and runs the show."

The terms 'deep,' 'vale,' 'flower-bed,' 'ravine' and 'the beast's lair' are all figurative names for the lower 'dan-tian,' also known as the 'Dragon-n-Tiger Cave,' the playground of sexual passion, located in the perineum. Dragon is the sexual urge of the male, and the tiger is that of a female. Obviously, this principle is not limited to marriage. The term 'marriage' is simply a metaphor for the gradual development of any relationship or situation. Don't take any conditions of combat; be like a changeable dragon and terrible tiger. Attacking your loving opponents, burst into their formations like a cannonball. It is commonly known that climb up of a mountain sometimes is much easier than to climb down from it. Once, despite a dangerous condition of uncertainty, you have to muster your courage and 'mount the tiger,' looking directly in the face of reality to go further and work diligently with your mind, your consciousness, in which the true situation gradually brightens up in all directions. Thus, you open the gate of being correct from within, taking your firm position, like a mountain, to the bitter end. Particularly, this regards the moment you need to dismount from the tiger's back and 'put your leg down.' Without any saying, the image of a tiger is merely a metaphorical expression for something larger. It is a symbol of the original Mother Nature, the ways of Dao, which, according to Lao-zi are 'the boundless mystery of all mysteries,' the hidden within each another the magic set of three to make the blend of threes. The pure Yin, pure Yang, and their blended union, also known as the magic square -- the gateway to all things with their generation and completion you can go through to become aware of the essence of the total number 81 or 'nine nines,' the correlation of Heaven, Earth, and the middle space between the two.

Sin, either in Zen Buddhism or Daoism, is not just a synonym for evil. It means explicitly an action that violates the sacred law, or is threatening to the very expression of humanity. It is an act of disloyalty, if not treason, against the norms of well-being. There is no such God in Daoism or Buddhism, but there is a predetermined moral order that is associated with karma. Desire seems to stem from inside the human being, yet most desires are external to the self and come from the outside world. Once the world is perceived as impure, salvation lies at the end of a long and painful process of purification. What a person does with his or her body is that person's own affair. But what is to be condemned is the harming or exploiting of another person, even if it is seemingly voluntary on the part of the user. Compassion towards others must not be abandoned for the sake of sexual desires. By the same token, sexuality, until then merely a technical obstacle, a potential stumbling block for ascetics, is here identified with defilement and is loaded with good effect. In other words, it becomes a form of vice. The line of the novice's poem, which says, "Don't let anybody else be involved in this my sin" can freely be interpreted as a cynical comment on the fact that Tian-tai's monks were more interested in boys than in their protecting deities and spirits, like the King of Mountain, as an instance. Committing one of the five sins and the ten evils is said to earn one a place in the lowest and worst layer of the hell realms. Therefore, the fear of hell arose in the young novice. He thought of Yama, the King of Hell, reading out the tally of his sins and virtues to the busy scribes and bureaucrats in hell. His life, a blank page with one dark graph, one blot, was the sin of this apostasy. This betrayal was handed then over to the demons who scrapped and bickered for his living heart, like scavengers for a piece of meat and threw his gutted carcass into the deep lake of excrement, where it rotted for eternity amid the slithering of a myriad of pink worms he often saw in his bad dreams. The dream worms, however, is said to have the ability to travel between one's dreams and reality. The Daoist theory holds that there are three sorts of worms (by the analogy of the main three 'elixir centers' of the human body) that control the bodily inside and, therefore, can remember men's wrongdoings and report of them to the Emperor on High while men are asleep. Furthermore, the upper worm is keen on gems; the middle worm is interested in delicious food; the lower worm enjoys sexual activity. The following verse also belongs to the novice who wrote:

"The way I live is not what is called 'life of dignity';
Still water of the lake reflects the principle
Of 'doing no further ado.' At times I climb up the peak
Of Mount Nirvana, or go to have fun at Xiang-lin.
As usual, I'm looking for idleness and carelessness,
Never ever talking about fame or wealth.
Even the deep Eastern Sea once happened to be
The mulberry field and orchard.
O my poor heart! Who will then take care of it?!"

Despite its more frequent association with the monks of Tian-tai sect, it seems that the phenomenon was also quite common in Zen tradition in general. Mount Nirvana, the highest in the area (3,420 feet), with Xiang-lin monastery west from it -- that was a shelter of the male love, if we were to believe the words of the following, refrain from a favorite song, which said:

"First the temple's youths and
Only then the King of Mountain
To be pleased with sacrificial ritual --
Monks hold the monastery's boys
Much dearer than they do gods
And deities themselves!"

There was on Mt. Huading (Flourishing Peak) a specific homosexual tradition associated with the awakening of the monks. In the same way that the novice immersed himself in 'having fun,' he could also ascend the top of the Nirvana Mountain where Xue Feng, his elder brother and mentor, used to practice in retreat. Likewise, those who could concentrate on all Zen Buddhist practices, as if just playing or having fun, would naturally obtain Dharma, or the ways of Great Dao. In the Book of Lao-zi it is said: "That what is not turned to ridicule cannot be considered as the Dao." Most likely, the playing for fun is only a metaphorical role here, but this metaphor is closely related to the other elements in the novice's thought. His play provides a necessary preliminary to understanding the non-duality between mundane and sacred. In his mind, the image of 'having fun' becomes tied not only to the idea of sexual desire but also to the study and awakening of the adherents. For him, love for homosexual intercourse is inseparable from the realization of the sacred act. Some can see in this his confession that making love played an essential role in the Tian-tai monasteries, and his 'having fun' is more than a mere metaphor. Whereas the literary "having fun" is represented as a passive victim, the development of his divine nature in the Tian-tai genealogical tales leads to a more dynamic and, at the same time, ambivalent figure, in which the sexual element becomes more visible. It is clear that salvation through sex with the monastery's novices was in accord with the will of the tutelary deity of Mt. Huading, the local King of Mountain, and, it seems, Foundling intensified himself the secret tradition of Tian-tai. Perhaps he was not always, as the legend seems to indicate, an active partner in his relations with other inhabitants of Xiang-lin monastery. In his dreams, at least, the roles were sometimes inverted. One day he told that in one of his dreams he had sex with Emperor, they were 'like husband and wife.' This dream, in which he played the feminine role, recalled another dream in which he saw the sexual union of the emperor with his Jade Maiden symbolically. In that dream, it was the novice himself who took on the role of the Jade Maiden, the sexual initiator of the emperor who was some decades younger than the emperor was. In another dream, however, the emperor was a young man, in his teens, and could almost have been a boy for love.

Xue Feng commented those dreams in the following way. "This is because of your previous life," he said, "in which you have been a daughter of a king in one of the distant kingdoms in India. You also had one elder sister, the incarnation of Manjusri, and one elder brother, the incarnation of Avalokiteshvara Bodhisattva, also known as Goddess of Mercy. . ." Xue Feng explained patiently that this was a necessary stage, which must be fought through if 'a new holy embryo' was to be conceived. He also gave good advice, saying, "If desire succeeds in gaining the upper hand in your mind, even for a few short moments, a new start of intensive respiration must immediately be made. This marks outwardly by violently expelling impure air from the lungs. Such violent physical motion would be a help psychologically to overcome temptation." Such things were usually described using spiritual words and concepts, as well as physical and physiological imagery. Xue Feng's descriptions were so interlaced that it was difficult to decide where the physical and physiological ends and where the purely spiritual began. As the quiet and deep breathing started again, a useful experience had been gained; there had been a strengthening of purpose. The day would, therefore, come when new and mysterious powers would be released from within. Hence the Daoists attached great importance to the true man being able to forecast confidently and explicitly his final retirement from the world.

One day, during his ascetic practicing in the mountains, Xue Feng ran into a blizzard. He had nothing to eat, and his body was freezing. Then he came upon his hut on the side of the cliff. It had walls, but a vast hole shined on through the roof. Nevertheless, he went inside and sat down leaning against the wall where there was a little less snow. Sitting there, he composed:

"In my house, there is a gaping hole;
In that hole, there is just nothing.
Pure and clean -- its hollow resembles a palace;
Beaming and bright -- its shining like the sun's.
Rude foods nourish this ethereal body;
Hemp robe covers this illusory substance.
I'd let you have your thousand saints show up
Against my pure nature -- a single buddha inside me."

Thus, he sat down preparing to die. The snow piled up higher and higher until he was surrounded by it completely. But at this point, he had already entered into Samadhi. Is there really such a thing as 'heat' and 'cold'? That is to say, does hell or suffering really exist? Depending on your mental state, you could say that there really is and you could also say that there really is not. When you feel subject to vexations, then heat and cold are very real. When you don't feel any vexations, then heat and cold simply disappear along with the hells. Most people are afraid to fall into hell and desire to go up to heaven. But, in reality, both of them are vexations, just as dreading cold or heat amounts to the same thing. So, if you get to Heaven out of a desire for happiness, that happiness will also be a vexation. Therefore, we can't have one without the other. If Hell exists, Heaven also exists. But when your mind is free of vexations both the hells and the heavens would cease to exist. From the standpoint of Zen, there is no heavens, no hells, no buddhas, and no sentient beings. That is to say, there are no vexations. In the Buddhist sutras, coolness corresponds to wisdom and heat to vexation. However, extreme cold also represents vexation. There are two categories of hells: some are boiling hot, and some are freezing cold. What is the 'hell'? It is the place of suffering, and suffering means vexation. Our objective is to replace vexations, which often caused either by over anxiety or laxity, with the cool refreshment of wisdom. At the level of 'prajna' (wisdom), there are no ups and downs, the heavens and hells. . .

In a couple of days, when the snowstorm blew itself out, the novice came to pay a visit to his elder friend in the mountains. Brushing the snow out of the way, he saw Xue Feng was sitting in the hut. Thereupon, he pulled some straw off the walls and made a fire. Then the novice took out a pot, melted some snow in it, and cooked up gruel out of some leftovers he brought with him in the bamboo tubes. When Xue Feng felt the sensation of heat, he came back to life. He saw his friend making food for him to eat. . . he hadn't died after all.

Chapter 3: A Monk Making

Soon after Xue Feng held the position of a senior at the monastery's granary, Abbot Zhao Zhou dropped in, making an inspection.

"We must be careful," he warned rigorously, "don't waste rice!"

Hearing this, Xue Feng became disturbed. "Nobody wastes rice here," he retorted.

At this Zhao Zhou picked a fallen grain of rice up from the floor. "You said that no one wasted rice," he jeered, "but do you know where this one came from?" Saying so, he pointed his finger at the grain just picked up from the floor.

Xue Feng was silent; he had nothing to say to that. Thereupon, Zhao Zhou concluded, "We shouldn't take this lightly. It is necessary to realize the fact that a great quantity of rice originates from this single grain!"

"But who knows," returned Xue Feng, "where this one comes from?"

Upon hearing this, the abbot burst out laughing and, feeling quite satisfied, went out.

As rumors went that from that very moment the abbot wanted to give him a promotion. It may well be wondered why a promotion? It sounds quite ridiculous behind the monastery gates: Big deal! A promotion! However, it is to be evidential that among inhabitants of the monastery, as elsewhere in the mundane world, there was a dual command hierarchy: one legitimate, based on seniority and ranks, another, covert, based on innate personal qualities -- charisma, intelligence, courage, inventiveness, and wisdom at last. Xue Feng naturally belonged to the second. He perhaps felt he had little to gain from a formal promotion -- additional headaches and responsibilities without an appreciable increase in real power, which was only available through self-cultivation, attaining advanced realization. The monk felt good with his current position, which placed him on one of the lower rungs of the monastery's ladder, but which allowed him to visit for some provisions exchange many other Buddhist and Daoist monasteries and nunneries that were studded all around the region.

Every time after several days or weeks of Xue Feng's occasional absence, the hungry monks started to vilify him mercilessly aloud, inspiring one another to impressive heights of virtuosity in inventing original and perverse new forms of character assassination. They said he went on a protracted spree, gambling all night at the brothels in Red Fort city, hiring courtesans to engage with him in unspeakable acts, during which time he was never sober for so much as half an hour. However, there was not the slightest evidence for any of this, except, of course, that which malice could supply. (Only once the abbot saw him unconscious brought back by villagers in the bed of a manure cart.) Whether this was true or not, the abbot made no effort to ascertain. In either case, whichever it could be sliced up, it was irrelevant to any association with Xue Feng.

The emblem of sexual transgression there was courtesans. From the outset the Zen Buddhist attitude toward courtesans is ambivalent; however, they are feared as a temptress, an emissary of hell. (Had not the Buddha himself, in a past reincarnation as the hermit Unicorn, been shamefully seduced by one of them?) Yet a courtesan is also a woman who, in a sense, has 'left home' for studying the bedchamber art and seeing the world through its vanity. She has awakened to the conventional truth because she can see behind appearances, through the veil of illusion. She is no longer bound by ordinary social ties and conventional norms because she can see through the men's games. She is not impressed by their social distinctions: priests, villagers, militaries, or nobility, at large, all are the same to her -- and she can, like a true master who knows one's business, manipulate them through her own 'skillful means.' At the same time, she, perhaps more than anybody else, is a prisoner in the net of Mara, bound by the world of desire. In a sense, she plays the evil role of temptress. In some corners of the world demons like Mara, King of Hell, are regarded as patrons of gamblers and prostitutes. A courtesan should also be an object of pity caught as she is in the transience of things. But orthodox Buddhism has preferred to emphasize her abjection, moral and physical. Taking of monastic vows, Xue Feng was never a purist. There was no need to raise a fuss about these apparent transgressions for. Despite all of his discourses on the identity of passions and awakening, he remained strangely virginal regarding his relations with others in the realm of the 'red dust.'

According to rumors, Xue Feng was a frequent guest of a courtesan by the nickname of Fair Lady Mu. She was famously known for her knowledge of three excellent recipes of love, for which men came from the farthest corners of the country, trying them on themselves; and upon their return home, they immediately trained their wives and concubines to what they had learned themselves. What could they learn from her? They could hardly love this already aged courtesan for her beauty, even in the days of her youth she wasn't reputed as a beauty. She did not have the talents that other famous courtesans usually have: she did not know how to play good music, or sing sweetly; she didn't understand the subtleties of good manners and secular treatment. However, though she was almost forty years old, her visitors invariably sought to win her favor. Among her visitors were many wealthy landlords and merchants, even some dukes and marquises ranked her above all the other courtesans. Those three unique recipes could be called her personal magic or just ingenuity, but they were extraordinarily useful because she understood every single visitor, even if she hadn't previously met him, in all details. Her first recipe she called 'Lowering the Chamber of Repose for Meeting with Ambassador.' Her second secret posture was called 'Raising the Chamber of Repose for Approaching to Ambassador.' Employing her recipe number three she could reinforce the masculine essence of her visitor so that he did not know fatigue, at all. As is said, Fair Lady Mu understood her men in fine details. All those who had already passed their period of youthful flourishing, she treated as their sacred mother, suggesting to have a good rest, getting relaxation after being so busy with so many heavy duties. Then she treated her client with a special tonic tincture, not so much to excite him, but to spunk him up. At that moment, she started to touch his Jade Stalk slightly. When he began to respond to her tender touches, she mounted him and quietly took his penis into her Chamber of Repose. Upon having made sure that the Tortoise Head was unlikely to slip back, she began to make rotational movements with her buttocks. Such her move she called 'the grain grinding,' and many then, driving at Xue Feng and his occupation, pretended to be in the know where this trick of the trade came from. Anyhow, she called this position so because, according to many clients, they felt at that moment as though they were grinding under the millstones. At that, she was so much insightful and experienced to use precisely that specific move from her rich arsenal, which was needed by her particular client. She began to hop so that the Tortoise Head hovered for a moment in between her Miraculous Gates, like a little mouse in the strong claws of a soaring eagle, never slipping out. Strangely enough, but this combination of rotational movements with hopping and jumping did not tire her clients; on the contrary, they felt an unprecedented surge of energy. It seemed that Lady Mu possessed such a huge reserve of energy that that itself, together with a client's sexual passion, became another source of his great excitement. When the moment came for the act's transformation into what was called 'Turning Clouds into Rain,' this allowed them to immediately go to her third recipe. She took her lower position, gaining, however, the upper hand and keeping the situation under her full control. She had an obvious notion of the importance of her attitude she called to herself ' maximal participation.' What did it mean? As is well-known, when a female takes her position below her movements have to correspond to those of a male. When a client rushed forward, as though pinning her to the bed, she quickly rose her lower part of the body, turning his furious attack into a pleasurable and smooth collision. In another case, she moved away from him in a wavy movement, which she had learned in her classes of internal style of martial arts, Taiji-quan, making him excited from falling into the emptiness even further. At that, he felt as if he was chasing in his dream, helping him to prolong the sweetness of a duel between the Yin and Yang forces. When other her 'sisters' told her that she was spending too much time on each and every visitor, she replied that otherwise, the female caresses would not be different from caresses of a wooden doll with a hole between the legs. That was the reason why she was nicknamed Fair Lady Mu or 'Wooden Fair Lady.'

Her last but not the least method, which allowed her sexual partners to feed each other with their vital substrates in such a way that they did not know fatigue, she worked out and developed, as they said, due to her communication with Daoist priests, including Xue Feng, who provided her with knowledge from the ancient treaties on healthful sex. From those texts, among which "Huang-di Nei Jing" (the Book on Internal Written by the Yellow Emperor) took the top position in the list, it followed that when the Yin and Yang forces reached the Great Extreme (orgasm), too much of their vital substrates (fluids) were wasted for nothing. For that reason, the sexual partners who were devoted to the joy of turning Clouds into Rain were getting tired more and more with every orgasm. Lady Mu's method reduced to making a close circle between the partners, achieving such an effect that every drop of the vital fluids flew from one partner to another without loss of energy. It gave them both enough strength for engaging in the next duel. She had learned how at a crucial moment of turning the Clouds into Rain to capture the Tortoise Head and direct it with utmost precision to 'the life-giving source' of her Upper Chamber. Upon doing that, she forced her man who was entirely in her arms to freeze entirely or move as little as possible. At that, his Yang substrate, ejaculating in a limited portion, met her Yin substrate to flowing together and blending with each other and exchanging with their vital fluids in circulation for their continued revival.

At the core of this recipe, there was a Daoist principle of 'returning the semen to its source,' which allowed prolonging one's lifetime and ultimate pleasure of both partners. Again, according to rumors, this method was introduced to her when she was young, seventeen or so, by a wandering Daoist-poet who never appeared again. In due course, she succeeded to bring this method to such perfection that she had a distinct sense of physical rejuvenation whenever the opposing substrate flows were directed towards each other with maximum precision, providing full effectiveness. And it was quite certain that after overnight in her company, a client woke up with his completely rested body and soul to be full of refreshed physical vigor. When asked about the cause of the miraculous effect of revival, Lady Mu's answer was always the same: she told that a white witch had visited her clients in their sweet dreams.

As a faithful adept of the Daoism, all Xue Feng's aspirations were directed towards the image of Ultimate Earth, the Sacred Feminine, Great Mother of the World, his ultimate ideal, most probably, was the unattainable quintessence of femininity concealed deeply in the masculine nature. At the same time, he wore his shabby robe of the layman; he could be on intimate terms with both nobles and commoners, yet lived impeccably like a religious devotee. To be in harmony with people, he associated with elders, with those of middle age, and with the young, yet always spoke in accord with the Dharma. To demonstrate a capability to gain the upper hand and control sexual intercourse, he used to enter brothels; to establish drunks in correct mindfulness, he dropped in all the taverns. He would even be honored as a eunuch in the imperial harem because he was master of a secret technique of pulling in his genitals to get access to 'the imperial treasury' (harem). Nevertheless, assuming the rumors had some basis in fact, however slight, all inhabitants of the monastery had often wondered where Xue Feng got the money for his spending. Hard cash was in short supply in Xiang-lin. Some of the more cynical monks hinted that the abbot himself subsidized Xue Feng's revels and, what's more, the money was diverted out of the slender reserves the monks set aside to purchase what they couldn't grow or produce themselves. As a youngster, his bosom friend Foundling disbelieved those tales; however, it was Xue Feng who covered the loss the novice brought once from Red Fort. Did the abbot willingly contribute to the delinquency of one of his charges? Unlikely. But later on, Foundling was not so sure. The subtlety and power of the master's mind sliced through conventional wisdom like a plain sailing through the pacified and flat ocean. The only thing Foundling could say with certainty was that whatever the abbot's reason for indulging Xue Feng, if indeed he did indulge him, it must have been calculated to bring a rich return on the investment, spiritually speaking, indeed. Perhaps, it was by this concession that he won the monk's confidence as a healer and skillful exorcist whose voice was miracle-working and who was equally good at brandishing his fly whisk of a Daoist boxer and brush of a poet. The following poetic lines were dedicated to his revealed talents:

"His spirit is rarely bright and clear,
And in appearance, he is full grand.
With his brush, he pierces thru seven writing boards;
In reading scrolls, he apprehends five lines forth.
For sleeping he pillows on the tigress's head;
He sits firmly for long, like ivory in gum.
It seems he has not a single obstacle inside—
Not even a speck of dust spots his mind;
He is cold, like the frost on the ground."

Furthermore, there were whispers that he was transmitted secretly with the abbot's robe and the bowl of Dharma so that he inherited the Patriarchate for his profound insight. As is known, after passing the robe and bowl on to Xue Feng, the abbot told him to leave the monastery for dwelling in a cave and practicing the Dharma singly to avoid frictions among his adherents in the temple.

As a famous creed of Xiang-lin monastery insisted, "A day without work is a day without food," the monks supported themselves in part by working in fields, chopping up firewood in the mountains, and cleaning inside the monastery's gates. In fact, this aspect of doing daily work between the sessions, preaches, and meditations was not something that Abbot Zhao Zhou created. Xue Feng himself lived this practice. Before becoming a monk, with his father and brothers, he chopped firewood for a living and worked in the field. Upon arrival at the monastery, he was first sent by the abbot not to the meditation hall, but to the granary to grind rice. While working in the storehouse for years, he cultivated his mind, teaching himself to maintain a stable and concentrated state of awareness. In doing so, he let go of the ups and downs of emotions and moods. Achieving this clear awareness was crucial because only in this mental state would he has a chance to become a sagely minded person. Of course, everyone who practices Samadhi, a state of intense concentration achieved through meditation, in intercourse, it is regarded as the final stage, at which a union with the divine is reached, needs correct guiding views. Even before meeting the abbot of Xiang-lin, the monk had experienced initial enlightenment, which occurred when he overheard someone reciting a verse from the Mahaparinirvana Sutra. From his experience in attaining enlightenment, he understood attachment and detachment, as well as the difference between 'self' and 'no-self,' between 'I' and others.' These understandings became his guiding views in all fields of his activity.

One day someone asked him, "For so many years you are an ordinary rice grinder, brother. Would you consider this job to be below you?"

Xue Feng replied, "If in your mind you are clearly aware of what is happening around you or with you, then it doesn't matter what others perceive or believe. You may appear to be foolish or jerked to others, but in your mind, you know you are not..."

Xue Feng believed that cultivating such a personality could also be transformative for others because people would eventually realize that you were not a fool and that in fact, you were accepting them. Such behavior gives others permission to be more honest and less pretentious. However, once you engage in the practice, you should put aside considerations of benefit. All you have to do is practicing with effort and consistency. If you have ideas of gaining or getting rid of something, you thus just generate more vexations. Yes, the ultimate purpose of Samadhi is to reach the final state of enlightenment, but though there are some talks about a kind of sudden awareness, the real progress is always to be gradual and involves stages.

It came to be that, for him, the sexual aspect of life was partly a ritual partly a discipline subordinated to the rules and regulations formulated by the ancients who considered sex as an instrument of achieving realization. He saw in this not merely a romantic and joyful moment of returning to the animal innocence and natural freedom lost by people a long time ago, but a particular kind of practice at setting the opposite Yin and Yang substances into the state of harmony. Both entities nourish each other with their vital elements to support the universal nature of the sexual act. For him, the ultimate purpose was to become worthy of it through perfect mastering sexual techniques. He always wore his rough robe of a layman and had his hair cut up to his eyebrows. His everyday duties were to supply the monastery kitchen with grain from the marketplace and to grind rice. By night he composed his mantras and chants with a cadence bolting in his cell. He never wrote down his miraculous vocal formulas, by which (but it was not the point of his compositions) he could help others, as the magic of his vocalization lied in harmonized vibrations he produced internally, from within, verbally, but not through his writing brush, by which he also wielded skillfully. He was an accomplished man in his own way. For him, at the time healing by incantation really was a form of meditation though. (It has to be mentioned here that composition of the graph 'zhou,' meaning 'invocation of the spirits,' shows two mouths on top and altar underneath them, strongly suggesting the participation of two individuals: one presumably a medium engaged in the task of invoking the spirits of a patient.) Isn't anything to which a man gives himself with the whole force of his being brings him complete satisfaction? Doesn't he makes himself as a star of its constellation and relying on its gravity as a form of discipline to compel him toward that vigorous, last orbit of perfection -- a form of meditative concentration? Meditation is what leads to awareness or Dharma in one of the Buddha's countless incarnations, also known as 'Achieving Perfection.'

From one's birth, a human being doesn't need to learn two things: one is breathing, and another is eating -- all the rest is the subject of learning. This means getting some knowledge to put it then correctly into practice; otherwise, how can one know whether he or she is a well-versed person especially in one's exotic, if not to say 'esoteric' skills. Many stories were told of battles, in which the black magic of one master had caused the illness or even death of a rival master with less powerful magic. And the monk spewed them forth like an inexhaustible fountain.

The expertise of an esoteric healer was judged by several criteria; the first one being his external performance of rite of curing. Learning to sing well, to perform the various ritual steps and Mudras, or hand symbols, memorize several hundred ceremonial texts, and many accompanying formulas was, of course, the primary goal of the young disciple in attaching himself to a famous master. Most of the Tian-tai sect adepts never went beyond this stage only because the ability to perform the standard repertoire of rite of curing would enable a Buddhist monk or a Daoist priest to attract a large enough, following among the pious faithful to earn an excellent livelihood. If he could write a stylish talisman to cure illness, exorcise evil spirits with ox-horn trumpet, perform ritual dances and acrobatic tumbling, winning a reputation for being a powerful magician, the demands for his services would be almost endless. Most disciples, therefore, studied with a master just long enough to learn the external rituals and enough of the esoteric doctrines to lend credence to their ritual performance. The second criterion for judging a healer, which determines his rank at ordination, was his knowledge of the esoteric secrets of the worship. This included the ability to perform the meditations and breath control techniques of internal alchemy (nei-dan) and to recite the standard orthodox lists of spirits, their names, and the mantric summons found in the Buddhist sutras and Daoist scriptures on alchemy.

To accelerate the progress of curing, some exotic medicine generally known as the Golden Elixir Pill, were often to be taken. For there were dangers associated with its practice; poisoning, primarily. Attempting to transform the corruptible parts of their natures, some monks (those of a more literal turn of mind) resorted to the direct ingestion of mercury and lead, small quantities at first, but gradually building up the dosage as the body's tolerance increased -- an alchemical mithridatism. As one imagines, this had a disastrous effect on the liver, and, in fact, generally proved fatal. Nevertheless, its adherents (the survivors) pointed with a certain satisfaction to the undeniable success of their technique in preserving the body in the grave. But there were dangers of another order. One monk who, through some carelessness or misuse of the methods, lost his soul, which flew out from between the ribs of his body like a songbird from an opened cage. For two days he could hear it singing in a treetop near his window. Then it disappeared into the blackness of the forest, and he wasted away and died of sorrow. Others that inhabitants of the monastery heard of were confined in the bodies of animals for their crimes. Some fell headlong into hell, but some of them relished these stories.

In the Daoist alchemy, it is the blood, and various sorts of fluids that interchange and produce what is called 'the Tiger energy.' It comes into existence in the trigram Li (Fire) and gets control over the inner essence nourished by the five Zang-organs. Once reaching the heart, this sort of feminine energy becomes transformed there. Then it flows around the Palace of Kidneys to produce the jing-substance and qi-essence respectively. This process is called 'the vermilion mercury's production.' One who spontaneously assumes the Tiger posture is unconsciously regulating the energy of the lungs (correlated with Metal, Heaven, air) supported by the kidneys (Water, clouds). There is an ancient saying which goes like this: "Dragons dwell in waters, while tigers hide deep in the mountains." (This is because the Tiger is a devotee of fresh air at the production of the pure essence). And it is essential for the advanced practitioner of ancient principles of sexology 'to fetch water from the mountain peaks' (which is the Baihui acupoint of the upper dan-tian) but "fire from the bottom of the sea" (the Huiyin acupoint of the lower dan-tian). All this was used to determine the procedure of 'moving backward' the male's semen and transforming it into 'the holy embryo' upon its entering into the middle dan-tian, the elixir field, right in the lower part of the belly. Whenever the tiger descends from the mountains, there is a threat to people. When the Tiger ascends the mountains, there is a threat to the Dragon designated by the image of clouds. The ultimate task of the Tiger (symbol of air, wind) is to transform the clouds into rain (sexual act), the Yin-Yang's interaction; hence an old expression "the play of wind and clouds," which is a euphemism for sexual intercourse.

The term 'tong-lei' or 'like attracts like' or 'harmonic resonance,' as it is termed in the Book of Circular Changes, supposes that the nature of clouds is to follow the power of dragons, but that of winds is to follow the power of tigers; thus everything follows its kind. Dragon (Yang) gives birth to the myriad things while tiger (Yin) brings them to their completion. The dragon's cradle is made of the intangible clouds while that of the tiger is associated with the 'tangible' mountains. What does the dragon's spiral motion mean? According to Lao-zi, "When wanting a thing to be contracted, first be sure to expand it; when wanting a thing to be weakened, first be sure to strengthen it" (Verse 36). Therefore, when wanting to move forward, a dragon first takes a move backward; when wanting to move leftward, it first moves rightward to gain a foothold in the center. As another saying goes, "Give me somewhere to stand, and I will move the earth." Once you take the central place using your proper spiral movement, you gain the upper hand and become a master of the situation. Not without reason, one of the emblems which designate the Center is the Yellow (terrestrial or earthly) Dragon.

The Fire-Dragon is situated in the trigram Kan (Water) and is the Root of the Life-Mandate. It is the mother of one's spirit. (When Master Zhang, the legendary founder of Tai-ji Quan, went to practice in the Zhongnan Mountains he met there with a Daoist by the name Huo Long or Fire Dragon who taught him 'to fetch water from the peak (which is Niwan center, or the upper dan-tian) down to the middle elixir field, acupoint Qi-hai.) As for the lower and the middle dan-tians (the elixir fields), the opening of the former and closing of the latter increase the Yin energy dramatically, producing the reservoir of jing-substance. Thus all and everything that is beneath the line of waist corresponds to the Yin energy (feminine) that gathers not only in the kidneys but in all five Zang-organs corresponded to Yin. For this reason, the Classics says, "Yin is collected in the form of Jing-substance (semen) and has a tendency to rise up to its extreme. Yang is protected from any sort of influences of the outer world and make one firm and solid in one's middle dan-tian." Once Yin reaches its extremity on top of the head, Yang starts to grow up, going down to the lower part of the belly. When Yang reaches its extreme point, Yin begins to consolidate in the lower dan-tian (Huiyin). Once the Yin-Yang relationships are harmonized in a proper ratio, the tendons and energetic channels become unified into one, the bones and marrow possess firmness and solidity, qi-fluids and blood follow each other in an adequately fast circulation.

Chapter 4: A Man Making

Xue Feng's natural talent for the curing art had landed him a job as a wandering healer in the neighboring villages and towns, combining with his monastery duty as a rice supplier. His healing method involved a certain amount of physical yoga, called 'qi-gong,' quite mature since this tradition was cultivated by Daoists from time immemorial and enlarged with what Bodhidharma, the twenty-eighth Buddhist patriarch and the first patriarch of Zen Buddhism, brought to China in the first decades of the sixth century. It was also recommended that one who meditated should repeatedly recite one of the short prayer formulas that contained the whole meaning and purpose of existence. The basic tenet behind such therapy was that everything in the universe was in a constant state of vibration. If true, the cells of the human body constantly vibrated, meaning that vocal vibration could relax or agitate, heal or harm. When men have an unbalanced emotional or mental attitude, a misalignment of the subtle bodies with the physical body can occur. When this happens, the body needs help to restore itself to its original vibration. When one focuses sound vibration to a problem area, balance to that area can be temporarily restored. When there is a balance, the body is more effective in eliminating toxins and negativities. Therefore, the sound is considered the direct link between humanity and the divine -- it is the contributing factor to the real states of health and consciousness achieved through subconsciousness. The most important healing principle of vocalization is the ability of vibration to reach out through vibrational waves to set off a similar vibration in another body. It triggered a response of similar frequency. In fact, every cell in the body is a sound resonator and can sound outside itself. By learning to direct and control the voice or applying tones and forms of incantation, sound healing could stimulate within the mind and body. In fact, the voice belongs to the body, but it is the instrument of the spiritual self. Voice releases power and the power is released in the direction of mind (thought), sending the energy to an appropriate area of the body. As an old saying goes, "All energy follows thought." It is the quick intake or grasp of energy that carries an image or thought to the subconscious. All aspects of toning are related to breath. Breath is life. When a practitioner becomes aware of his breathing patterns, he has greater control over himself. As one becomes more balanced with toning, one's breathing becomes more fluid, healthy, and harmonious. From of old the repertoire of symbolical vocalization, a combination of breath and sound had a spiritual significance, which was applied similarly to Heaven, Earth, and Man. It sought to unite men and spirits into a single state in emulation of the perfect harmony of Yin and Yang, or of Heaven and Earth, as well as the cavities of rock-formations could also symbolize stars, which in turn represented lamps of dhyana, wisdom. Harmony, a particular combination of two or more tones in a spell, affected subtle and spiritual energies. By finding the right blend of sounds and rhythms and their harmonies, the healer could trigger a powerful resonance that corrected and eliminated imbalances.

But let's get closer to our theme. Since the human body is a highly organized energy system, it can be altered, strengthened and balanced through the use of hand touching. It creates the mystic, as well as the artistic framework to blend the feminine with masculine at the physical level in the exact complementary manner of the miraculous interaction of Yin and Yang. Thus intercourse becomes real acting in this art; a mystic interaction of Yin-Yang, skillfully represented by the opposing elements in real life through the obscurity of a destiny of both partners, the conditions under which they come to be together. The pauses between intercourse, the momentary stillness between orgasms, or the enclosed emptiness in blending composition, all became an inseparable part of the whole. Since the feminine Yin or the masculine Yang alone could not form a complete interlocking symbol of two, representing the Taiji motif called 'Ultimate Extremity' (two fish-like halves in the Daoist symbol of Yin and Yang necessarily complementing each other), it means that once a thing reaches its extreme point of transformation, it turns into its own opposition.

As it is stated in "Huang-di Nei Jing" (the Book on Internal Written by the Yellow Emperor), there are two sorts of numbers regarding the sexes: 7 and 8, which, according to the Book of Circular Changes (Zhou Yi) correlate with young Yang and young Yin (unchangeable Yang and unchangeable Yin) respectively. Thus the fundamental dualistic outlook, with the differentiation of the Yin (female) and Yang (male) principles, went back to the "Zhou Yi" which was later formulated by Confucius. But let's first talk about the odd number 7 (7x7=49), which, however, characterizes the sexual life of women. By the age of seven, a female has her teeth wholly established; her hair grows rather long, and some moisture appears in the vagina. At the age of a double seven (14), she has a period and thus becomes fertile. At the age of three times seven (21), her body fully ripens, her limbs are filled up with energy, her hair reaches full length, and the last of her teeth appears. If during coition her pulse is steady and even, her children will be healthy. At the age of four times seven (28), her muscles and bones are healthy, she gives birth to children comfortably, and her Solar Valley, as never before, is full of light. When she reaches the age of five times seven (35), her pulse is no longer so intense, her face begins to become wrinkled, and her hair loses its brilliance. At the age of six times seven (42), her pulse in the three regions (the chest, abdomen, and vagina) weakens, the face is completely covered with wrinkles, and the hair begins to turn gray. When she reaches the age of seven times seven (49), the monthlies stop, the pulse no longer appears in the vessel, and the Yang (masculine) power is no more so joyfully welcome at the Jade Gate as it was before.

As it has been mentioned earlier, everything in life is formed of vibes. This is a result of the movement of every particle of every substance. Vibration exists in objects, animals, humans, and atmosphere. The vibrational frequencies of animate life are more active and produce fluids. If the human hearing were to possess the necessary sensitivity to perceive all ranges of frequencies, people would be able to hear the music of flowers and grass, mountains and valleys, the singing of the sky and stars and symphony of their own bodies. All organs, tissues, and systems of the body have similar vibrating bits. A saying goes, "The Buddha's light illuminates everywhere and rectifies all abnormalities." This means that cultivators of good laws carry immense energy in themselves. Wherever they pass by, they can correct any abnormal condition within the area that is covered by their power. Similarly, when partners of the same fluids meet together, their coition is like a tight ball of string marked out on the guide-posts to the sacred mountain peak becomes a magic line on the chart to find the spiritual harmonization. At another level, such a union reminds the sacramental word 'aum.' It has resounded in India down through the ages should be pronounced as a three-syllabic word, 'a-u-m,' in such a way that the vowel sounded imperceptibly merge into one another. An impressive articulation of the monistic view of the world meant: a—the point of departure; u—the differentiation, and m—the reunion. Inaccurate pronunciation is of grave concern as it will affect the effect of mantras.

But let's return to our numbers. The even number 8, however, correlates with the masculine code of men's sexual life till the age of 64 (8x8=64). At the age of eight, a boy's teeth begin to change and establish, the hair becomes thicker, and the testicles secrete the first drop of 'the liquid pearl.' At the age of double eight (16) his Yang outflow becomes plentiful and speaks of maturity; he is ready now to connect with his Yin partner in achieving peace and harmony. At the age of three times eight (24), his muscles are hard, the bones are strong, the outflow from his testicles is strong and frequent, and his last teeth sprout up. At the age of four times eight (32), he reaches the peak of manhood; his body is strong, and fire is constantly burning within. At the age of five times eight (40), the testes produce less sperm, the hair begins to fall out, and the teeth start to be damaged. When he turns six times eight (48), the strength of Yang is much reduced, wrinkles appear on his face and gray hair on the head. When he reaches the age of seven times eight (56), he ceases to be the source of the vital substance, diseases attack him like a swarm of wasps, his strength is coming to an end, and his five internal organs start to dry up. To prevent fast development of this process till the age of eight times eight (64) some energetic exercises called 'qi-gong' should be put into practice on a regular basis, the main point of which is to open up the central miraculous energy channel, or meridian, called 'ren-mai' at the front and 'du-mai' at the back of one's body to allow ф proper flow of qi-energy. When one increases the flow of energy through the central pulse, then he also protects his condition of quick-wittedness. Many of the works that set forth the advice and instructions of the legendary Yellow Emperor on the technique of sex were, in fact, the work of the Tian-tai patriarchs and masters. They believed that living beings had truly great potential and that if they could use wisdom to mobilize their potential, they could transform their vital forces and help themselves constantly to move toward a more energetic state of practice, including sex. The energy state of sexual practice was one in which practitioners were diligent but did not worry about how long it took them to accomplish attainment. Therefore, adepts of Tian-tai did not worry about whether they would have genuine attainment in their lifetimes. All they did was to strive constantly to be energetic and diligent. Then they moved steadily forward. One in meditation, who could maintain this kind of energetic diligence, was considered a strong adherent on the natural path. An environment, no matter how bad that was, and no matter how deep the suffering was, could not enslave a healthy practitioner who would fearlessly strive to make progress. This was undoubtedly the most important and the most widely used method in tantric yoga practicing. Its popularity was due first to the fact that it was an effective method, and also it was completely devoid of loose associations and effects. The breathing exercises were believed to accelerate the cleansing and purification, which was so essential to becoming more ethereal and spiritual. By developing the embryonic or cosmic breath, men laid hold on the spiritual-physical substance, which, more than anything else built up the energetic body as a tool for achieving the Yin-Yang harmony. An adept started to become a sagely minded individual. The graph for this dignity, which was so strongly craved among hermits, was composed of two main elements: a crystal, known as 'Clay Pill,' and four hands around it (two of a master above and two of a disciple below) to express the idea of purification and self-cultivation under directions of one's spiritual guide. Later on, another two elements, a man, and a mountain were added to shield the primordial concept. It was especially by becoming a hermit living in the mountains or woods that this process of purification can take place; but not exclusively so, for the cells of monasteries and airy pavilions built on the banks of rivers and by the seashore were also suitable for this highest idea. The main thing was that the air should be clear and that there was stillness. To begin with, the breath strokes should be deep and quiet, and so hushed and noiseless that if a small feather was placed on the upper lip, no movement was noticed. Definite rules were given as to when the deep breathing in and out was to take place, and when breathing was to be reduced to a minimum. Every time a practitioner entered in copulation, he should close his mouth and calm his breathing so that the energy converted into saliva and then returned to dan-tian, the middle elixir field in the lower part of the belly. He should keep the sperm inside and not allow it to spew out. To achieve this, he had to let his exhalation get out through the nose. Otherwise, the clean energy would easily slip out. And if somehow the energy got into the bladder, that could give rise to many diseases.

To reach the highest purpose of attainment in copulation that stood for in Samadhi as well, the practitioner should follow a unique sequence of training incorporating these skills, according to which he could prevent illness by facilitating the unobstructed circulation of the vital energy and the blood. The forces and nature of invisible energy currents, also known as 'the dragon's veins.' They were determined not only by mountains and hills that matched with the Yang power, and valleys and watercourses corresponded to the Yin, but also by the movements of the heavenly bodies (stars, planets, constellations) from hour to hour, watch to watch and day to day all around the year. Thus, during intercourse made in springtime, the head should be directed to the east, in summer to the south, in autumn to the west, and in winter to the north to support the most favorable conditions for copulation. The odd dates, especially in the morning, are convenient; the even dates, and mostly in the middle of the day, can be harmful.

There is a more profound meaning here. When the sex practitioner listens to the sounds uttered by a woman, he interprets them according to his nature. When he observes the forms of her pose, he likewise creates a full image of her sexual abilities. But such ideas that he has are not the actual reality. The real nature of her sounds he doesn't hear due to his oppositely disposed of nature, and the exact form of her postures he is unable to perceive appropriately. In that, he doesn't grasp reality, when one looks at things he is as blind; when one hears things he is as deaf. Understanding the illusory nature of experience, the practitioner should not get disturbed by whatever arises. The lines in the Lao-zi (Verse 40) read like this:

"To grasp the way of great Dao is like to be in the dark;
To advance in the way of great Dao is like to move backward;
To sail smoothly in the way of great Dao is like to ride out the gale."

After years of sex diligent practicing, the practitioner reaches a state of 'forgetfulness,' a country in which he thinks and does not think at the same time, he copulates and at the same time does not copulate. If the practitioner reaches such level of sexual development, he then becomes a master of the vital substance, dwelling in an intense state of Samadhi, the divine wisdom; his or her body becomes a small universe in itself -- the energy inside the body circulates, supports, and nourishes itself.

The monks of Tian-tai monasteries had some other remarkable methods to accelerate respiration and circulation of the blood. These rules were strictly observed, according to which the breath through the nose belonged to the lungs, while the inspiration of the mouth belonged to the spleen, the central organ of control all the other organs. All these regulations were necessary to learn through continuous contemplation, as the monasteries offered some advanced courses for high-ranking officials in retreat and some devoted pilgrims. So, some rules were mandatory for observing correctly. Before starting a love battle, it was necessary to sit in a lotus-pose for meditation, concentrating the spirit and, streamlining the energy flow along the central energy channels 'ren-mai' and 'du-mai,' allowing a free flow of qi-energy. The practitioner should inhale clean air through the nose and exhale foul breath through the mouth; then he clicks several times with his teeth and collect saliva in the mouth; he makes some physical stretches and then, without any haste, gets down to sexual intercourse. As soon as the sexual desire is wakened up in a female, the male should embrace her, clinging to her tongue and drinking the saliva accumulated in her mouth, absorbing her feminine energy concentrated in the saliva. Then, without losing his state of calm, he slowly enters his magic tool into her vagina to produce his pushes in such a way that nine shallow dippings are followed by one deep; two quick jerks he makes after eight slow. Having done such movements up to one hundred times, he has to swallow the saliva in the manner indicated earlier to repeat the whole process for another hundred times, swallowing the saliva as described above. Upon doing through this procedure several times, he reaches the state of inexplicable bliss and happiness. The ultimate task is to keep the sperm inside his body, not ejaculating it out by all means. For this, he takes his tool out of her vagina, making a deep inhalation. If he does not interrupt coition to catch his breath, he simply has to press on the channel of the semen flow in the crotch (on the spot right behind the testicles) with three fingers put together to prevent ejaculation. In such a case, his semen will not be lost, and the Jade Pillar will preserve its hardness and strength in the further battles. To get the feminine energy, he has to be a true partner and wait till the passion inflames within her, and her Magic Gates will be opened and moisturized with her juices all over inside. Letting her be slightly in motion, the male remains at rest without entering into her vagina deeply, but, clinging to her lips, man soaks up the divine moisture which is accumulated under her tongue. Thus, his masculine energy grows stronger in a natural way, by itself, and he gets the true fit of energy. Having three or four gulps, he ultimately takes his magic tool out of the pussy. Upon finishing the act, it's not good for him to fall asleep immediately. He needs to sit down and take a lotus-pose for meditation, while swallowing the saliva more than thirty times; and then, using the method called 'the upstream moving along the Yellow River,' he lets the energy spread throughout the entire body, employing the central energy channels 'ren-mai' and 'du-mai.' Then a pleasant sleep will be provided for him without delay. Wishing to reactivate the love battle again, he should start acting over again as it was described earlier.

In a case a female loses her seed, he needs to stop the coition and let her regenerate her energy, clinging to her lips in deep kisses up to five times; otherwise, if not to revive her strength, she can fall ill in the aftermath. He who does not follow these instructions can lose his spiritual power in the period from ten to fifteen days when his face becomes covered with boils. This fact has already been verified; so, everyone is warned to be careful of that.

According to this technique, the ancients not only used the inner energy circulation method within themselves, but could even listen and see the state of the internal energy in their partners: when it rose or lowered, moved to the front or back, shifted left or right, up or down, affecting both outside and inside of the body. This kind of supreme technique was never achieved until after many years of good practicing, in which some specific sounds were incorporated into sexual intercourse also known as 'the battle of Yin and Yang.' These sounds were kept secret for long, appearing only in old poetic lines. Some of them read like this:

"Hold your 'lower elixir field' (dan-tian)
While practicing the internal 'gong-fu';
'Heng' and 'Haah' – two syllables,
Which have miraculous power in sex.
When both lovers are in motion,
They tend to be separated under the vigor
Of 'heng,' but when they come to be at rest,
They're combined under cover of 'haah.'
In other words, we're talking about 'closing.'
And 'opening' respectively. Rend and stretch,
Let your true nature take its course freely;
Respond slowly but follow quickly
After your mate's bodily movement.
Thus you come to know every tiny detail
About the secrets of sexual intercourse
From within the soul, your released good Self."

The two sounds 'heng' and 'haah' were produced when inhaling and exhaling during copulation. Good partners, when they make love, produce these two sounds naturally for three reasons. Firstly, it makes internal energy smooth and comfortable; so, the internal organs cannot get hurt by the pressure. Secondly, internal power can be released completely; none of it remained inside the circle created between the partners. Thirdly, it sometimes can shock a partner. If the partner experiences fear, his or her mind gets lost and, therefore, becomes unable to control a situation and oneself; so, another one has a chance to correct the condition of 'two bodies as one' through building up the 'heng-haah' balance. In other words, it can be used for breaking up energetic stagnations and muscular stiffness. It requires to project the sound vibration through the partner's ears to his/her mind and then deeper into his/her cells and tissues. When a resonated sound penetrates the partner's body, it causes massive chaotic vibrations that disrupt the body's normal energetic flow. This energetic disruption, however, softens and liquefies the partner's stagnant qi-energy and this is the primary reason why sexual intercourse provides a healing therapy effect. According to such an attitude, once the lovers cease to regard copulation as an interaction, the contact between them becomes a dialogue at the level of qi-energy, sometimes beyond any physical contacts. Hence, they have to work purely from within, waiving their own intentions but following the energy of each other. Only then intercourse becomes an immediate attempt at an experience, in which the mind plays no part and does not try to explain it. When one of the partners utters the sound 'haah,' another one starts to follow him/her as if on command, inhaling the energy and filling in the circle between the two. The sound 'heng' is usually produced when one of them 'grabs' his/her partner's inner energy with exhaling it and washing away the contaminated energy as a result of produced physical or mental stiffness. This has to be cultivated a lot. It needs to be taught verbally and secretly, from a mouth to ears, in order 'to open then the crimson door and see the azure sky.'

The origin of these sound-exercises is lost in the mists of ages but has been claimed to go back as far as the sixth century BCE. The 'heng' and 'haah,' exhaling the old and inhaling the fresh, imitate the image of a bear climbing up on the tall tree and the bird calling for a responded mate. These sounds are for long life and only that. This is what the sages of old exercised, and who nourished their bodies, and who studied the secrets of longevity endowed on them by immortals.

Before the common era, seekers after longevity used a variety of approaches, including incantations and sacrifices to the spirits, as well as drugs (pills of immortality) and breathing exercises to prolong their lives. But afterward, men cast off their dependence on the spirit world and relied more and more on their own efforts, resulting in an expansion of knowledge about drugs and therapeutic exercises. Practitioners termed these techniques 'nourishing of qi-energy,' and the non-medicinal methods included both breathing control and sexual activities.

By tradition, there were six ways of entering a male tool and nine basic love postures that beared a very unusual for hearing allegorical names, such as " the dragon's tumblings" or "the monkey grasp" or "the turtle's leaps" or " fish touching with scales" or "two cranes twisting with necks," and so forth. All those postures denote various forms of energy and its articulations evidenced by the very nature of their names, indicating a certain quality of the action. Such stylized or, it's better to say, the typical forms of human practice, make the legacy of Daoist tradition. From there a matrix of sexual culture was formed, ascending to the pure and immaterial structure of the Great Void of Being. As a supplement to those love movements, the postures were added with some additional elements for healing many various ailments.

During intercourse, a man should absorb the energy of his partner from the mouth, nipples, and vagina. Partners have to change the rhythm and nature of their movements that require them a creative and ever fresh perception of life, suggesting an extraordinary sensitivity and clarity of consciousness, nourished by the peace of mind and contentment of soul. Such coition supposes a full reproduction of energy, ever-renewing reality of the great Dao, which boils to a thousand changes, even further, ten thousand transformations. Of course, in this unstoppable flow of life, there are so many patterns and musical orders that they can be perceived only in a natural way. The changing of sexual postures and movements of partners reproduces transformations of the eight trigrams, the trajectory of the heavenly bodies, the various cycles of the internal alchemy cultivated by the Daoists. Literally, copulations between a man and a woman are treated as the prototype of the universe. That is the course of upbringing and self-improvement caused in the human personality, in society, and in the world. That is a real workshop of morality, a masterclass of mystical enlightenment, a projecting of the physiological act into the realm of socio-cosmological and mystical symbolism that make the sexual activity, among many others, a pure game with its strict formularies. On the other hand, there cannot be universal rules where your action becomes your creativity. What's more, the parallelism between sexual intercourse and the Dao allowed, under certain conditions, to abandon physical intimacy completely. In some cases, there were some concrete indications that partners who were able to correctly tune in to the music of the ways of Dao could exchange vital essences and create intercourse even from a faraway distance.

This is quite a complicated stuff for intellectual perception but, when one comes to an understanding of the main principles of making love, it is only a matter of a touch or a glance to know what is going on with the partner. Combine this with mental training to supplement physical practicing, and the partners get a pretty good design for improving their sexual health using their mutually supported abilities united into one. Besides, there were another four magic words in Xue Feng's repertoire which he used in his sexual practice. The word 'spread' pronounced in flat upper tone was used to circulate the energy within him and his partner. He spread it then upon his strength so that his partner couldn't move freely. The word 'cover' uttered with entering tone was used to cover the point of the partner's orgasm. The word 'swallow' with its upper sound he used to receive back and transform his masculine power completely. The word 'confront,' with its entering tone, was used to match his approach to that of the partner's precisely. These four words seemed to be formless and soundless. Only those who were able to understand the strength and achieve the most exceptional level of energetic regulations could know the meaning of the energy circulation along the circle created between the partners. Only those who cultivated their qi-energy and nourished it correctly, so that it spread to all the bodily parts evenly and entirely, could respond to the soundlessness of those four verbal formulas at the level of pure spirit.

The ritual of tantric sex was esoteric; it was not meant to be directly understood and witnessed by all the faithful. The interplay of Yin and Yang elements was represented and celebrated as a sexual union. Some scholars believed that the tantric schools, which later were absorbed into Zen Buddhism, evolved first as the Daoist outlet. The esoteric meaning of Tian-tai's rituals and magic was concealed from all but initiated; only after many years of training and a gradual introduction to religious secrets was a disciple deemed worthy of elevation to the rank of master and full knowledge of the esoteric meanings of the tantric ritual of sexual intercourse. For this reason, the aspirant disciple tried to join the entourage of a famously known master, so he could learn the formulas for the ritual intercourse and gradually gain access to the hidden aspects of tantric sex. A more fantastic scene than the preparation for the ritual could hardly be imagined. At nighttime, a whole crowd of monks in wide robes, beneath the dim light of the round lanterns, were racing around at high speed in the monastery courtyard with dust whirling about them to clean their breath and bring accumulated energy to the sacred Oneness. After such rituals, the deeply impressed by them a monk-poet completed the following poetic lines:

"We view the deep, so somber and dangerous,
The valley where the Dragon is softly humming its song,
The gloomy ravines where the Tiger patiently
Waits for its prey with roaring and growling.
Behold, here is at once man's most precious possession,
And passion's flower-bed, a lair for the beasts.
Just here is the place where life's primitive forces,
The Yang and the Yin, unfold themselves.
Here is the place where the chief of the underworld, too."

The deep, the valley the flower-bed, the ravines and the beast lair are all figurative names for the lower dan-tian in the crotch, the play-ground of sexual passion. The Dragon is the sexual urge of the male, and the Tiger is that of the female. This practice was related to alchemy and attempted the compounding of the Golden Elixir Pill, the fusion of Yin and Yang, attained through a regimen of rigorous, highly formalized sexual intercourse, undertaken at certain times and seasons following astrological configurations and the oracle advice.

The methods of sexual activity were usually kept by Xue Feng quite secretly, and he did not reveal his recipes and techniques willingly. Moreover, he had in his repertory the knowledge of herbs and other sorts of medicine, and how to use them to stimulate his partner's sexual activity. These medications were also taken by him internally to strengthen his body, improve the blood circulation, break up clots, stop internal bleeding, and heal the musculature of injury. As usual, those medications came in the form of decoctions, powders, pills, and wines. Some medicated wines could often be used both internally and externally. The use of internal medications often required a clear understanding of the internal condition. The so-called secret formulas were often tailored for a specific individual to suit his or her body make-up. So, no secret recipes were presented there because of this consideration. From the beginning, all seemed to be empty and dissolute, but because the thirst for life still persisted, and because the consequences of the partner's actions couldn't be erased, both created for themselves new forms of existence where the wheel of births and deaths, happiness and ill fortune run their course.

Here I should explain Xue Feng's attitude toward sex in general. Like most of Daoists, he considered sex not in connection with procreation or as the receipt of sexual gratification, but as the precept of maintaining a healthy state of the body and mind. A thousand year question and dispute between Daoists and Buddhists whether to deprive themselves of sexual intimacy or not, for Xue Feng, was definitely affirmative. Daoists believed that a man was symbolized the Yang or masculine power while a woman the Yin or feminine, and their union allowed them to benefit from each other and prolong lifetime. According to this viewpoint, during sexual intercourse, a man and a woman mutually reinforce each other. A man who is able to repeat this a dozen times without ejaculation won't be ill and will live a long healthy life. On the contrary, the Orthodox Buddhists considered that sexual proximity of men and women must be limited for procreation only.

Sexual intercourse provides an example of the individual becoming one with all. Two individuals are physically interacting, each taking both a passive and an active role. Through this interaction, one experiences a sense of abandonment or chaos (correlated to the second stage). This feeling takes over the body as a whole in a manner that the rhythm and pulses which were harmonized in the preliminary stage now become like a stream of music flowing through the whole being. Then, amidst this experience, there is a feeling of upheaval or orgasm, and the one is born (the third stage). At this point, the individuals have shifted from two separate entities to one being (a holy embryo). Now the diagram is completed.

As a person who had achieved enlightenment, Xue Feng believed that everything under the heavens was well harmonized between the Yin and Yang opposed forces. However, the most beautiful thing among the others was a man who differed from all living things with the unique nature of sexual desire, which occupied not the last place in achieving harmony between Heaven and Earth. Passion for procreation is the physiological instinct of man in the process of his evolution from birth to death. His sexual and reproductive energy depends on the vital abilities of the kidneys, which is subordinated to a life cycle. The fact that the essential power of the main ten internal organs is concentrated in the kidneys leads to understanding that the state of their life force affects the overall activity of man and is a decisive factor in the state of health and aging of the human beings. If a person follows the laws of Nature and understands them, he remains to be the source of Vital Substance, knowing a full sexual satisfaction until the dying day; otherwise, his vital substance will be depleted long before his untimely end.

Xue Feng considered all physical and mental desires in addition to all emotional problems originated with the vital substance imbalance at all three levels of elixir fields (dan-tian) within the human energy microstructure. These imbalances and impurities manifested within the third dimension as physical, emotional or mental challenges to experience and learn from within the experiential path of life. He advised men to restrain ejaculation until female approached the moment of orgasm. When a woman is ahead of a man, he has to move easier and produce the lighter jerks, as though playing on lute strings. When a man is ahead of a woman, he has to water his lips with the tongue, breathe through the swollen nostrils, and raise his head up, thus straining his shoulders. Having mastering such a trick, he can be sure that his seminal fluids will not be ejected more than two or three times during a dozen amorous engagements. For a man who was preoccupied with something and too worried, he recommended a rapid penetration, which in such a case has certain advantages. This way, a man gets rid of a hundred worries and cares at once, instead of forgetting about them slowly. At that, he should immediately reach the Upper Abode, moving on the way there to the left and to the right and varying the movements quickly. This will make a woman confused and lost in her own sensations, while he gains the upper hand and full control over the situation rapidly. However, it's not enough to be the master of a case and win the upper hand. The retreat should be taken immediately after the coming, and before the Jade Peak falls off. To leave the battlefield in a miserable and wilted state indicates that the fighting spirit of Yin (feminine) has overcome the morale of Yang (masculine). The practice shows that a twenty years old young man can ejaculate once a day. If he is thirty, he can do it once in eight days; if forty -- once per every sixteen days. At fifty, he can ejaculate once per every twenty-one days; at sixty, it is the best to exclude ejaculation, at all; but if his body still has enough strength, then he can ejaculate once per month. There are some whose breathing and inner strength support each other and, therefore, they are full of energy. Such people cannot abstain from sex for long, and if they do not ejaculate, they have chirps and abscesses on the face and other parts of the body. If a man of sixty and more does not have a contact with a woman for a long time, his thoughts then calm down, and he can exclude ejaculation at all. In a sense, sex was considered by Xue Feng as a therapy for the human light body that transferred benefits to the physical body through the energetic channel network and that used new discoveries that were not for common knowledge. The best description that could come up with for intercourse is a similar frequency curing the problems of vibration and the Yin-Yang energy exchange. In other words, man, as described by the ancients, is as a related field of vibes and intercourse capable of facilitating normalization and purification of this human field of vibrations with qi-energy generated permutations in the human body at the cell level (DNA), which is an excellent indicator of vitality. Sex, one of the most powerful avenues of human expression and as such, provides a handy analogy for the systems of the body and mind. According to an old statement, the human body is unable to reproduce what the mind cannot imagine. Perhaps, the body cannot perceive what the mind cannot generate, and vice versa. There often are pieces of evidence that the mind, in addition to being a master-conductor, is a very complex generator and commanded the systems of the body through frequency. From a spiritual perspective, thinking of sex as a health-improving message can slowly enhance one's mental capabilities and improve one's abilities to deal with daily challenges on the way to final realization. Consequently, the fundamental view of traditional Chinese medicine (TCM) on sexual life is that one should not lose intimate relationships or indulge in them. If one adheres to moderation in sexual activity, understanding its principles and improving the sexual techniques, he or she can maintain a healthy state of the body. To show restraint in sexuality means that the male and female should adequately make love with a perfect harmony of rhythm and movements when sex is based on the mutual desire and passion of both partners. The sexual harmony is directly related to a knowledge of the physiological characteristics of a man and a woman. For the sexual relationship, which helps to maintain a good state of health, it is necessary to attach importance not only to the mode of action but also to sexual hygiene. In view of such circumstances, the ancient Chinese raised intimacy in the rank of art and, like any other arts, the way of making love had to be exercised to learn all its subtleties and facets.

These educational and evolutionary processes dictate changes in the conscious living habits and choices to a lifestyle of a higher more mature order. Changing, however, is not a smooth process neither for laymen nor for monks, as the conscious part of them has a definite tendency to resist change and clear of vibratory imbalances because it may release control to varying degrees, depending on the significance of the vibratory impurity, emotional block being cleared, and so on. In a nutshell, physical experiences are merely a reflection of some portion of the human light body's non-physical energy structure, as long as people are living in a dimension of cause and effect. If one elects to improve, heal, and purify the human energy fields via sexual act, he thus chooses to change some portion of the experiential path. Often, with consistent use of sexual intercourse, one gradually sees life's challenging process clearer and therefore less stressful. Progressively and relatively speaking, one's life complex process starts to be simplified. Consistent sex used to provide benefits that most humans are not used to observing or experiencing via a therapy directed at their vibes structure. Therefore, if the monk set about doing something, the obstacles he encountered did not appear as problems to him. If something couldn't be accomplished, he did not waste his time trying to finish it. If something could be achieved, then it was a matter of discovering how. In neither case was there a problem, following an old precept of 'dealing with a problem starting from its easiest end; and accomplishing a great deed in small details.' Later on, the following poetic lines were devoted to the master of Zen healing.

"O living beings! There is no way to persuade them.
What's the meaning of their perverted upside-downs?
On their faces there are two evil fowls: eyes and ears;
In their hearts—three vipers: greed, anger, and illusion.
This only pose for them hindrances and obstructions
To make you be involved in all their cares and troubles.
But you raise a hand up and click your magic fingers,
Just chanting, 'Namas Amitabha Buddha,' and that's it!"

Usually, when a man thinks he has finished dealing with a problem, it can reappear in another form, or in many other ways. As an old anecdote goes, once, upon cutting a worm with his ax, a monk said to Zen master, "I've cut a worm into two pieces, but both pieces are still moving. I just wonder," he said, "in which piece the worm's life still remains?" Instead of a reply, the master took the ax and cut both pieces once again. Thereupon, he bit on the space between the parts. So doing, he threw the ax down and went away. However, such a method of problem-solving refers to a kind of intellectual understanding. But what object did it take in Xue Feng's meaning of the self-cultivation? The purpose was what the Buddha saw and knew, exposing all-encompassing wisdom of everything. The reason was that in all his practices the master believed that he discovered the image of the original nature of his self, as well as of life in general. He perceived the essence of his real and lasting quality, which was described as man's original countenance and, in accord with which, he who had passed over to the other side, the liberated and spiritualized devotee, would have many new encounters then.

Chapter 5: Tigress's Roar

One day, performing on his daily duty on supplying the monastery's kitchen with rice and delivering it from the marketplace in the town named Red Fort, the monk was passing over the mountain ridge when suddenly heard a tiger's roar thundered in the misty thicket behind. The roar was so dreadful that the monk became frightened to death. On the one hand, even the mighty roar was only a roar, yet not the tiger itself. That was just an indication of the tiger's existence somewhere not far away. On the other hand, since the roar was delivered from not afar in such a powerful and violent manner, the monk had a chance to estimate the distance between him and the fierce beast, as well as degree of danger he could be involved in shortly. As the roar sounded extraordinarily thundering and threatening, in no time the proper direction and his destination receded into the background, the path became a maze, the purpose of his passing immediately sunk into oblivion. Doubts and fear of losing his life burnt within his mind like hell; uncertainties about the right and the wrong assailed him -- he was standing motionlessly, like a frozen pond in winter. For a certain while he just turned his back on his true self -- the tiger's roar shocked him, he was shattered and razed to his heels. He could see not a thing through the dim screen of his excited and, therefore, unclear mind, like a doomed quarry, which smelt upon the wind the slightest scent of its predator, pricking up his ears, nostrils dilating, alert, uncertain what it was. Recognizing it not from memory but by instinct alone, he detected the scent, which had come to him over and over, making him trembled at the faint thrill of anticipation. All of a sudden it came home to him what it was, that scent. It was the scent of wildlife -- the real one, which waylaid then crouching and watching him from some spots behind the nearest thicket. The monk squatted down and gazed into the flow of a tiny brook, letting his past life passed in quick review. The whole experience was seen in its rise and fall, then all became empty and dissipated. But owing to the thirst for life still persisted, and because the consistency of thoughts still was intact, with that stream of ideas arose another -- both on a single source: the view of the temple, what he had to do with his mission there; he would have been hard-pressed to specify. The scent had grown stronger. The monk became a little bit farther strained in his way when he, at last, recognized it as the salty scent of his own blood. His nose was bleeding.

Zen teaches us that a lot of stressful doubts will finally result in great realization. This marvel is beyond any description and can be approximately compared to a sudden leaping up from a state of being frozen inside a deep well with ice-cold water into the condition of scalding hot and then to some freezing cold once again as if your whole body has been burst into thousands and thousands of bits from within. Due to the considerably stressful situation, which provoked his nose bleeding and which then led the monk back to his own true self, he launched to trust in himself even more strongly than ever. Armed with his trust, he rode on condition to move in accord with his own will. He became a true master who was standing beyond the nets of circumstances. Upon discovering the fact that his original self had still been within him, and due to his starting from doubts and fear, he investigated the situation and his own person in it, employing entirely focused spiritual power. What he found there was his capability to hear well every slightest sound all around. However, for the whole of the night he harkened no signs of life, but in the early morning, as he was walking along an extent of stillness and quiet flowing brook waters, he suddenly heard the sound of rustling and crisping behind him. He turned round to face his pursuer to discover that that was nothing; at least, it could be something that still had been hiding in the dark bushes. Yes, at first he saw nothing; then his glance slipped forwards and, to his complete astonishment, from around a bush appeared a creature, which treading soundlessly toward him over the thicket, like a floating dream. In an instant he made out the muzzle of a massive beast; that was a tigress. The animal was like a swirl of black and orange strips burning in the morning sunrays, the whole bunch of primitive energies yearning for a return to the depths of the chilly piny forest. As the tigress paced, she turned her terribly massive head from side to side and scrutinized the bushes thoroughly. Her green vertical pupil eyes flashed with a curious and impersonal fury. The monk's 'gong-fu,' the level of his self-cultivation through performance of his daily toil, was good enough to gulp his agitation and calm down in mind as fast as it was possible and, as a result of his internal efforts, the clouded screen fell then from his eyes and he caught a sight of the tigress's eyes fluoresced through a layer of misty morning. Though it was very dangerous to meet the tigress's gaze in the deep mountains, he, summoning up all his willingness, encouraged himself to look directly in the face of reality in order to go farther and exercise diligently with his mind, in which the real situation started to brighten up in all tiny details.

Very soon his trust in his good self became stronger. He even started to chant and vocalize his internal spiritual forces so intensively that the wild creature was given a chance to realize on its own its spirit interlinked with the all-embraced Dharma, the real way of Nature. Still, the monk's conduct was pretty shallow and vacillating. Aiming at that submerged but ineradicable human instinct of self-preservation, he quickly climbed to the top of a huge stone and, all the while stupidly smiling and bowing with humility, he emitted quivering sound of his incantations, one by one. Upon hearing this, the bewildered animal sat back on her haunches and pawed the air like a house cat, sweeping with her tail around. The tigress then fell to the ground at the foot of the boulder where she was lying panting on her belly. But presently she roused herself to try the same upright pose again unable to resist her blind submission to her conductor. And thus the 'dance' accompanied by spiritual chants went on a circle by circle.

Apparently, the monk preached the words of illumination to the tigress used in the Dharma sense, but not in the sense of intellectual understanding. He, most probably, taught her that all living beings, however, varied in shapes, were all of the same corporal material, and that everything was composed of the same substance. He recounted the pattern called 'One-in-All and All-in-One,' which was then solidified by his famous saying that every sound or color or fragrance was none other than the Due Mean. He taught that every dharma thus was an embodiment of the real essence of objective reality. There might be a similarity in understanding without similarity in outward form; there might also be the similarity in form without similarity in understanding. He said, "Those creatures that resemble them in the shape they love and consort with; those that differ from them in the shape they fear and keep at a distance. A creature which has a long skeleton, arms differently shaped from legs, hair on its head, and an even set of teeth in its jaws and walks erect is called Man. But it does not follow that a man may not have the mind of a brute. Even though this can be the case, other men will still recognize him as one of their own species in virtue of his outward form. It followed that all living beings and creatures had the Buddha-nature lay in hiding deep within them and thus could be saved." He also told the tigress that the Buddha was one who experienced reality as it was, one who realized the truth and was an example of Truth and that all beings that practiced the truth were those who were genuinely compassionate. He mentioned the gist of all teachings of the ancients that 'a violent would come to a violent end.'

"The intelligence of animals is innate, even as that of man," he added. "Their common desire is for the propagation of life, but their instincts are not derived from any of the human sources. There is a pairing between the male and female and mutual attachment between a mother and her young. They shun the open plain and keep to the mountainous parts; they flee the cold and make for warmth; when they settle, they gather in flocks; when they travel, they preserve a fixed order. The young ones are stationed in the middle; the stronger ones place themselves on the outside. They show one another the way to the drinking-places and call to their fellows when there is food. In the earliest ages, they dwelt and moved about in company with a man. It was not until the age of emperors and kings that they began to be afraid and broke away into scattered bands."

This willing subordination, and the idea that the female would allow herself to be thus used by the male in his quest to elude death, very poignantly suggested to the monk by the tigress's doomed affection. Perhaps even more than her exploitation, the idea of her vast, passive power, the inexhaustibility of her vital feminine essence, excited his attention of a male. As he toyed with that notion, a startling thought occurred to him. He thought to himself, "It is recorded in mostly all sutras that there is a kind of creature in all the three realms which has the bad habit of not paying attention to what it is listening to. As a result, it has to drift along in the world of suffering. If you can practice the ways of good conduct that you learn, you will progress on your self-cultivation rapidly."

In some degree, he was a tiger as well, an incarnation of Amitabha, the Buddha of the Pure Land of West, while the west, symbolically, was associated with the image of the tiger. Anyway, dealing with the feminine beast, he was not close to a conductor than to the tiger. Perhaps, there was a little bit of both in him. On the other hand, finding her way by listening to the monk's preaching, she faced to the gate of the Buddha's teachings and, stretching out her neck attempted to see what was behind the gates to realize the gist of the teachings. Her all senses became then concentrated and harmonious in the state where her great spirit was depressed, as she performed her obedient behavior. Verily, as the saying goes, "When the inner eye is focused, one can see that everything is of the same nature."

Again, he could preach using his vocalization of internal spiritual strength to explain the Dharma of emptiness, selflessness, and suffering. Conceived as an ecstatic manifestation of Amitabha Buddha, the monk embodied the forces of insight and compassion beyond any logic and convention. Invoking in the beast's spontaneity of the awakened state, he transformed his own hesitations and attachments into enlightened activity towards the tigress, which signified the latent power of the intrinsic Buddha nature.

Thus, being in the very core of transformation, the monk seemed to have the appearance of sick, mentally disturbed man, just like a sage who appeared to be crazy in the eyes of ordinary people. Following the beast's spontaneity, he merely became a genuine act of offering himself to the passive feminine power when on his way he forgot where he was going. Sometime later, upon his 'recovering,' he confessed to himself, "Before I had plunged in forgetting and in that confused state of floating, I did not know whether Heaven and Earth were real or not. From now on, upon my recovering, generation and destruction, gain and loss, misfortune and happiness, right and wrong will trouble my mind in the same way as before. Will I ever be able to regain the forgetting, which I enjoyed for a short while?"

The tigress, though she had entered the teaching, she couldn't distinguish yet between good and evil, blessing and disaster, the right things and false ones. Still, she did not enter the world of the bodhi-mind; she only was given a chance to discover the gate tentatively, holding fast to the scent and trying not to hesitate to enter. Being so different, the monk and tigress embodied the going out and coming in, both ends of the same thing called Oneness. Even though they acted as a master and a disciple, the substance of the self-sufficient bodhi-mind did not have the character of the distinction between the two: all was everywhere and undifferentiated, without coming in or going out the gate of Enlightenment. It was like a dashing wave in the Void, through which the sun and moon shedding their lights. To destroy any distinctions by attaining freedom from consciousness and from all dualities, the two sank into the fathomless depths of self-consciousness, actually, its absence in the form of dreaming: their minds became as calm as the fathomless ocean, all thoughts vanished utterly; there was no pressure or stress; hence no nose bleeding. Every single corner of the entire universe became familiar and meaningful, as their interpenetration into everything was absolutely total. Astonishment with which they embraced every single thing that came across their way, every transformation, did not proceed from alteration induced by fragmentation, from a distance between their selves and world or the discrepancy between interior and exterior, but just from the innocence of forgetting. In fact, this was the great awakening, living life to its utmost, the devotion which melted every moment in a mixture of life and death. Life was thus the becoming, the driving motif of transformation and end of every moment, like the ocean which in the meantime swallowed and brought out each wave. Though the waves might cease to exist, the sea was still there. The sea had neither life nor death. So dreaming, the monk strove for dwelling himself in an unchanging state of inactive activity and non-duality. Though the picture of the landscape changed on each occasion, one element was constant: always in the background was the sound of running water, sometimes nearer, sometimes farther off; sometimes percolating like a brook or rivulet, sometimes a hellish torrent railing down its course. Through high meadows thick with uncut grasses, starred by the blue mountain gentian, or in cloud-forests where the sun shone like a huge, pale gas lamp floating in the mist. The sound of water droplets pattering on the leaves of rhododendrons drifted to his ears. Sometimes through snowfields, sometimes in sultry heat through the slick clay of a rice paddy; sometimes in deserts, sometimes over an interminable plain, through salt marsh and estuary, into remote caverns underground, he followed, arriving at last, always, at the ocean, where the sound of running water merged with the sighing of the waves time and again. From this perspective, the image of death was the quiet ocean, the place where the spirit found repose in the middle of emptiness, in the tranquility laying beyond the boundaries of extraordinary things. Dreaming, as a superior way of knowledge, was defined as a form of wandering of his spirit, while actual activities were the result of the contact with her (tigress) form. Thus the spirit revealed itself in dreaming, the formation attracted to action. This is why, when the spirit was concentrated, all dreams and thoughts disappeared by themselves, giving way to forgetfulness. Men cannot express in words the experience of the true awakening; their ideas cannot penetrate the most profound dreams, as they are the result of arrival and passing of transformation of the spirit and formation.

As for the tigress, most probably, she dreamed of learning to get more experience on her way in understanding her true nature, flowing in the sea of perfect knowledge. But even the complete knowledge is not the bodhi-knowledge, at all. She, like all the other living beings, had her potential to become a buddha but, since of her purposeful learning, the realization would never appear properly. Most likely that was the reason why she was reduced to the form of a wild beast over and over again. It is hardly possible to say something definite about the tigress's dreams. Perhaps, she headed to the west to pay homage to her ancestor, the sacred White Tiger, a symbol of the west (direction to India). Perhaps, she dreamed of attaining to the highest worlds, much like the concept of rebirth in the Pure Land of West, or the like. Generally speaking, the contemplative forgetting or forgetting of knowledge represents a form of self-cultivation, attainment of wisdom. This implies full experience, a way of reaching beyond the phenomenal, a transgression, not just the void, emptiness, dark space, or lacking significance. This refers to a second forgetting, the forgetting of forgetting, the forgetting as a form of self-dedication, of mirroring the universe. This is the self-forgetting equivalent to dreaming, which overcomes the character of this story.

Suddenly, the monk turned over and awoke; his awakening gave rise to ignorance or uncertainty, it was difficult to determine; in reality, he was dreaming. His awakening to ignorance also demonstrated a claim that all activities were nothing but dreams. From this perspective, awakening acquires a double sense, just as dreaming. First came the awakening from sleep or from dreaming, the awakening from illusion; another, a negative one, was the awakening from forgetting. The latter represented a decline on the spiritual level. It may be noticed here a double inversion, as awakening, in this case, describes a form of falling asleep of the spirit. It is the awakening to actual, concrete reality, which is a subject of transformation, dominating by emotions and their harmful consequences upon the mind they endlessly trouble.

The objects of the material world include the boards, setting, and characters of a dream-drama; when one awakens, the stage vanishes; the players and the audience too, disappear. Hence, much one has practiced, whether for ten years, thirty years or two days, when one wakes up it takes a couple of moments. So, what is the use of all those years of practicing the self-consciousness or its absence? Why not wake up immediately, without foreplay?

Upon waking up, he addressed to himself, just thinking loudly: "How do I know that he who is afraid of death is not like a man who was away from his home when young and, therefore, had no intention to return? How do I know that the dead will not repent of their former yearning for life? Those who dream of a banquet at night may wail and weep the next morning; those who dream of wailing and weeping may go out to hunt in the morning. When we dream, we do not know that we are dreaming. In the dream, we may even interpret our dreams. Only when we are awake, do we begin to know that we have dreamed. By and by comes the great awakening, and then we shall find out that all life is a great dream. All the while, fools think that they are awake, that they know something." Then he had a look at the tigress, saying, "Either the sagely minded Confucius or you," and he pointed his index finger at the beast's nose, "you both are in a dream. At the moment when I say you are in a dream, I am also in a dream..."

Thus, the monk and the tigress were in a dream, the dream of reality, and all these preoccupations, relations, preaching, and hunt made one ceaseless dream. What actually happened at the moment of the dreamers' awakening? At that moment the monk already knew emptiness, and when the tigress fell into it together with him, the minds of both became one, and that one was called Emptiness. Then they both saw it. The monk's mind was empty; he became a carriage run through the emptiness, and that carriage rode his mind. Deep karma of many years was standing; on awakening, it was all cleared up. But what if the two go to sleep again? Staying awake is not an idle practice, it is continuous of realizing the Truth. Continuous realization requires full attention. What happened at the moment they fell again into a doze at midday? What happened when they gave it all up? What was this giving up?

There was no need to hold anything on. Other than the imputed, there never was a reality, past, present, or future. So, what was it?

At the time the monk and the tigress were absentminded, they had accomplished something without even knowing how it was done. In fact, it was his consciousness that played the whole part. At the moment he awoke he was filled with a very firm perception that the complete realization was just comprehension that he was not bound. Such freedom was the awakening. Nothing else had changed. At last, all the dreams were over; ideas of sagehood were gone too. At ease, he was no longer concerned with finding or losing his state of tranquility produced in full accordance with the principle of inaction or doing no further ado. Since he had realized the Buddha-nature from within, nothing with gain or loss could touch his purified mind any longer. Humming a simple song of kids, he perched then on the tigress's back. Her eyes were fixed ahead, in the direction towards the gate of the Buddha's teachings, and nothing could impede this. The monk and the tigress started to become one or, saying precisely, two sides of one single formation. The monk pointed out at the 'stream,' causing the tigress to trace it until she reached the 'source.' While the tigress traced the stream, she found out that there was only one source named the Yellow Spring.

Entering the monastery gate on the back of the tigress, Xue Feng started to make his rounds back and forth along the temple's veranda, singing his simple songs and vocalizing some queer syllables. Seeing this, all inhabitants of the monastery got scared to death. Since their minds did never linger in the state of contemplative illumination, they hastily scattered. Though the monk was left alone in the monkish quarters, the ten thousand pairs of eyes of all buddhas and bodhisattvas couldn't find him attached to anything. He did not identify himself even with the self-sufficient bodhi-mind; so why should he strive? The door of his cell was closed, and even saints were unaware of him because his purity was such that it left no mark on him. At midnight, sitting alone with his tigress in the moonlit cell, he composed a verse, which he then scripted on the wall of his cell, reading as follows:

"Originally, there is not a thing;
Much less any dust to flick off.
Once you can comprehend this,
You needn't sit still any longer."

Just think of a fisherman with a net as a tool of fishing. His instrument, the net, is his method of making his stuff for a living. He casts out his net, but he should also drag it then back in; whether he has caught fish or not, he must do it anyway. If he does not collect his net, it means that he does not intend to fish anymore. So, each time he finishes his work by hauling his net in.

The experience is like gold extracted from ore; the efforts become forgotten when the aim is achieved. Before one is realized, when one sees a mountain it is a mountain, and when sees the sea it is the sea. Upon becoming realized—the mountains are still mountains, and the seas are still seas. But the make-up of the hill and sea are different, depending on whether one is finally realized or not. After the realization, the mountain, sea, buddhas, beasts, and the entire universe become one with the true self-nature. There is no more extended practice or no-practice, wisdom or vexation. Everything is complete; everyone is a buddha, and the environment is the Pure Land, the blessed Western Paradise. Then where should one go to search for a master who clean forgot words to talk to him of everything?

Afterward, because of his extraordinary pranks, Xue Feng was forced to leave the monastery. Seeking confirmation of his illumination, he made a pilgrimage to the sacred Wu-tai Mountains (present-day Shanxi Province in Northern China) to pay a visit to Manjusri, the chief of the Four Great Bodhisattvas and foremost in wisdom.

* * * * * *

Originally, Mount Wu-tai was a Daoist sacred mountain known as "Zifushan" (Purple Palace) and was believed to be the abode of numerous Daoist immortals. Wu-tai encompasses some different mountains, but long ago Buddhists chose five particular flat-topped peaks as the perimeter of the sacred area; hence the name, which means Five Terrace Mountains. The highest peak at 10,033 feet is called Northern Terrace and the lowest Southern Terrace (8,153 feet). There is a distance of twelve miles between the two in the form of a steep mountain range stretched out from the north to south. The flat peaks of Wu-tai and all the surrounding temples were dedicated to Manjusri, Bodhisattva of

Wisdom and Virtue. The Buddhist monks trace the beginning of Manjusri's association with Wu-tai Mountains to the visit of an Indian monk who visited Wu-tai in the first century CE and reported a vision of the Bodhisattva. Manjusri is believed to reside in Wu-tai, and a great many of legends speak of Bodhisattva's apparitions usually riding on a blue lion in the deep mountains above numerous temples and monasteries.

The path the monk took through the large and small towns, villages, fields, and forests was long and difficult. Overgrown pathway lay before him, but he stubbornly pushed on, thinking to himself: "He who has attained the essence of wandering does not know where his steps will lead him; he who has attained the essence of contemplation does not know what he is contemplating. Each thing is a good occasion of wandering; each thing deserves to be contemplated." For him, wandering became an opportunity of dissipating the illusion of security and stability, which he acquired using settling in a determined place. Being free in his wandering, Xue Feng thought to have reached a superior modality; it seemed to him that he had integrated himself in the flow of transformation. The danger of identifying himself with reality, with a place, a time, and circumstances did not exist anymore. At that stage, the only thing missing was the identification with the whole to hide the universe in the universe. He did not seek a place which could offer him shelter, he was not a point lost in the torrent of transformation anymore. It did not drag him along in life, as well as in death; he was not a spectator who contemplated the current from a certain distance, he had become one with it. He could then experiment simultaneously two complementary aspects of the modality manifested as life and death. For him, external wandering became useless because he had already identified himself with the universe and could then find in the very core of his mind everything that the world contained, or it became one, in which any single thing might turn into an object of contemplation.

On the sixtieth day, he stood at the foot of the Wu-tai Mountains. As he looked up, he couldn't even make out the peaks. Nonetheless, he started up. It was colder than he had been, and he nourished only by the berries and water that had been so abundant on the slopes. Up and up he went. The path grew continually more difficult until he wasn't sure of his way. Guided only by his urgent need to complete his mission and the general knowledge that his goal lay somewhere in the upper reaches of that huge rock mass, he plodded slowly on.

Next day he was climbing right through the middle of the clouds massed about the sacred mountain. He was so tired, but the summit seemed yet so far away. Thoughts of turning and heading back down flitted through his mind but, as he remembered what had driven him to undertake his journey, he made a resolve to continue on. There was much to be done. The air nearing the summit was quite rare. His lungs labored as he plodded ever upward. It was the afternoon of the third day, entirely a day and a half in clouds, not sure of his way, summoning his strength and courage just to purchase the next step. . . And then, he was out of the clouds. Sunlight wrapped him in its radiant arms and drove the chill from his damp bones. Where he had to suck with all his might for a lungful of air, he suddenly found his breathing calm and relaxed. And to his amazement, before him, not more than the distance from the granary to a Jade Buddha Hall at the Xiang-lin temple, was the flat peak: not cold and barren, as he had imagined it. It was lush and filled with fruit trees of many varieties, some he didn't recognize. And there too, on top of the peak, a lovely spring winded down and through the grove, splitting into smaller brooks that ran and gurgling down a multitude of paths to the valley below.

He experienced that once at twilight, standing on the crest of a high ridge and peering down into a gorge where the black cord of the river uncoiled, falling two hundred feet over a broken scarp and sending up a fine mist of spray on the grey slopes. He dropped, facing down, and gave thanks. He hugged the ground to him. Actually, he could almost feel himself, becoming one with it and he prayed and thanked the magnificent Heaven for helping him do the arduous climb. For a long while, he lied there, almost overcome with his achievement, wondering what he had survived at all. Then he rose and went to seek a shelter for the night.

Next morning he started to search out the master, but Bodhisattva was not to be found. He searched with great diligence and considerable patience but to no avail. As he walked through the groves, he stopped and looked out over a fantastic view that opened before him. He marveled at the beautiful scene; it was hard to imagine now the awfulness that left somewhere below. All seemed so peaceful, so quiet and so beautiful in broad daylight. At night the heavens were a playground for his eyes: the stars he had never seen before blinked back at him, as if in welcome.

The following few days turned insensibly to decades and the decades became months. Still, the monk continued to seek Manjusri; and always he was disappointed in his quest. One bright morning, as he stared out over the valley below, he thought he heard something. So far away, so light on the wind, it might have been nothing more than a slight gust on the steep surface below. Still, he wondered, if it came from Xiang-lin temple in Tian-tai, from its cells or granary, was there anything left. . . was the apprehension still awakened. . . A multitude of disturbing questions awoke for an instant in his mind. And then he realized the most profound revelation he had ever known, or would ever know. The real flavor of that state couldn't be described; like someone who was drinking water -- only he knew how cold or warm it was. Once you reach this state, you naturally understand what it is all about; if you are not at this state, no explanation will be adequate.

Soon after that, in one of the numerous caverns that dappled the mountain, all of a sudden he encountered with someone who looked like a deity, rushing to ask him straightaway: "Are you Manjusri Bodhisattva?"

The spirit-like person replied, "How can it be that two Manjusri bodhisattvas exist all at the same time?" Then he added grandly, "I am the divine child of the floor and roof, of Heaven and Earth. I am the god of Thunder and Wind who controls the fundamental destiny of all beings. I have three names: the God through Whom All Beings are Born Alike, the Ruler of the Revolution of the Fundamental Destiny of Beings, and the Master Who Provides All Beings of Ten Directions with Food of Dhyana. Besides, I am the Master Who Ties Karmic Affinities for the Future and Who Can Teach Simultaneously All Living Beings."

Upon hearing this, the monk knelt respectfully before the saint, but all of a sudden the divine vanished into the air without leaving a trace.

It turned out that in a few days he was visited once again by the same divine who wondered, saying, "The deep mountains are so quiet and solitary, the true abode of dragons and tigers. How is it that you, who are so virtuous, have strayed so far to come here? What brings you here?"

The monk said, "I am not virtuous. I have come to see you, Master."

Upon hearing this, the saint thought to himself, "This monk is lying when he denies his virtues." Xue Feng knew immediately what the saint was thinking, and the latter regretted it, apologizing for being so stupid. Then the divine imparted to the monk his robe together with the Tripitaka Scriptures and sacred Law (Dharma), transmitting the great Mind-to-Mind Seal to the monk who thus received the complete precepts. At the same time, he explained to him how the sacred Law had been transmitted from one patriarch to another. That was reminiscent of the way Shakyamuni Buddha had passed it to his disciple Mahakasyapa when, instead of speaking to the assembled multitude, he had held up a lotus flower. While the audience awaited teachings, Mahakasyapa alone had grasped the essence of the Law, just producing a smile. . . Finally, the deity got up to escort the monk down the mountain to the river where, as they got into a boat together, he picked up the oars. The monk offered to row, but the saint denied, saying, "No. It is only right for me to get you across the river" (that meant an allusion to the Buddhist teachers helping their disciples reach the 'other bank' of spirituality).

But the monk insisted, reflecting, "I have had the honor to inherit the robe and Dharma from you, Master. Since I am now completely enlightened, it is only right for me to cross the stream of birth and death by my own effort to realize my own essence of the Mind."

After that, the saint gave him the oars, and they reached the opposite bank safely. There they bade each other farewell.

Chapter 6: The Real World

It happened that Xue Feng went continually on his own way, turning from the beaten paths of the earlier patriarchs. Though he dwelt in the midst of the twofold truth, he was ever able subtly to reject existence and non-existence, to strike the mean in his acceptances and rejections and not to run counter to the principles of the Dao. After a few months of staying in Wu-tai, he, carrying just only his rattan staff and scrip with the scriptures and robe of succession, headed back to Tian-tai unencumbered with any worldly possessions.

Begging on his way, he came late one afternoon upon a navigable river settlement -- a collection of huts made of shingle and mud and perched on stilts above a broad white spur of sandy beach. As he made the rounds, one fat fellow with his bald head winked and motioned him over with a few quick sideways jerks of the head. Encouraged by his manner, the monk approached and, stopping before him, bowed respectfully, holding out his bowl.

"Alms for a poor man," he said, invoking the ritual petition.

"In reply, he heard a lubricious gurgling followed by a short roar. Looking up in amazement, he found green-brownish spittle, floating like a massive silkworm in the bed of his bowl. The fat man smiled at him with unbelievable shamelessness, his eyes reduced to dark slits, his lips filled up with expressive defiance. The monk felt the blood rush to his face; his hands started to tremble beyond his control. Then the fat man's grin suddenly vanished and was replaced by a look of sober malice; his hand lay on the hilt of a dagger he had thrust in the leather waistband he wore. Mastering himself, Xue Feng wheeled and stalked off to the edge of the water, where he knelt down and immersed his bowl in the current, scouring it with sand.

"Cool down," he whispered savagely to himself.

This retreat set off a rude chorus of derision among the gapers on the river's bank. All eyes regarded the monk. He was hissed at, hooted, and jeered.

"Puffing himself up like a toad, the fat man called after him, yelling, "Hey, chicken-heart, you forgot to thank me!"

Closing his ears to the abuse, the monk stole quickly through the crowd. Possessed by he didn't know what inspiration, probably, because that guy was the only one who wasn't showing signs of active enmity, Xue Feng walked up a few feet behind a wandering swordsman who was lounging idly in front of a small teashop. The monk addressed him. At first, the swordsman appeared not to hear him. Then at the second repetition of his greeting, he turned slowly in his seat and stared at the monk. A thrill of horror tingled down Xue Feng's nerves at the sight of him. There was something decidedly hellish in the view, like a corpse's that made his blood run cold.

"What do you want?" he asked, in a rasping voice, just one degree above a whisper, so soft that it took the monk by surprise.

"I haven't eaten in two days," he said. "If you could spare me something. . ."

The warrior turned and to his horror reached for his sword. Picking it up, however, he merely laid it aside and delved into a bag, which was resting underneath it. Taking out two rice balls, he tossed them to the monk in swift succession, then turned his back and resumed his resting. This small kindness moved the monk deeply. Prostrating himself in the dust, he thanked him in the most generous terms. This the warrior acknowledged no more than he had the dog's affectionate tail-wag. Putting one of those balls in his scrip, Xue Feng sat down and, composing his mind, proceeded to eat the other, taking small bites, chewing slowly, savoring. As he ate, the fat man came to him, asking, 'You want to eat?'

The monk nodded.

"But maybe not exactly what you had in mind? Ha! Ha! Ha! Could it be a little more than you bargained for? But who's laughing? I hadn't bargained for it either. Anyway, you'll get no alms here, damn you! We don't believe in charity, for that matter!" he said petulantly. "Then you can carry a load for me, ah?"

'I'm not afraid to work,' the monk replied, nervously defiant.

With a quick jerk of his head, the fatty summoned over a man who was bent double under a load of hemp. As the man approached, he continued to probe the monk. Rolling out from underneath his burden, the carrier dropped it at his feet.

'Shoulder that,' the fat man said.

Throwing off his own pack, Xue Feng reached down and strained to lift it. The hemp was heavier than he expected, but he managed to get it up on top of him. For a second he tottered and came close to falling.

"With us," the fatty cried out, "if a man wants to get something, he works -- just like that. This is a true man's statement, remember? But perhaps you aren't a man. . ."

The monk heard a few snickers from the crowd. The sweat from his forehead ran down into his eyes. He tried to look up, but he could see only ankles and calves. Suddenly he felt the fat man clutched him tightly from behind.

"Let's have a look. What have you got underneath those clothes, anyway?"

The monk felt the bully thrust up powerfully against him. Taking advantage of his bent position, the man grasped him by the hips and started making crude motions, trying humping him like a puppy for the amusement of the crowd. Something in Xue Feng's heart went wild. With a violent effort, he drew himself upright. The load hit the fat man in the chest, knocking him backward. Dropping it in the dust, the monk wheeled to face the bully, clenching his fists. One look at the toad-like face, however, was enough to chill the heat in his blood. There was a look of insane pleasure on his features, which short-circuited his anger. The whites of the fatty's eyes had turned a shade of blood red, as though from heavy drinking. He also gnashed his teeth in eager anticipation of a fight. Xue Feng tried to block his fist as it came down, but it crashed through his uplifted arms as if they were paper. The fat man's fist smashed into his face, sending him heavily to the ground. The world zoomed in and out of focus; then he lost consciousness completely. . . When Xue Feng opened his eyes again, he was staring directly into the sun. There was a salted, brassy taste in his mouth, and when he spat in his hand, a piece of broken tooth came out with the dark blood. The fat man was standing at his feet: legs spread wide, fists on his hips, lowering down at the monk.

"Get up," he said.

As the monk made no move to comply, he straddled him and, bending down, grasped the front of his jacket. Twisting it, he lifted him up, intending to drop him then down again. As he did so, the monk noticed a figure of a man standing behind the fatty. His dark, slim shape eclipsed the sun briefly, throwing a long shadow over the scrappers. Through the scales on his eyes, Xue Feng recognized the swordsman. With an agile movement, his sheath was pressed against the fat man's thick neck from the right side.

"What the hell do you think you're doing?" the fatty uttered distinctly, stopping himself, frozen.

"Let him alone," the man said in his soft, rasping whisper, and with the gentle pressure of the sheath, he urged him inch by inch out of the monk. Standing so at his peril, the fatty's breast puffed up, his nostrils dilated with an excitement that was part anger, part fear, part surprise.

"Listen, a soldier of fortune," he said in a low voice, tremulous with suppressed emotion, "I have no quarrel with you."

"Most fortunate for all concerned," the swordsman replied. "In that case, you will leave the monk alone."

"Why defend him? What's he to you?"

"That's my affair," the swordsman replied curtly. He fixed on the fat man's face a moment, then turned to depart.

"You, filthy bastard," the fat man spat after him. As the swordsman did not respond, he grew bolder. "Who do you think you are here? I'll teach you not to interfere." Saying so, he drew out his dagger, whether to fence or merely intimidate.

"Watch out!" the monk cried, warning the swordsman.

But the swordsman had wheeled already, drawing as he turned. His eye stared straight ahead in the trance-like fixity of concentration: his back was straight, his stance fixed. A glint of light passed along the length of the unsheathed blade, lighting it with the lightning speed. He held the sword a moment high above his head, parallel to the ground, grasping the ribbed handle firmly with his right hand, tip projecting forward, edge to the sky; his left hand supported the right one with two fingers resting on the right wrist. Taking the second step, he came down swiftly and moved ahead; his rear leg, describing a crescent in the dust, swept inward, then out again. At the same time, he brought the blade down before his face perpendicular to the ground, edge forward. In the third position he snapped his wrist sideways so that the tip pointed to his left, the blade again parallel to the earth but transverse to his direction of motion, instead of in its line. As he did this, he drew his rear foot even with his front one and again went on point, only without rising, coming down into a bent-kneed crouch. Though each movement was precise and separate with the severe elegance of dance, the whole transpired in the time, it took to breathe once profoundly and exhale. In his final crouch, he was no more than a yard from the fat man, who was only then swinging his dagger free of his waistband into the fencing position. Precisely what happened next, it difficult to say precisely, but the swordsman moved his blade with such speed that it literally disappeared. There was only the whoosh -- the sharp steel made as it sliced the air. Then all heard a click, as of metal against metal. The dagger dropped with a soft crunch in the dust, and along with it, four finger bones of the fatty's right hand. In no time his face turned red as though with embarrassment. He hesitated as if trying to decide what had happened and what to do. Then he began to scream like a pig. Falling to his knees, he clutched his injured hand, gathering it to his belly. Hunching over it with his head down, he began to rock in his own blood.

The monk watched with disbelieving horror as the swordsman raised the steel again into the first position -- tip forward, edge to the sky, left hand with two fingers resting on the right wrist. Taking a breath, he prepared to bring it down.

"No!" The condemned shouted, throwing himself at full length at the feet of the swordsman. "Please! Spare me!"

The warrior hesitated without breaking his fixity of gaze. A large vein stood out in his forehead.

"Heed me well," he warned, addressing to the crept fat-guts. "If ever again on your account, I'm forced to draw this blade, you will not live to see it sheathed. I swear it."

With this, he looked directly at the monk for the first time. His face no longer pale, he seemed years younger.

"Come with me," he said, starting off with a deliberate stride, humming a tune, the words of which said:

"I have just bought me a five-foot saber,

I swing it with a gleaming cadence.

I fondle it three times a day,

I won't change it for fifteen maidens!"

Uncertain what he wanted of the shocked monk, filled with awe and terrified that he might somehow arouse his wrath himself, Xue Feng followed him at a little distance. When they had gone a small way, the warrior stopped. To Xue Feng's complete astonishment, he laughed and blushed like a young lady.

"Why are you walking so far back?" he called behind him.

"I am. . . I'm. . ." the monk stammered.

"But, of course, you disapprove of me! Saving your life, I've offended your moral sense." He laughed. "You must show compassion."

Cleaving through his irony, Xue Feng gravely bowed his head. "I owe you my life."

The man shrugged and frowned, saying, "Perhaps I've done you the greater disservice." He studied the monk. "What's your name?"

"Xue Feng (Snow Peak)."

"Well, Xue Feng, come and walk with me," he said, becoming agitated again. "I can see that you are green and have a small experience of the world. You wouldn't be safe back here. Such men would eat you alive. But I'll watch over you. Who knows,... we may even become friends. At the least, we can kill a few dull hours over a friendly cup of wine. . ."

"Thank you," the monk replied, swallowing hard, "but I don't drink."

The man laughed, a short, sharp burst, then suddenly frowned. "You are in my debt," he replied peremptorily, "and that is my pleasure."

"After all, you were not going to kill him, were you?" the monk inquired with great caution.

"Why not?" He replied heatedly. But in no time he added, "You are right. That fat guy was quite ridiculous to die from my sword. The experts of my trade know that the intensity of the experience is directly proportional to the risk. Only in the pursuit of an equal adversary does one come into the higher reaches of this mastery. And that means killing men. Not murder, which is done in stealth and from advantage, the lowest form of meanness and dishonor, but fighting battle. In truth, this is why the great sacrament was brought into the world, so that man might come to know himself, his fundamental essence. All the platitudes of justice, sovereignty, self-defense -- these are just the excuses invented by those who are not strong enough to stomach the truth or think that the rest of us aren't strong enough to stomach it. Fighting battle is the highest expression of human aspiration, the final truth and end of human life that pushes us beyond our limits into our divinity. The fact that we kill, not out of grim and unwelcome necessity, but because it refreshes and invigorates us because the spirit craves it and because only in the moment of taking life are we truly alive ourselves, brings us to awakening. For the rest of it, we are always half asleep. That dull, gnawing restlessness pervades. If you think I'm joking or insane, ask any man who has tasted it himself, who has known the savage joy of fighting hand to hand against an enemy in battle. Whoever you are, but you will note that with the passage of the years, after all else has faded, this memory remains. The only moments in my life when I've known respite from the emptiness were in the heat of battle when I've looked into my adversary's eyes and slain him without malice. Why? I can't tell you, monk."

Whether the swordsman said this only to shock him, difficult to say, but the monk was appalled. He continued, saying, "From the time I can remember, I cared for nothing else -- neither fame nor money or power as the world understands it. There is only one true form of absolute and final power for a warrior, and that is taking lives. Giving life is a power too, but that is the privilege of women and their burden. Only in these two activities are the deepest passions of the soul aroused. When a man has known the taste of blood, it's not a simple matter to forget."

"What forced you to become a mercenary?" at last the monk dared to ask.

Seeing the look on his face, the warrior laughed. "What forced me to become a mercenary? My fate brought me to it, and my fate then took me out. Enemies, once vanquished, were then gathering armies making scattered attacks along the frontiers. Many were savage and brutal stealthy campaigns against the guards and the boundary settlements: the voice of fire roaring uncontrolled, the sound of women wailing, cattle lowing in terror, wood hissing and popping in the flames, the intense heat of thatch raging in your face singeing the eyebrows, cracking the lips, blacking the skin, the smell of burning flesh. . ." The warrior paused; his glance seemed a bit shined with a challenge. He started to recall in a brown study, "When I last time got out of the action I was at the end of my strength -- barely a bag of bones. By that time I was half crazy. My nerves were shot. I was suffering withdrawal syndromes. My service in the guard wholly exhausted me, both spiritually and physically, I was completely diseased, my clothes hanging off me in shreds, the hair matted on top of my head. I looked like a beggar, worse than a beggar. Worse than a leper even, but still alive unlike hundreds and thousands of the others. . ."

So saying, the warrior stood up, and they both continued on in silence toward one of the stone dwellings higher up. Without any previous clue, somehow the monk knew that was their destination, for alone of all the houses in that settlement, it had a thin wisp of smoke curling above the roof, evidence of a fire within. Besides, as they neared it, he discerned an odor emanating from the place, a peculiar and equivocal sweetness, as of wildflowers and dung. Crossing the threshold, they entered a dimly lit room. It took a moment for Xue Feng's eyes to adjust, then by the light of the small channel fire heaped in a stone well in the center and the forest of oil lamps scattered like a random constellation in the darkness, burning as though in a vigil, he began to make out the scene around him.

Everywhere men were sitting or lying about on the floor or on the wooden ledges built into the walls, some of them resting their heads on pillows of white porcelain.

A withered old man with dugs like a woman's sat intently roasting a small black pill of something that looked like pitch in the flame of a lamp nearby, regarding it with a fixed stare like a hungry man reverent before a meal. It was spitted on a long needle, the dipper, which he turned slowly and evenly until it began to sag and ooze in a viscous boiling and the smoke began to rise. Placing it in the bowl of a pipe as long and thick as a bamboo flute, he gently inserted the stem between the lips of the reclining man beside him, then went off to serve someone else. Some of the men had curled up on their sides like fetuses, as though asleep, only their eyes were open, staring with the same glazed expression. Those in the upper levels were almost invisible, ghostlike in the milk-white cloud of smoke that hovered near the ceiling. There was no talk, no socializing. No one laughed or smiled. All smoked in silence, oblivious of their neighbors, their surroundings, even themselves it seemed. Except for the occasional flaring of a match, the settling of the coals in the fire, or an interrupted sigh, there was no sound at all.

"You are a monk, you said?" the warrior asked as though seeing him at the first time.

The monk nodded.

"A Buddhist?" He smiled and made a sweeping motion with his sheathed sword.

"A Daoist."

"Welcome to the Yellow Spring, the Source of Life, the Realm of Repletion. Here you see the concept of 'wu-wei,' the pure inaction in its most precise formulation."

His laugh was shrill this time, a little mad.

"They are addicts," the monk said gravely, reproaching his irreverence. "The pleasure of opium is an insidious and ultimately debilitating parody of the intoxicating bliss of enlightenment."

"Maybe," the warrior said, "but as they are, so am I."

"How can that be?" the monk demanded.

The man smiled. "You are thinking of what happened on the beach?" He shook his head. "That simply shows your inexperience. Opium doesn't necessarily induce a state of torpor -- only in those whose souls are torpid already. The mud makes each man more himself. That's the mystery of it. But you're right -- 'ultimately debilitating.' For in the end, each man is alike. . ."

He pointed with his chin to the man lying nearest them on the floor. "Regard the thing itself. I know one day I'll end like him. If not today, it'll happen tomorrow. If not tomorrow, ten years hence. The sooner, the better, as far as I'm concerned." He laughed and invited the monk to sit.

As he prepared a pipe, he continued speaking. "Though you do not say so, you are wondering at my mood, why I'm laughing, what has given me such pleasure." He paused, his glance expressed a challenge. "It is the taste of blood, monk. It has a tonic effect on me."

Whether he said this only to shock his company, it's difficult to say, but Xue Feng was appalled over again. Seeing the look on his face, the warrior laughed. "That's what I lived for once, why I became a mercenary? Again, my fate brought me to it, and I've followed it diligently."

Saying so, he lifted his head up to notice a light shade moved in the far corner of the room veiled with a painted curtain. In no time he discerned a lady's figure behind it, which looked vaguely familiar to him. To resolve doubts, he beckoned the man; they respired for awhile. Then he addressed to the monk, saying, "See, how small this world is!... But once a whore, always a whore, that's what I say. Isn't that right, monk?"

Xue Feng didn't know what to reply. Not waiting for the answer, the warrior grabbed him by his wrist and bear-led to the veiled corner. Removing the curtain, he uttered, "Good to see you, my darling! Still, miss me?"

The woman turned around and through the shadow lay on her face the monk saw how it stretched down, turning pale. "You?!" she mostly squealed out.

"Ha! Ha!" laughed the warrior, with a glance at Xue Feng, guessing playfully, "Maybe, it's me. . . Doesn't seem so long ago, does it? But it must be almost eight or seven years, isn't it? You're changed a bit since then -- better dressed." He nodded with approval, then, like an astute consumer, added disparagingly, "Not quite so young." He said and his face belied by his ironic smile.

"What the hell do you want from me?" She gave an inaudible mutter.

"Look how proud she is now!" he said, turning to the monk. "See how she preens and spruces!"

"I just dropped in," she excused.

"You weren't so proud in those days! You knew me well enough when I found you in that soldiers' brothel in Xianjing." At that, insolence darkened his features, then disappeared beneath a smile of brilliant lust. "Like I say, once a whore, always a whore. . . Isn't that right, monk?"

And even in the dusk of the corner where she was sitting, it was noticed clearly how her face flushed with fury, but she forced her lips to smile and replied with restrained emotions, "This time you have to pay," she uttered quietly.

"You OWE me your life, remember?" he emphasized this word with a serious note in his voice, breaking up all the following arguments even before they arose. "You must display gratitude."

"Don't YOU remember? I've paid you in full, and even more!" She retorted. "Whatever my former ways, I have mended them all. . ."

"It's not about me, . . it's for him," saying so, the warrior embraced the monk friendly by his shoulder. "I merely want to leave some of my kind footprints in the fate of this saintly man. Actually, I've already left some, disinterestedly, but anyway. . . Today I'm well disposed to charity." He laughed once more.

While waiting for the woman at their berths, the mercenary continued talking excitingly, "You may know your sutras and scriptures, but not women. Look at her, how she's done her hair, fixed herself up. She's always, hungry for it, I can tell. She is still in good shape, still something fresh, red meat with real blood in it. You'd better check her up tonight, and tomorrow you'll wake up refreshed, like a newborn baby."

He looked into Xue Feng's eyes, said, "She may act disdainfully, but for all that snort and fussing, I can tell she's dying for it. She truly knows her business, I ought to admit. Ha! Ha! Oh, boy! I couldn't forget it -- that first time with her, true bitch!" He grasped his pipe suggestively and caught the monk's eye. He started to have the bit in his teeth, more and more excited. "But I haven't told you yet about that trip, the time I brought her from Xianjing. That must have been -- what? -- the tenth, eleventh time we did business?"

"Please!" Xue Feng implored, putting his hands in a pacified gesture. "Not so loud."

The warrior went on, ignoring him, addressing now the monk now the crowd on high at large.

"She didn't have to be 'good-looking,' as long as she had 'a strong back.' Ha! Ha! How I laughed at that!" His talk started to be more entangled with each moment. "Remember! One of the rare lapses in your business is judgment, monk. Never jump to conclusions, man. . . You must have been a little nervous. Women could be had for nothing in those days, and I bought the cheapest thing in town. Still, she was strong, as I requested, and not so bad really, if you didn't look too hard. . . I didn't realize what a hellcat I'd acquired until I got her on the boat sailing out of Xianjing. By the time we got fairly under way, she was all over me. I tell you, at the end of the first day I didn't have a hair left on my stalk. Later she felt remorse. All that night she wept and tried to scratch my eyes out. I had to lash her to the mast and gag her before I could shut my eyes. That did the trick though. I left her there all night, and in the morning she was tame. The rest of the time she did exactly what I said. That was quite a trip! She was young then, you have to remember. Her tits were firm and high. Not like today, I guess, but still. . ." He spat on the berth as though to commemorate the spot. "She squealed and grunted like a pig, kept crying out for more; begged me to take her back with me. But I'm not a fool. And business is business, right, monk? We had a deal. Ha! ha!" His mirth turned once again. "Mind me, monk. You'd better have her tonight. There're a lot of men here who wouldn't turn their noses up at it. They get tired of fucking sheep, mountain rams, bloody goats," and he glanced at the piled crowd all around the place, "dogs, pigs, horses, each other's butt-holes, whatever else they find to stick it in out here. Don't you, folks?!" There were a few sniggers. Some scowled.

"Please, please. . ." begged the monk. But the mercenary registered no reaction.

"Don't you know the old saying: What's one more slice off a cut loaf? I wouldn't mind pumping her myself, just to see if she is still spoiled. Ha! ha! . ."

When the woman was ready with her stuff, she hastily went the haunt out, storming into the darkness of the muddy street. The monk tried to slink away as inconspicuously as possible, but the warrior cried out from the den's threshold, "Where are you off to, saintly lover-boy? Follow her and be brave tonight, fighting it out to the utter coming! Ha! Ha! It's worth a final realization, I mean it, saintly man. . ."

Chapter 7: The Bedchamber Art

Her room was utterly silent, except for that faint pit-a-pat cracking, which might have been the sound of her own thoughts. "If I were you," she said, "the question I would ask myself if rather, Do I want to?"

"What is that supposed to mean?"

At that very moment, their eyes met of his scrip, which her maidservant, a mute girl, tried to wipe, drying the remains of the drizzling rain outside, and inadvertently drawing out the robe, folded in a rectangle size of a small box.

"Hold it up," she commanded the girl. Her attention turned to the robe. "Unwrap it," she ordered.

With the elegance and disdain of a magician, the maidservant allowed her the back panel, the clouds, the tree, the two great beasts wheeling high above the world in the endless fighting of opposing forces. The monk became absorbed in it as well. It was the first time he had seen it in a while. The details enlightened by the fitful gleams of a lamp amazed him genuinely. The whole picture was displayed in motion. His eyes passed quickly beyond the scene into the rare regions of sacred art. High above the earth, two great beasts wheeled vertiginously in the air, their talons booking as they crushed together, whether to terminate or copulate, one couldn't say. Teeth bared, jaws clamped tight together, each appeared to suck the life-breath from the other's mouth, and then resuscitate him with a savage kiss. These monsters were, respectively, the Dragon and the Tiger: the first with eyes reminiscent of emeralds and a golden body flecked with blue-black satin scales. The second, the Tiger: ghastly white with the blackish strips till the end of its tail, except its mouth, dripping blood from its opponent's throat, or from its own broken heart. The Tiger's eyes were blue, as blue as space, the color the sky should have been. As Xue Feng changed the angle of view, the tiger turned his terrible, massive head from side to side and glared at him with its green, vertical eyes bright with a curious, impersonal fury, not at all like human hatred, and somehow beautiful. The blood streaming from the monsters' wounds converged in a single torrent flowing down the sky, washing the dawn, or sunset, with its hue, falling to earth like drops of bitter rain, a rain of blood, under which the whole of nature had been blighted. The rainfall reminded him of the beasts' symbolic meaning as primitive forces, clouds and winds: the one swirling and transmogrifying in the heavens, assuming fantastical shapes at will, as the wingless Dragon magically could; the other, silent, invisible, swift, like the Tiger springing out of an ambush. These two elements, warring, or mating, bred the rain which nourished the earth; hence an old expression "the play of clouds and wind," which was a euphemism for intercourse. This revealed for her the hidden story of her private anguish. She might have had some exposure to the mysteries of 'dual cultivation' even if only through reading or conversation. In fact, what she knew about the technique she learned from her master, who was knowledgeable about all Daoist schools, ancient and modern, and their secret practices concisely embodied in the sacred robe conjured the rites too pointedly to have done so accidentally. These primal beasts cleaving in their equivocal embrace were the images of destruction and generation, both. At the same time, in the robe the outcome of the battle between the most powerful denizens of the Oriental zodiac was still undecided, and would remain so; there was a dead heat for eternity. There was an insidious variation on the White Tiger and Green Dragon sexual practice in which the woman set out to subvert the man's intention, attempting to excite him to that pitch of passion where self-control became impossible, making him spill his load in her vagina, garnering his Yang-fluids to enhance her own longevity. It was by this means that Xi-wang Mu, the Royal Mother of the Western Heavens, attained her immortality in the process using up a thousand young men's lives. Incongruous as it might seem, that was what flitted through the monk's brain as he contemplated the sacred robe handiwork the saints wrought. The stories of young men who had been seduced out of their self-interest by powerful, conniving women, young men who had spent themselves for love, ejaculating load after a load of their sweet sexual albumen into the empty darkness, until their lovers' bodies were replete with it. Such tales resonated for him for a while. The whole appeared altered somehow, more vivid, purified, as though the interval it had undergone a further distillation, its physicality enhanced, solidified, until it crossed a magic threshold into immateriality and became pure essence, the spirit, a thought, a vapor, aura, whatever, and even more. His wonder was increased by what he saw when he emerged from that brief rapture, which was bittersweet to him. He looked at her. She was sitting as before, crying. Two tears had trickled halfway down her cheeks, small quicksilver runnels sparkling as they course through the parched deserts of her face.

"You're crying," he said.

"You seem surprised," she remarked. "What do you think of me? Am I so horrible that I may not shed tears? What woman could see this and not weep?"

Not knowing what to say, he kept silence. But with this recognition, in a sense not far from the literal, the courtesan had seen herself into the robe, and that the robe was her prototype, as surely as if the silk were her flayed skin, her tattoo, inseminating an indelible dye. Yet how she might have wished that the robe to have served her as a shield able to cover her hidden self entirely and protect each piece of her wounded and tearing apart at the seams life.

"Mei, bring the pipe." She said with tears in her voice and turned to the monk. "I have never seen such a handiwork, and I collect -- for myself and others."

The maidservant carried a tray with a lamp, a dish of black, gooey opium, and a pipe with a chased silver bowl. Breaking off a pellet, she shaped it into her fingers, then spitted it on the dipper and held it to the flame.

"Would you care to join me?" she asked when it was ready, offering him the pipe.

He waved his hand, declining.

They fell silent as she smoked awhile. When she had finished, she rose and crossed to the armoire. "Come and look," she said, inviting the monk with a sweeping gesture of her arm.

Inside he saw a cache of silken treasure: damasks, gauzes, twills, robes of every color, from palest shades of gray and pink to black and red, deep purples, mauves and indigos, a rainbow of vivid, deep-dyed hues, each one surprising and a little strange, as though implemented only once.

"This is Japanese," she said, flicking one with her long fingernail, her pride expressed almost disdainfully. "It was worn by a famous courtesan in Nara and Kyoto. . ." Her voice had dropped into a rhythmical, incantatory cadence, as though she were reciting poetry, or performing some ritual which she had celebrated many times and mastered long ago. Mei, her maidservant, tiptoed up beside the monk and was looking on, as though for the first time in her life. And it really was so. She seemed almost sweet. There was a look of childlike awe on her painted features, like a small girl experiencing a treat she's waited for so long, her dreams have made it magical, almost holy.

"This belonged to the abbot of a monastery," she continued, pointing to another. "It is said he wore it on his deathbed that on the last night of his life, the watchers, exhausted by their vigil, fell asleep. In the morning they awoke and found him gone, and this in the bedclothes."

She touched a third. "This is from the Imperial court. It was worn by a young Maid-in-Waiting, a noblewoman said to be a favorite of the Dowager Empress of the Wei dynasty. Though well-born, she fell in love with a servant in the palace, a boy of common birth. They were discovered. He was executed for his presumption, she locked up to prevent her from doing herself harm. But she refused all food and water, committing suicide employing a remorseless passivity. See the sad blue-eyed phoenix.

"These are my best pieces," she went on. "But today I've lost my relish for them, seeing this."

The monk was impressed by the majesty she'd taken on, almost afraid of it. But even as he watched he saw it disappearing, faded in the air. Her features hardened. "I must have it," she insisted heavily, picking up the sacred robe again. "Name your price."

He stiffened and appraised her coldly. "It's not for sale."

"Come, come," she cackled, shriveling up before his eyes. "I won't cheat you. I don't scrimp on quality. I pay top. I have clients who would kill for this." She smiled cryptically. "I might do it myself. . . Ha-Ha! But all joking aside, what is it to you? You are too green to appreciate it. Not to insult you, but in your hands, it's like 'a diamond in a sack of grains.' Besides, you have your youth. The world is open to you. For me the scope if pleasure narrows daily, hourly, contracting like the pupil of an eye. The thing itself, life, has become too brilliant for my eyes to bear directly. I must take it all at second hand, in small, medicinal doses, through such as this, . . or this." She indicated the robe with her first gesture, with her second, her mute maidservant Mei. "If for no other reason then, like charity, let me have it. I won't quibble over price."

"Some things cannot be bought and sold."

"Hist, hist," she said. "In the real world, that's mere sentiment. Everything has its price, its matched season. If not today, tomorrow. It's all a matter of timing, circumstance, and a quirk of fate."

"If that is true, it is a worldly truth."

She smiled cynically. "You know another sort?"

"I am a monk," he said.

She shrugged dismissingly. "And, as you know, I am a courtesan who's able to provide unearthly bliss and pleasure. . ."

What was next is difficult to describe. Usually, a master teaches the practitioners to learn the sexual technique in two aspects: the internal and external. The inner is breathing and the way of moving the qi-energy and jing-substance from perineum up to the crown of the head and then down into the middle elixir field (dan-tian) in the lower part of the belly. As to the external aspect of the sexual practice, it's all about postures (actually, there were nine key sexual positions to be exercised together, one by one). If both parts are taught simultaneously, and the practitioner is unable to get it right, then there would be complications. Therefore, the beginner should let the breathing be natural and not emphasize the method of distributing the qi-energy all over the body.

Through all the night she showed him her best qualification of a courtesan who is familiar with the Daoist Tiger-Dragon Zen Yoga, performing a set of all the nine love techniques, one by one. First, she tried to check up on his store of Yang-fluids, which, supposedly, was small and quickly depleted. For this, she started with the position called 'the Dragon's tumblings.' After spending some time foreplay, she lay on her back and moved with both hands the gates of her vagina apart so that his Jade Stalk could be easier accepted inside. At that, he knelt closely to the edge of bed mat and entered into her slowly; all his thrusts were directed upwards to reach her Upper Chamber. His tool, not well calibrated yet, moved slowly and quite freely. She directed him with her instructions, telling him to produce eight shallow jerks followed by two deeper thrusts, repeating this set of twisted dragon's movement several times. Moving forward like a drill, his tool was mostly dead, while moving back it became as though revived. How come that having no wings dragon is able to fly above the clouds? How come that getting no fins it swims throughout the seas and rivers? This is owing to its ability to take rotary and spiral movements to advance and retreat, zigzagging to the left and to the right. To move forward is not enough; simultaneously, one has to take a rotary movement to proceed effectively, like a drill; hence the position's name. As a result, slow but sure, his instrument started to be stronger and harder to move to the second position called 'the Tiger's tread.' For as it is said, 'Only the Dragon knows how to rise on the clouds to heaven, but to produce the fertile rain one needs the feminine power of the Tiger.' Now she wanted to support him with her Yin-fluids, which women possessed in inexhaustible quantities. Frankly speaking, she had little to gain from that exotic practice known only by Daoist alchemists (except perhaps some pleasurable sexual activity in a charitable cause or a second thought, like in the case), but being under the influence of the sacred handiwork, which evoked her deeply concealed emotions, she was willingly subordinated in the act of 'sexual noblesse oblige.' She lay with her face down and rose her butt up. He remained to have knelt and, embracing her belly with both hands from behind (hence the name of the position, so long as the tiger uses to make a surprise attack on its prey from behind), pressed tightly to her buttocks, and entered his solid now dick inside her as deep as possible. He moved his instrument back and forth five times, each time producing a series of eight deep thrusts; hence she asked him to observe the measure with that position properly. Very soon her vagina opened up wide so that her sexual fluids, literally, started to splash outward as if from the mountain spring. As for him, she commanded him to keep his semen within himself, concentrating on counting the thrusts. The act run smoothly but very intimately. When he suddenly felt that the sperm was about to eject, he quickly removed his Jade Stalk out and squeezed the tip of its head. At the same time, he was told to press forcefully with three fingers of the right hand on the acupoint called 'Haidi' (Sea Bottom) located in the crotch, just behind the scrotum. At that, he threw back his head and took a long deep inhalation to cleanse his heart and calm the mind. "Freeze," she ordered resolutely."Now take your time and, squatting as though you want to relieve your bowel, put your tool up, forward." Doing so, his energy immediately rushed upwards, along with the spine, to reach the crown of his head and thus prevent ejaculation.

"Your sexual energy is the greatest treasure of the body," she said, "don't waste it! My master used to say, 'If to seek only pleasure, squandering all the reserve of the masculine substance (yang), it would be the same whim as if to throw a precious Mani pearl into the sea. Who will be able to find and get it back?'"

Upon having a short break, the act was going on, moving to the third posture called "the monkey grasp," which reduced to the following disposition: lying on her back again, she lifted her hips and knees upward so that they leaned against his chest. This position resembled the monkey climbing up a tree; hence the name. Thus her buttocks became slightly raised, hanging over the bed mat. When he entered his tool inside her at the maximum depth, she started swinging, imitating the monkey picking fruits on the tree. As a result, her seminal fluids were emitted abundantly, like the shower. . . When the turn came to the fourth position called "the clinging cicada," again, she lay facing downwards; her body became erected and elongated as though the golden cicada clinging to the trunk. He lay prone on her back and entered his stalk into her but not too deep. She slightly lifted her buttocks to grab his 'red pearl,' the head of his dick, telling him to produce a series of nine thrusts six times in a row that made her extremely excited. As a result, his slight movements within her vagina opened the Jade Gates outside to the fullest extent. According to myths he had learned earlier, the golden cicada was a symbol of a restless, yearning mind, a heart still passionately attached to the world of senses, the marketplace, afraid to let it go and plummet, like a stone into the bright and shining realm of the Void. Besides, due to its onomatopoeic aptness, this image was appropriate in other ways too. For the dreary, mechanical whine of male cicadas in the forest of a summer night, keeping the cravings of the flesh, that monotonous, obsessive music of a diseased appetite which could never be satisfied and so might be appeased, or mortified -- in this poignant image was adumbrated the carnal hell of a man. The return to the still source of being was an attempt to allay this 'music,' to quiet the cicada that was always singing in the temple of the heart. The fifth posture called "the turtle's leaps" boiled to her disposition on the back with knees bent so that they could touch her nipples when he pushed her from behind. At that, she, enjoying herself, began to sway from side to side with the whole body, rising slowly upward. Again, he was nearly coming, but she insisted on blocking his semen channel by pressing on the 'Hai-di' acupoint in the crotch. After sending his energy upstream to the crown of the head, his power increased so drastically that he felt the faint current running through his temples. It was an ethereal strain touched with joy; yet it was neither joy nor fatigue, not in the common understanding of these words. Through some deep impulses coming up to his temples, he started to hear a songbird's singing somewhere out of the impulsive current. Its song provided a pleasant excuse for the act's procrastination. Listening to the bird's performance, he fell into a meditative state. Though neither alerting nor restful, the trance was exceedingly delicious, shot through with trembling of nervous ecstasy -- unlike anything he'd experienced before. By turns his body burned as with fever and tingled with chills, he started to fathom that the bird's song appeared to come from no particular direction, or from all directions simultaneously. As he went deeper, it seemed to come from within his body, entirely. For, though beautiful, the tune was as cold as starlight and lacked a human meaning. . . or else, perhaps, contained a meaning too deep for his soul to digest. Feeling that his condition is on the climb, she moved to the next posture called "the soaring phoenix," which she used to produce a high tide of the whole performance. Remaining on her back, she lifted her legs so that his knees came to be placed between her hips. Leaning with both hands on the bed mat, he thrust his dick. By then his tool was hard and hot to produce the pulling movements inside her; she responded rhythmically with her counter motion. This act was carried out thrice with eight jerks each. Then her butt was pressed down tightly, her Jade Gate opened widely to emit the seminal fluids out to her full satisfaction. As for him, being slightly lost in himself, he forgot of the songbird and almost believed it was his own soul singing while soaring in an unknown height, straight to the seventh heaven, the realm of mythological critters and immortals. From there, he had to descend to the solid ground to reboot his corporeal self. Through the window that was opened on the courtyard, a fluttering of darkness against the silver horn of the new moon convinced him that he had been deluded with Phoenix -- the real songbird had lighted in the upper branches of the peach tree where it performed its serenade. At just that moment the branch quivered like a bowstring as the bird stopped singing and sprang off in the dead night. With his eyes, he followed the trajectory of its flight across the sky until it darkened the bright horn of the new moon and disappeared, as though swallowed up in the blue-dark vault of heaven. Exactly in the place where it had entered or had appeared to enter, there was a blue discoloration in the crescent, like a shadow, an adumbration of a new form, he recognized this blemish as the foot of the Celestial Rabbit. The seventh position called "the rabbit sleeks its fur" was performed like this: he lay on his back, stretching his legs along the bed mat. She mounted on him, facing his feet; his legs were placed between her knees. She bent so that her head touched his legs. At that, his Jade Stalk penetrated inside her, resembling the stretching of zither strings. Experiencing great pleasure, her seminal fluids were secreting in plenty. It gushed abundantly, as if from the mountain spring. In joy and merriment, in harmony of satisfaction, his spirit and flesh became excited and resurgent as well. He dived into that celestial silence, listening to the stillness with pleasure. Outside the stars were winking into life; they hung like the luster of a lantern, shivering in the ecstatic crystal darkness of the night sky. As his eyes were becoming accustomed to the gloom, he made out the Rabbit, which, night after night, as in a spotlight, could be seen bounding across the sky in the face of the moon, running for its life, then diving into the black hole of its burrow to emerge timidly again with a new month. Each night it skulked in the darkness of the universe, foraging for existence, fleeing every time the sentry swept it with the hot light of the flood, fixing its silhouette in that crisp aureole which marked it as 'a fair game' -- the bridge to the eighth position called "fish touching with scales." He lay on the back; she mounted on him, stretching her legs forward. He slowly entered his jade stalk on a shallow depth and stopped moving, standing by. This act resembled a newborn baby grasping his mother's nipple with his jaws. She was the only partner who produced short and intermittent movements as if scaling. For his ultimate task was to avoid ejaculation as long as possible, taking his instrument out of her once nearby the coming. . . Very soon he came to be firmly convinced himself that she was a sort of witches, the true lady of pleasure, and might work a fearful metamorphosis on him. For a moment he thought to himself, "Had I not heard that the fresh, unpolluted blood of a virgin was always in demand among alchemists and wizards -- an essential ingredient in the compounding of the Golden Elixir Pill? . ." He remembered how some of the senior monks had been so cruel as to tell him that that was why they had kept and fed him so many years, as a sort of sacrificial pig or fish. All of a sudden, he made a guess, "Perhaps she would have me suspended by a hook over a flame to cook out my vital substance, as the sap is drawn from birch and mulberry trees. Then she could distill it into an alembic and quaff it off heartily, like a ceremonial cup or a jug of spirit, belching and wiping her mouth on the long sleeve of one of her collected in many robes." This or a similar scenario seemed to him, not at all improbable.

Yes, she was at her best that night. To perform the ninth and the final posture called "two cranes twisting with necks," she let him sit down on his butt, stretching his legs forward; she sat on his hips and armed around his neck. His Jade Stalk entered into her Divine Gate, filling up the inner space entirely. Simultaneously, he clasped her butt with both hands, helping her to sway up frequently. Once she started to experience indescribable pleasure, her seminal fluids were spilled abundantly to his fullest satisfaction; he absorbed her fluids with his solid dick, sending the transformed energy through the upper elixir field on top of the head back to the middle elixir center in the lower belly to his great benefit. Upon finishing the act, she said, "You did well, saintly man. Once you become able to seal up your Jade Stalk's spitting out, you can achieve the highest grade of enlightenment. As I was taught, the ability to make love and avoid ejaculation can improve your hearing and eye-sighting dramatically. If you can do it twice in succession, your voice becomes clean and strong. After making it three times in a row, your skin becomes smooth and shiny; after four copulations without an ejection, your bones strengthen significantly. Five-time ejection-free intercourses can make your buttocks and hips filled with solid strength; after six non-ejaculations your urethra cleanses up completely. Your willpower becomes strengthened after your seventh non-ejaculation, and the spirit will be liberated after eight intercourses in succession without sperm depleting. Starting from the ninth ejaculation-free copulation, your lifetime will be prolonged critically to become similar to that of Heaven and Earth, and after the tenth making love in succession without losing any drops of your semen you will attain a final enlightenment of a sagely minded man to be recognized as an immortal dwelling on earth. . ."

Ultimately, the opium did its job, and she went down like a felled trunk. When finally the night was mostly over, the monk felt oversaturated with new impressions and knowledgeable possessions: love, dread, guilt, hope, madness -- multiple cross-purposes drove him mostly killed. She lay next to him, like a prodigal planet come home, at last, attracted by his pure heart's gravity. At the end of the night, he started to be like everyone else, he had initiation; he was a human; he was a monk; ultimately, he was a mortal. As to what that meant, he wouldn't have dared venture an opinion, too newly initiated into the practical mysteries he had learned about theoretically. He doubted before if he could have any, had he tried. Now he worked. The truth was, that night he was fit for much of anything, virtually insane.

Packing the robe into his scrip, and having exhausted its possibilities, he felt himself out of further unequal bargain of the divine and mundane, and began to hit the road, bidding goodbye to the wick with all its sinful contents he went through in such short time with all these begging, fighting, fucking -- all mostly at once. Passing by the peach tree he had seen last night through the window, he made out its real fruit, the tiny unripe pills against the blue sky at the early dawn -- the fruits of darkness counterpoised against the seed-buds of twinkled light. The songbird started to sing again and had been all along. Its song drew him back to the Tian-tai Mountains. As he paced his way, an old story came to his mind about one monk whose injured soul flew out from between the ribs of his body. Like a songbird from an opened cage, it flew out, lighting in a tree to cry its grievance to the world and sing its master a long, sorrowful farewell, then disappeared into the forest for good and all. Likewise, his virgin which he had lost that night for getting something dangerously huge instead.

Chapter 8: Alchemy of Love

He followed his path diligently. Upon reaching the monastery in Tian-tai, Abbot Zhao Zhou asked him, teasing, "Tell me, brother, what didn't you have before you went to the remote Wu-tai Mountains?"

"I had nothing I didn't have before," was the reply.

"Suppose it was so," agreed the abbot, "in such a case, why did you head off for Wu-tai?"

"If I didn't do that," the reply came immediately, "then how could I be sure I had nothing I didn't have before I set off for Wu-tai?"

Hearing this, the abbot remained to be very pleased. "Once long ago there was a tradition of religious pilgrimage among us," he said. "For there have always been a few for whom, due to a quirk of fate or temperament, the 'hundred paths' were not sufficient, men who through some curse, or spiritual distinction, could not journey in the wagon ruts of tried and traveled ways. For these, the journey inward led out into the world. You, I sense, is temperamentally aligned with these. Seeing it in you, I can't help but seek it in myself. I always expected that one day you would leave us and go out into the world. That day has come. Remember, all the hundred paths are hard. All require risk-taking and sacrifice. But this is the hardest. In the hundred tracks at least there is the comfort and support of fellowship, a community of like-minded seekers who can share their enthusiasms, their doubts, and so find some degree of solace. In the monastery, too, there is a relative absence of temptation. But the way that leads back into the world is a lonely and dangerous one. The people of the world will not understand your passion, or if they do they will be frightened by its implications for their lives, and so despise you for it. And the risk is higher. For the unredeemed world of the marketplace is rife with dangerous passions, circulating in the air invisible and virulent as the germs of pestilence. It is difficult to go into the cities of the plague and not receive contagion oneself. Of those who leave, some return, but many more find the world too succulent, too beautiful and creamy and prefer to spend themselves upon the acquisition of what, by its very nature, diminishes contentment the more of it they acquire. This is not to be condemned. For these men of sorts are inextricably involved in the ways of Dao."

During his practice in the Wu-tai Mountains, Xue Feng aroused his Bodhi-mind, the aspiration to attain the higher enlightenment for the sake of all humans. Once he had done this, the local deity taught him a method of contemplation and practice using the energetic centers of hearing and visualization, employing which he became able to enter the spirit of Void. What does it actually mean? It means such a realm, in which there is purely nothing. By knowing existed things, the sagely minded man can understand what does not exist. This is what is referred to in Zen as 'illuminating the mind and seeing one's original nature.'

To attain the way of great Dao as emptiness, the monk went through his daily life, accumulating practice and upgrading his 'gong-fu' day by day without deviation even a little bit from the original nature of his true self. As a result, he made his spirit become not in the least clouded. When, at last, the slightest cloud of his original innocence cleared away, there was the true emptiness appeared as the way of Great Dao. Whether he gave Dharma talks, or helped living beings, or meditated, or made trades in the marketplace, or engaged in any other activities, he remained to be empty in his mind. He then found himself on the brink of the Gate of Void, through which he saw at a glance his own world, other worlds, the Buddha's world, the demon's palaces, the Pure Land, all and sundry in ten directions. He observed the mundane world of Three Realms as if he was looking at his own reflection in the bright mirror of the three thousand universes. Entering the Gate of Void, he realized that the magnificent mirror, which was boundless, as it had no frame, never had dust alight; it reflected impassively all that was passing before it, but remained itself clean and spotless evermore. It remained nothing and thus was empty of illusions, free from consciousness and from all attachments ever possible. Due to the virtual mirror visualization, the monk attained the supernatural power of seeing anything anywhere. He saw that the Void was filled with virtues and that wisdom had existence and that the principle had existed and that the ways of Dao had existed and that the spirit had the power of Nothingness.

Upon attaining the complete realization of Dharma, he returned to Tian-tai to spend the rest of his days meditating and practicing in the deep mountains. His famously known verse sounds like this:

"Originally, I've come from the Tian-tai Mountains
To make a hundred of thousands miles route of return.
All my life I roam like a drifting raft or clouds
Scudded across the sky -- my back and forth floating
Lasts for long. Wandering leisurely and carefree,
I meet no troubles; keeping myself aloof from all dust,
I ascent the way of Bodhi-mind, which is the Emptiness."

And then:

"The worldly pathways lead to the forked roads;
Hence all folks suffer a lot of vexation and hatred.
Mastering the state of rest, I sink into the sea waves;
Wandering about, I wheel thru all the Three Realms
Of the mundane. O heavens! It's pitiful indeed that
There's not even a single soul that is born in the world

Just not to be then buried. Lightning flashes --
For an instant they blaze up; life and death --
A swirl of dry dust, wet dirt, mud, and dry dust again."

Such a perspective was nothing more than a free point in the middle of a stream that flew eternally. For him, the foundation of the universe and the fundamental principle, on the ground of which it functioned all the way, was a plunge in the middle of a process of transformation. Passing from one level of existence to another, from the existent to non-existent, from life to death, he went on and further beyond the limitations that different realms applied.

As legends run, Xue Feng returned to Tian-tai to dwell in a cave he found to the south of Xiang-lin temple. That was a mutually rewarding decision for himself and for the monastery's abbot who was quite happy when the pilgrims and all ranking officials at the retreat that came to pay homage to the sagely minded master also dropped in the temple, every time leaving some donations.

One early morning a pilgrim paid a visit to the master, asking of the true meaning of the term 'the innermost mystery of all mysteries' was.

Instead of replying to him, Xue Feng silently lifted his index finger up. Seeing this, all of a sudden, the pilgrim attained realization.

Actually, the profound mystery of all mysteries is the most critical and highest principle of all teachings. It is the essence of attaining the nature of the self. By lifting his finger up, the monk prompted the guest to realize the fact that the profound mystery for him was his true self-nature: the state of his body, his soul, and his good self, all in all.

In a while, upon advancing in his mind, the pilgrim said quietly, "I've heard people say you are an expert in what is called 'filling in the Void with the Yin (feminine) power.' I beg you to provide me with your wise instructions, Master."

Xue Feng said, "This method is known by Daoist alchemists from time immemorial, but today most of them ignore its cleverness and benefit. To fill in the Void with the feminine power you first need to warm up your 'kiln.' For this, you should choose a young woman with radiant eyes, white teeth, beautiful lips, clean face, smooth skin, a sonorous voice, and pleasant manner of speech -- such sort of female fits most. If a woman is weak from birth, her skin is dark and pimply, and monthlies happen irregularly, then for the fourth decade, she is no longer suitable for appropriate sexual intercourse. Choose also a pleasant day when the weather is fine, and establish calm and peace in your heart before being engaged in a love battle between opposing powers, the Yin and Yang. As for hours, take your time in the period from the midnight to noon when the power of Yin is on declining, while the Yang is on rising. At the start of copulating, drop your clothes and sit in a pose for meditation, concentrate your spirit and pacify the qi-energy. Your belly should be empty to make the energetic channels open for smooth circulation throughout the entire body. Otherwise, if you're full, it is difficult for the energy to circulate freely. Do some warm-up -- it will be helpful a lot. Sealing up all the nine openings, you will thus be able to direct the qi-energy exactly to the spot of its destination -- the middle elixir field in the lower part of your belly. Once the energy reaches your Jade Stalk, in no time you start to feel some heat growing in the center of your palms, acupoint 'lao-gong.' Grab your scrotum and penis with your right hand, bringing all the three parts together. Use the left palm to produce the circular stroking in the area of the lower part of the belly, heating the elixir field. Perform two series of nine circulars of stroking in opposite directions to make the total number 18 (9+9=18). Then, having changed the hands, do the same procedure to get in the complete 36 circulars. Upon finishing with the stroking, pat on both thighs a couple dozens of slaps to make your Jade Stalk rise itself without delay.

"First embrace her precious vessel and talk to her tenderly, saying some pleasant words to touch her heart with your fine complements; then try to awaken her passion by touching three sacred peaks, which are her tongue above, her nipples in the middle, and her Divine Gates below. When you caress these three peaks a woman becomes excited -- her vagina comes to be moistened, and passion awakens in her to the fullest. Then you hold her firmly to your body, caressing her entire figure and letting her mind follow her lust. Upon entering your dick into her vagina, produce nine shallow thrusts upon one deep. The precept says: "There's no place for haste on the battlefield, there's no way for fuss in endearment."

Make sure that your jade stalk produces more shallow thrusts and less deep ones. With the shallow dives the Yang power becomes stronger, and with the deep ones the power of Yin comes to be strengthened. With a shallow dive, you secure a victory for yourself, while with a deep one you inevitably suffer defeat. Be careful at this and differentiate appropriately! Enter into her vagina slowly but quickly get out of there; don't be in a rush to prevent disrupting of your spirit. After a long battle, take a break and have a little rest; calm down your fighting spirit and pacify your heart to continue then with your refreshed abilities. As it goes:

"Close your mouth, grit the teeth,
Look up at the top of the summit
To be efficient and battleworthy.
Breathing through your nose,
You thus inhale the pure wind;
This makes you open the golden well
Of your sagely mind.
Grab her arms with your palms,
Weave her legs with yours,
Be like an ape and thus
The highly treasurable black pearl
Will rise to the very top of Mt. Kunlun."

In a while, the master added, "There's a battle strategy, you see?" He said this eagerly, searching the pilgrim's face for a sign of proper understanding. "What else? There's a tactical inspiration, a gift from Heaven, which reduces to the ability to avoid ejaculation as long as possible to absorb the feminine essence as much as possible. For this reason, the greatest figures of old used sexual intercourse as the way of mastering their 'gong-fu,' checking up on a constant basis and demonstrate to their subordinates at which level they were at that moment about the ability to absorb the feminine fluids (the female power) for their own benefits. Of course, there should be a certain sequence of action to observe. Start with foreplay. First press on her gently and leisurely and remove your own haste and extreme excitement. Generally speaking, you shouldn't ejaculate before she comes to extreme excitement. Once some saliva accumulates under her tongue, and her perineum becomes moistened, it means that she is ready to throw up her energy in the blast. At that moment, if you touch her tongue with your tongue, and press her right thigh with your left hand, her sexual energy stands out in abundance. This energy can be drunk or absorbed with your Jade Stalk immersed deeply into her inner space. Swallowing her accumulated salvia is known as 'drinking the waters from Celestial Lake,' while what is absorbing with your solid dick is called 'drinking the pre-birth or universal wine.' Once you have mastered both ways of exploiting the lower and upper elixir fields, you can be as though a bit tight without drinking wine -- continuously on the high person, as they designated such a state of body and mind. And these words are not idle to be proved by the following short verse, which runs from olden times, saying:

"To crop the feminine power in plenty
You have to find a duly worked fertile field:
A young and pretty fair maiden, from eighteen
To twenty-eight years old is a perfect match
Who has to be neither skinny nor fatty,
With clean and smooth skin, like white jade,
With her face of a white lotus flower, preferably,
To proceed without any sort of aversion.
If you can breathe with your abdomen part,
Your whole inside is boiling with pure mercury,
But if the Gate of Life (acupoint Mingmen)
Is shut too tight, the lead, the opposing ingredient,
Will not be able to properly reborn. When both,

The lead and mercury, start to be well accumulated,
They push you straight away to the coast
Of the Primordial Ocean; and the marvelous spot
Of the Mid Elixir will elevate you to the upper stage
Where all celestial beings and terrestrial immortals
Are in bliss to hold celebrations and fun; a lot of fun."

"Making love with a woman, start from producing one deep dive per every three shallow ones and, gradually, go up to one-to-nine proportion. Take about three hundred thrusts in one-time copulation. Your ultimate task is to avoid untimely ejaculation by all means. Once you feel that the semen is about to erupt, quickly remove your Jade Stalk out from vagina and squeeze the tip of its head; at the same time, press forcefully with three fingers of your right hand on the spot called 'hai-di' located in the perineum, just behind the scrotum, to block the semen channel of the lower dan-tian. According to the Daoist tradition, the old name 'Hai-di' or 'the Bed of the Sea' is also known as the Dragon-and-Tiger Cave, where the Yin and Yang powers are released for the masculine and feminine compounds. The posture called 'Piercing with a Needle to the Sea Bottom' means that you use your instrument as if a needle to stimulate the lower dan-tian (elixir center) for activating interaction of two opposing forces. When you do it precisely, and a true fashion, as long as the whole link of postures is well performed and truly understandable, it becomes a transformation of the body at the level of cells' continued renewal, in which one finds a fundamental source of creative inspiration and time-proved practical wisdom. As an old verse goes:

"To know how, being full of lust and desire,
Remain free from desire is a great virtue;
To live in dust being never stained with it
Is also the greatest of all attainments.
Be gentle and slow in your movements,
And thus a hundred ailments and illness
Will never touch you, passing you by."

"Next, using your imagination, direct your sexual energy from the perineum upward along the spine to the crown of the head, and then downwards again to the middle elixir center in the lower part of your belly. Meantime, try to feel duly this gently circulating energy as nourishment for the reproductive organs, an important aspect of the kidneys' system. Simultaneously, take a deep breath and hold it for a while, cleanse the heart, and calm your mind. At that moment, take no move, just freeze to make the impulse pass over. Upon having a short break, repeat the coition again, as described above. Having reached the state of excitement, take your time and, squatting as if to relieve your bowel, and direct your solid dick upward. At that, your qi-energy rushes upwards to prevent ejaculation. Your sperm, as the original substance, is the greatest treasure of the body; if however, to seek in each intercourse some sort of pleasure only, squandering all the reserves of your original masculine (Yang) power, it would be the same whim as throwing a precious Mani pearl into the sea. Who will be able to find it then? As an old song runs:

"Wanting to realize the secret of long copulation,
Take the posture of a turtle. Thus, you will be able
To direct the treasurable Yin energy from the depth
Of her vagina straight to your elixir field (dan-tian).
All the three peaks: her mouth, breast, and jade gate
Are the source of both partners' miraculous instincts
And desire that always run prior to proper sex."

Then he continued, saying, "Ultimately, if we are talking about a true accomplishment, the non-ejaculation is not yet a real attainment; the true achievement is to return the semen to the middle elixir field in the lower part of the belly and thus improve the vital energy of the whole body, distributing it accordingly. That's the true way of the great Dao implemented in the number 60! What does it mean? If we take the distance between the lower dan-tian in the crotch and the upper elixir center on top of the head and designate it by the correlated number 36 (3+6=9), we get it masculine character of the Dragon, which climbs up along the spine to grab with its mouth the treasurable crystal but called Clay

Pill. Accordingly, the distance between the upper elixir center and the middle one in the lower part of the belly correlates with the number 24 (2+4=6) and, therefore, is represented by the feminine image of Tiger. As a result, we get the number 60 (36+24=60), the number of complete circulation and closed circle; hence it is said of closing all the nine openings to properly accumulate the qi-energy in the body. When the number of produced thrusts reaches tens of thousands, a woman starts to get her rocks on the other three spots, which are the nipples, thighs, and kidneys. In between, pay attention on her look and the timbre of voice, gently stick to her lips, touch her body to calm her excitement down; at the right time take your tool out of her jade gates, do it quickly and then squat down, taking the turtle posture for absorbing her substantial fluids, her vaginal discharge, with your stalk. This is what is poetically called "the black dragon drinks the sea." This way, you first accumulate your own masculine strength originated in your body to achieve then a chaotic mixture of both sorts of energy, the masculine and feminine. Again, the mixed energy rises up to the crown of the head and then descends from there to the middle elixir field in the lower part of the belly. This is the way the male cultivates the right energy in himself to benefit himself considerably. As an old song runs:

"Seal up your Jade Stalk tightly first
To maintain and support the authenticity
Of vitality in yourself.
By recovering your semen,
Improve the vital energy of life,
Accumulating it diligently
In your middle elixir field.
Once you clean up your energetic channels,
The black dragon drinks the whole sea,
Enriching your body with the miraculous power
For gladness of both partners
And improvement the bedchamber art."

"When your Jade Stalk is erected but does not increase in size, it means that it has no muscle strength. When it grows in size but does not harden, it means that it doesn't have the force of the tendons. When it comes to being hard, but is not hot, it means that the vital energy does not penetrate into it. The absence of muscular strength in it implies that copulation is impossible; if there is no essential energy in it, there is no other way but to refuse from intercourse.

The real art of making love is deep and dark, like the waters of the Yellow River. It is free from extremes of cold and heat; it is like the weather in autumn and spring, to judge of which one can only in springtime or in autumn. He who does not practice the Daoist doctrine of the Middle Way cannot reveal for himself the secret of real interaction between man and woman. It should only be comprehended throughout one's lifetime and treated with a certain caution. This is the matter that requires divine enlightenment. In a word, the pivot secret of a proper sexual activity reduces the ability to prevent ejaculation first. He who is able to seal up his Jade Stalk and bring the semen back to the middle elixir center (dan-tian), producing the golden elixir pill, can achieve the highest grade of enlightenment. Upon attaining the highest degree of pleasure, bite your teeth tightly, pick up your abdomen and take a slow inhalation in order to collect all "the three flowers" (the spirit, essence, and substance) on top of the head (the upper dan-tian); thus, all the five sorts of energy will return then to the primordial state of subsistence. Secondly, keep yourself within limits and follow the golden principle of the Middle Way, which means, to desire without desire, and enjoy but keep yourself out of the extreme joy. As the poem runs,

"Holding in hand the Golden Seal, employing which
You've blocked the semen track to prevent ejaculation,
You thus mount on a water buffalo, sitting backward
To reverse the qi-energy along their channels
Throughout the whole bodily structure. With only one
Single blocking in the perineum, you are able to turn
Waters of the Yellow River upstream to reach its spring.
The Dragon (Yang) moves backward too, starting from

The trigram of Heaven (spirit) to that of Fire (substance),
Utilizing dividing the middle line into two separate parts.
Once the bottom line becomes divided too, you get your dick
Up to the top of the Mount Kunlun -- the symbol of the essence
In its entirely masculine (Yang) manifestation ever produced."

As is said, ability to make love and avoid ejaculation ten times in succession, without losing a drop of male semen, would allow one to attain complete enlightenment of the sagely minded man to be recognized as one of the immortals dwelling on earth. . ." Saying so, the master retreated to the far corner of his cavern.

On another day, a Daoist nun came to visit the master. Entering the cave without permission, and not taking off her straw hat, she proceeded to walk with her staff around the seat on which the monk was sitting in meditation, exclaiming, "Tell me the meaning of this move and I will take my hat off." She repeated her offer thrice, but to no avail; the monk kept silence, uttering no answer. At last, she blazed up. Waving the sleeve of her robe, she was about to leave the cave when suddenly the monk said to her, "It's getting dark. You'd better put up for the night."

"Explain the reason for that my move and I will stay overnight," she offered again.

In no time the monk started from his seat and pinched her butt heavily, instead of reply.

The nun was most indignant at that saucy action.

"Do you still have this in your mind?" She exclaimed.

"No," retorted the master, "it is you who still have this in your mind!"

Upon hearing this, the nun thought to herself, "They were right saying that this monk is an extraordinary person."

"How long is it since you became a nun?" The master asked her after a short pause.

"Enough of this jeering," she suddenly cried. "How stupid this is! My only question is about the meaning of my moving around your seat but, if you're unable to find a proper answer, just admit it. That's why I'm going to ask you one more time, "Will the day ever come when I'm a monk, not a nun?"

"Who are you now?"

"I'm a nun. Who doesn't know that?" She scoffed.

"But who knows that?" In no time retorted the master.

By pinching the nun's butt, the monk prompted her to realize the fact that the reason for her movement is in her own self. Saying, 'Do you still have this in your mind,' she thus proved her blunder of dividing people into male and female, as well as all other things into two distinct halves. One who has achieved complete realization cannot have any opposing concepts of duality in one's mind. The enlightened mind doesn't discriminate between male and female, me and others. The monk proved the impossibility of attaining the deep mystery while attaining the opposite halves of duality. Zen masters of olden times were fond of saying, "A pure mind will produce a pure land." Those who seek from within attain final realization, their pure land. His provocative action served as a means of purification to destroy the opposing concepts of 'the male-female' in her still immature mind. The mind of an adept of Zen is so different from that of an ordinary person that the latter can neither judge nor understand the former anyway. When, through purification, one's pure mind achieves the final state of enlightenment, all relative concepts of male and female become integrated into one. Thus, a man is again a male, and a woman is still a female. The pure mind becomes unified with the environment, perceiving things as they are.

Ultimately, the nun decided to stay the night. She thought to herself: "The subtlety of Daoism is profound and inconceivable. Originally, it does not matter whether you are seeking the truth or not. My living in the mundane world was filled with revels. . . Now, my life is boring and dull. Oh, well, I have done some practice to realize the true ways of Dao. I'm trying so hard, don't I deserve some merits? Who does so much for attaining enlightenment as I do? This sagely minded monk is well-known all around the Tian-tai region. I must stay the night to learn from him of the unity of opposing Yin-Yang powers."

"May I know where you are coming from?" the monk continued asking in awhile.

"I'm coming from the Daji Mountains," she replied.

"Has the sun risen yet?" (This means, "Have you attained realization?")

"If the sun had risen," she said, "the snowy peak (Xue Feng's monastic name) would have melted." (This means, "If I were enlightened, my fame would have surpassed yours, and I would not need to come here and learn from you.")

"What's your good name?" the master tried to question politely.

"My name is Xuan Zhi (Miraculous Sewer) of Wenzhou."

"How much do you sew each day?" (This means, "How do you practice every day?")

"I do not even have a stitch on." (Meaning, "Since I've reached an advanced level of realization, I don't need to cultivate myself anymore.")

Saying so, she tried to pay the master her formal respects and bowed twice to be stopped by a loud cry of the master. He exclaimed, "Your robe is caught on a rock!"

Xuan Zhi turned around to look down. At that, he broke out in laughter.

"And you said that you don't have a stitch on yet?!" he scoffed.

Upon hearing this, the nun attained her true realization.

Being thankful to master for his attempt to ruin her exaggerated self-importance and hyperbolic level of 'gong-fu,' she bowed twice again, saying, " I've heard some venerable patriarchs stated that by taking only the sitting meditation, a practitioner of the ways of Dao couldn't obtain peace and bliss in one's mind. Is it true that through the self-cultivating, one is able to perceive all things as Oneness? Besides, they said that men and women were able to be spontaneously united at the spiritual level and daily experience the state of bliss even without any physical contacts. They called it 'following the heart to achieve bliss of all the thirty-two heavens.' May I know your highly esteemed opinion regarding that, Master?"

In reply, the monk recited his verse which read like this:

"Beware of cunning and malice --
Don't let the vain world devour you; be above all.
After a hundred thousand tries
Of your devoted efforts, the spirit will soar up
To the thirty-second heaven in a twinkling.
Be quiet, sitting stiff, with no embarrassment,
Directing your thought toward the Truth --
The earnest of your inevitable realization.
Let the bodies do not merge into Oneness --
The spirit of both partners makes a great union!"

Silence fell. The monk thought to himself. "Perhaps she has no lover, and she does not quite know what ails her. Perhaps she is not interested in any particular man, but she is in love with an image of Man she has in her mind, and being in love with Man she is in love with life. That makes her be a little bit more neatly at her sewing and imagine she is in love with the rainbow-colored embroidery itself, as symbolizing life, which seems to her so beautiful. Very probably she is embroidering the design of a pair of mandarin ducks for someone's pillow, those mandarin ducks which always go together: swimming together, nesting together in pairs, one a male, another female. If she stretches her imagination too much, she is liable to forget herself and make a wrong stitch. She tries again, but it goes wrong again. She pulls hard at the silken thread, a little too hard, and it slips out of the needle. She bites her lips and feels annoyed. She is in love. That feeling of annoyance at a vague unknown something, perhaps at spring and the flowers, that sudden overwhelming sense of loneliness in the world, is nature's sign of her maturity for love."

Thinking so, he, however, started from afar, saying, "A female body refers to the Yin power, and only her spiritualized vaginal discharge refers to the Yang; hence, it is called "the Yang element of lead dissolved in water." Another name for it is "the Red Mother." The male body belongs to the Yang, and only his sperm energy refers to the Yin to be called "the Yin code of mercury buried in the sand." Another name for it is "the Gray Father." The red is the color of mercury, while the gray (white) is the color of lead. Once united together with the two form an elixir of authenticity which, upon reaching the crown of the head make a person feel good, like a youngster, all the rest of his life till the dying day. Saying so, he sang his couplet, the words of which sounded as follows:

"To everyone who wants to exercise
What gold dissolved in water truly means,
The Red Mother opens the secret
Of two quick thrusts on every eight but slow.
Thus, the warm and pleasant season will be last
The whole lifetime to make one happy
With the true self-nature revealed to the full."

Then he continued, saying, "In fact, excitation is all-inclusive. You have to thread your path at every single move. A man is considered by a woman as a manifestation of a certain kind of energy. Even her erotic visions and wet dreams serve her as a form of energy substitution: they help her to activate internal energy and eliminate different blocks in different parts of the body. If a woman keeps control over her dreams, her well-managed erotic dreams can help her to form a single center, around which her internal energy strengthens significantly. Her sexual energy is the driving force; it connects her with the universal law. Orgasm is the highest manifestation of her primordial energy; to go through it means to upswing the inner forces, becoming connected with the original vital source. The state of orgasm is never limited by the realm of sexuality, and this is an important aspect of a women's development. Regardless of the degree of her sexual activity, she needs to realize the inner mechanism of close relationship with a man; this will allow her not to muffle the great forces contained within her feminine self. . ." In the end, regarding her query about a possibility of her conversion in a monk, the master told her the story of the beautiful nun by the name of Huli Wei. She was standing on the doorsill of enlightenment, at the last threshold, where utmost concentration is required, when she was violently abducted by imperial troops and commanded to compound the Golden Elixir Pill for the emperor, the Son of Heaven. In vengeance for her disappointment, on the day the emperor had appointed for his apotheosis, Huli Wei bade him dismiss his guards and servants, then served him 'the Heavenly Banquet' she'd prepared by her own hand. The banquet, whose main course served in a covered dish, contained the still-smoking head of the emperor's baby son with its boiled, staring eyes. For this enormity the gods imprisoned her in the body of a fox, where she had to remain for all eternity, only allowed to assume human form at certain seasons, when she became a lovely maiden who wandered the countryside at night, preying on unwary travelers whom she seduced and then devoured. The fox shrines, where offerings of raw meat or live chickens were often left, were intended to appease Huli Wei and the other fox fairies of whom she was the Queen. "My counter-question is: Would you like to be simply a nun or a queen? As is said, 'If not for me, whom the hell is created for?'"

Instead of the answer, she put her teacup away and stretched her arms -- there was a resignation in her gesture, as though she realized the night had gone against her. But her dignity was unimpaired, and though she'd lost her battle, the larger war was far from over -- her face had started to congeal again into the mask that it had been before. "I'm deeply grateful for your hospitality," she said formally, bowing to the master, "and for your teachings, of course. But time presses on. I must leave before the dawn while there is dark enough to see me down the mountain. For the 'pathway' is treacherous." Allowing himself one last jibe, the master said ironically, "And I will not feel safe until you reach the high road." Saying so, he retreated into the depth of his cave.

Chapter 9: Marketplace

At Xiang-lin monastery its inhabitants' time was divided between meditation, attending Dharma talks, and daily work; morning and evening were spent in meditation, daytime was for working. Meditation and Zen yoga were referred to as 'gong-fu,' or truly diligent labor, otherwise known as 'cultivation of internal energy and spirit by occupation.' It was the most real, important, and profitable work that could only be performed in this world. This included physical exercises: stretching, breathing, specialized massage that today would be called 'qi-gong,' including mental exercises, such as visualization, dietary practices, consuming special essence enhancing foods and herbs and avoiding those which were thought to harm the vital essence. Some esoteric rituals were thought to bring the practitioner in touch with the heavenly dictates and alchemical practices -- a range of activities, including ingesting the substances involved in transformation and final conversion. Everything else, which didn't answer to the purpose of upgrading to immortality, was regarded as mere recreation and meaningless pastime, transient in nature. There was also an important practice called "universal invitation." This was a time when everyone was invited to do work outside, or beyond the monastery gates. This was sometimes called 'going to the hillside,' but it did not necessarily entail field work. It might include various chores around the monastery. Under certain circumstances, attendance at Dharma talks might be excused; however, 'the universal invitation' was mandatory for all monks without exception.

On the way to Xiang-lin temple, there sited a town named Red Fort, the market of which was frequented by Xue Feng. One night, just two days before he had to go to the market for some procurements, he saw a strange dream as he was a sailor who was returning to the capital when a violent force-eight gale sank his boat. Everyone died except for him who was miraculously stranded on the shore. His cries attracted a giant ape who then fed him roots and fruits. For ten long years, he was nourished by that monster until Guanyin Bodhisattva, the Goddess of Mercy, who was nominated as a protector of the monk, discovered him and took him to his monastery in Tian-tai. However, for being well protected, he was required for his prior suffering.

Through the first decade of his living at Xiang-lin monastery Xue Feng was ordered to attend to duties in the cloisters, cellars, and kitchen, which he did among the other monks. That was a period in his life story when the youngster at the first time took stock of his position in his conscious life and experienced all the hardships, felt the briefness of his prime and the transience of being profound. It was the self-awakening as he approached manhood and acquired his first awareness of being. When he entered the monastery at twelve, he could already know something of the reality. He couldn't read, but only in a few years, following his good tutors, he began to compose his original verses. Where did his knowledge come from? In fact, he did not just work and learn by studying commentaries on the sutras and scriptures but by somehow catching the essence of things around him every waking moment. That was a meditative absorption of experience, rather than erudition. Moreover, he enjoyed putting himself through hardships as a natural part of life. And once he developed this habit of enduring difficulties, he began to learn and enrich his experience. He succeeded fast because facing challenges with fortitude came to be a natural part of him as an individual.

The pine and cypress trees that can stand the cold and those who can stand hardship are sure to become the material of which beams and pillars are made. Nevertheless, even quality wood will not show its fine grain unless it is worked on by a good carpenter. Even a warped block of wood, if handled by a good carpenter, will soon show the results of excellent craftsmanship. That's why his brush for writing his verses and the fly whisk were instruments not to ignore the conventional world. Like the sages in olden times, he used it to perform his relationship with the world, sweeping away all the mundane and untrue things termed 'the red dust,' symbol of the worldly profit and desires, throughout his living and everywhere in Red Fort with its reddish dirt. Even less ochre he could observe around the town where the local villagers had cultivated mountain terraces, brighter red swatches from the iron oxides in eroded and exposed patches.

As is said, his monastery's duties were laborious, but the real hardships he went through were his dealings with the 'red dust' in the market. As soon as he became adult enough to buy some products for the monastery's kitchen, he often was sent to the nearest marketplace in Red Fort, the only 'remarkable sight' of its reddish ochre location. The bazaar was littered with stacks of exotic merchandise, most of it a half-finished material of one sort or another, gathered from the remotest crannies of the mountains to be sold for exorbitant prices. There were crates of bird eggs carefully wrapped in leaves, heaps of pelts of every color and description, downy fur for the tips of calligraphic brushes, baskets of unusual plants, roots and mosses, which grew only under the eaves of seaside cliffs. The monk's glance frequently tarried on the lumps of uncut jade and river pearls, sacks of brittle sun-dried bat wings gathered by hunters in caves beneath the earth, live bats in cages, too. There also was plenty of vegetable oil, ramie, wild honey, tea, rice, and medicinal herbs, of course, in great variety. Entering the marketplace, the young monk attained the common truth as it was founded in reality and which he mostly forgot behind the monastery's gates. He came to the picture of the mundane world of profits and desires, fame and gain through his insightful vision of the healer to be.

Since from early childhood he contracted a disease that had grotesquely bloated his face and had turned his skin a sickening bluish-yellow color, when he went to buy rice from peasants and wholesale suppliers, he frequently got into rows with the snot-nosed little savage-kids who followed him around, ogling him, sniffing out his difference like animals.

Next day, as he strolled through the counters out of the wilderness of his tangled impressions and emotions, one thing had seized him entirely with obsessive force. It was a bronze statue of Manjusri he saw selling in one of the trade seats. The bronze image tantalized him, exciting all the passion and enthusiasm of a young monk to pursue and simultaneous dread of the encounter. There was an element of reverence in his feeling, but it was compounded with, perhaps, confounded by -- something of a very different sort. Part of him wanted to retire and dwell in it in privacy, like a tiger skulking away to the darkness of its lair with a marrow bone.

His appearance among the trade people did not inspire them with a mutual delight. As he planted his staff and entered the trade seats, a silence fell over the rows, broken only by the anxious cheers and cries of sellers and buyers that dammed up the place. The first few peddlers he approached shooed him away with scornful gestures, frowning and hissing. He might have regarded this as a presage and retired discreetly from their territory, but with the instincts of a lousy gambler, he persisted, keeping moving deeper between the seats. Passing the straw-roofed greengrocery, he cast a glance at the woman who eyed him boldly and smiled, as he thought, with a lewd suggestion. Attributing this to his own sinful nature, he quickly looked away. She beckoned him with 'psst.' But remembering the abbot's advice, he kept moving and pretended not to hear. The clumps of men standing about and talking also cast suspicious glances at him over their shoulders, and in response to his broad and friendly grin, scowled and spat, then turned away resuming their conference, as though already satisfied that he was not worth their attention. Deeply abashed by this reception he stood apart, shuffling nervously.

"Psst," he heard again. Looking up, he saw the woman nodding him over with a rolling motion of her head and a coy smile.

At last, he dared to approach, bowing respectfully at the base of the deck.

"I haven't seen you here before," she said with an attempt at nonchalance, through which eagerness glinted like a blade in the dark.

"You're a handsome guy -- and manners too! What do you want to buy? Confide in me, I can help you."

Not knowing what to say, he blushed and averted his eyes. Then he plucked up his heart and, pointing at the bronze statue at next counter, pronounced, "How much is that one?"

"You must speak to my husband," she nodded in the direction of a man who was absorbed in a transaction and who was running from place to place.

As the monk stood aside, the old merchant came close to him in the course of his route, shooting him a suspicious look. Meeting his eye by accident, Xue Feng tried to brazen it out as best he could. The old man's face was red with irritation, but he forced his lips to smile and, addressing to him, asked with restrained discontent, "How I can be helpful to you, young man?"

"I come to buy some spices for the monastery's kitchen," he said calmly.

There were a few sniggers. Some scowled.

"I'm a monk," he said, attempting dignity, exaggerating slightly in a small voice.

"A what?" the merchant shouted.

"A monk," he repeated.

The merchant stared at him in disbelief, as though waiting for the punch line, then threw back his head in a laugh. The men around the counter began to laugh too. At that moment the woman spat and stormed away into the crowd.

"If you're a monk, how come you haven't shaved your head?"

"I'm a Daoist, not a Buddhist," he replied.

"A Daoist! I thought they'd all died out. More is the pity."

"And how do you suppose to pay for it, eh?" There was no quietening him.

Upon lifting the sleeve, Xue Feng searched carefully in it to prove his responsibility, but discovering a cut instead of money, he flushed with embarrassment.

He turned to the merchant, whispering, "Everything was in the right place. Believe me, I can vouch for it. I checked it out beforehand, and after too! . ."

Upon hearing this, the merchant's hilarity was sated, he began shouting orders again, ignoring the monk, as though he had become invisible.

Ashamed, he tried to slink away as inconspicuously as possible, but the merchant suddenly noticed him and cried out, "Where are you off to, monk? Come back and entertain us. What do you want to buy? Or did you come to help us to show the merchandise? It's worth a meal, you know."

He cackled at his own joke. "A monk, eh? How do I know you're on the level? What kind of magic can you perform? Can you tell fortunes, change the weather, or raise the river? If so, then perhaps we can transact a little business." He smiled at him through narrowed eyes.

"Such feats are beneath the dignity of a true adherent," he replied coldly, by rote.

"Ho!" the merchant grunted, frowning. "So that's how it is! Something for nothing, right? Seems that's always the way with monks. But if you ask me, if a man can't perform some useful service in exchange. . ."

Sad as it was to be squirming on the hook of his malicious inquiry, it was almost worse to be dropped and left to fend for himself. All of a sudden he found that those who hadn't deigned to notice his existence before, now ogled him shamelessly, some with hostile suspicion. Afraid of betraying his anxiety, he swallowed hard and, assuming a mien of piety, made off, trusting to meekness as his best defense. He might at least expect the legendary generosity of thieves. For if these men were not the rural folks he took them for, they then were surely robbers. That was the function of this bunch of piratical looking fellows crawling around him in the dust: to distill life for others, at some risk, but for high profit. And in their ignorant and dangerous faces, he detected the lineaments of rude thinkers initiated into a privileged intimacy with nature. Who were they but the real Daoists the abbot had spoken of so often, those who understood the way of Dao directly, through firsthand experience, unencumbered by the excess baggage of ideas and talks.

"Around here you don't come for purchasing but making eyes at the women. Got that, monk?"

"Woe betide you!" he challenged. "Haven't you heard of an old saying that 'lighting the fire of anger in one's heart, one can fire the holy wood of virtues. . .'"

With that, as though on cue from him, the merchant eyed the monk exultingly and cried out to someone in the crowd, "Your wife has found a playmate!"

The old man, who was absorbed in a transaction, started and cupped his hand to his ear. "What's that?"

Apparently, he was partially deaf, for his buyer, tugging at his robe for attention, turned him toward the merchant. Seeing who it was, the old man bowed and simpered with fulsome deference, showing his blackened, rotting teeth.

"I didn't catch that, sir!" he cried officiously, as though it were some great joke upon himself. "What did you say?"

The merchant didn't bother to reply but directly pointed in Xue Feng's direction.

Seeing him, the old man's false smile broke into a thousand pieces strung across his lips, like beads quivering on a thread. Wizened as he was, he blushed. Raising his scrawny arm in the air, he shook his fist.

"Didn't I tell you to stay in the house!" he screamed, in a high, eunuch's voice.

"Did you, husband? I don't think I remember. Anyway, why get yourself worked up?" the monk heard female voice uttered behind him. He turned round to see the same youthful woman he met earlier and who, he suspected of stealing from him the money. She narrowed her eyes with dispassionate contempt, replied to her husband, "You know you have a heart condition. What if you died? Where would that leave me? Think how sad we'd be, no one to make us any money."

"Cunt," he lisped witheringly, "crow, viper, slut . . ."

"Ha! ha!" the chorus of idlers roared, breaking in.

"That's right, old man," the merchant edged in. "You've got a whole menagerie there wrapped up in one. I always said you got a bargain on that deal. She's worth every penny you paid for her. How much was it? Let's see. . . I ought to remember, but I don't. You remember though, don't you, my dear partner? You never forget a sum. . ." The merchant turned to him and smiled with impotent hatred. "No need to hash out that old tale again. It's stale enough by now. Everyone here has heard it from your lips at least a dozen times."

"Nice to see you again, ma'am!" Xue Feng tried to hook her correctly.

But the woman raised her chin and turned her profile to him. Refusing to acknowledge his address, she suddenly slipped into the crowd, as she did it before, sinking into oblivion.

He tried to chase her, but all his swiftness was for nothing -- she vanished into thin air.

Remained to be with neither money nor provisions, the monk wished the earth would open beneath his feet, swallowing with him all his losses. He squatted on his haunches in the dusty curb and inspected his both sleeves again -- the upcoming wind swung them. The sun was setting into the trees of the horizon, running like a silent tear of blood down the gray-bluish face of heaven. There was a feeling of perplexity and frustration at having lost the game, and yet the sky, its broad expanse spreading out and out above his head, soothed him with its majestic impassivity, its complete lack of all complexity, all damned detail. That gray and somber peace, as of the end, or the beginning, distracted his mind from the failed chase compensated him somehow. The next instant, since returning without provisions was inconceivable, he decided to borrow some in the neighboring monastery, the senior monk in the storehouse of which was his old friend.

Telling what had happened in the marketplace, the monk wondered, "But how could they steal from me?"

"Ah! That's what I once was told myself," the storekeeper lamented expressly.

"It's better to be rich and have money; a lot of it. That way you could buy them off with cash. But when they find that you are poor, having nothing else to take from you, they'll steal your heart with all your bloody guts. It is said that one has to share others' woes if one has a debt of gratitude and that one has to help others in trouble if one has accepted others' favors or bounty. The rich can repay others with money; the poor have to repay with their loyalty and obligation. If you accept the men's money, I am afraid you have to repay it with your life someday." At that Xue Feng wanted to laugh, but his elder friend spoke in such a lugubrious tone that his rising from nowhere mirth, though highly strung, popped like a bubble. Yet he refused to leave him on such a sad note, saying, "If so, why to go into the marketplace of the defiled world, exposing oneself to the contagion of lust and greed, if the answer lies within and can be retrieved through meditation?"

"You must be like the lotus," the storekeeper said, "which grows in mud and yet retains its purity. Take with you your three treasures, which are mercy, frugality, and modesty, or daring not to go ahead of the world, and you will need no others. As Zhuang-zi states, those who strive to be in front always find themselves alone and behind. When Lao-zi speaks of staying behind, first of all, he means non-striving behavior concerning others. Inspired by desperation, you persevere in resisting this stern mandate, but Lao-zi said:

"Only without going out of his door
A sage can comprehend the earthly events;
Only without looking out of his window
He can observe in full the ways of Heaven."

The monk laughed loudly. "Would that be that there were more sages! Unfortunately for the rest of us, the way is often far more devious and convoluted. There are no hard-and-fast rules, no dogmas to rely on. Remember, Lao-zi also said, as a commentary on his own sententious utterances, 'He who speaks does not know; he who knows does not speak.' And again, 'To remain whole, be twisted!' and 'The more you clean it, the dirtier it becomes.'

"The Way is water, my friend, not stone. Like water, it flows on and on, and merely fills up all the places through which it flows; it does not shrink from any dangerous spot nor from any plunge, and nothing can make it lose its own essential nature. . . . Thus, likewise, if one is sincere, when confronted with difficulties, the heart can penetrate the meaning of a situation. And once we have gained personal mastery of a problem, it will come about naturally that the action we take succeeds. In danger, all that counts is indeed carrying out all that has to be done, thoroughness, and going forward, in order not to perish through tarrying in danger.

"It is only when we dare to face things exactly as they are . . ." said the monk. He smiled, and on the instant, taking a deep breath, faced things precisely as they were.

"Right, to gain something, you must lose something. Reflected in real life, you may experience a little suffering in the physical body, or feeling uncomfortable yourself. Conflicts suddenly arise because of personal gain or emotional friction, the goal of which is to let you improve the true mind. However, if you remain calm and unruffled, if you are able to do that, your mind becomes improved through this tribulation. Correspondingly, your level of 'gong-fu,' your skillful effectiveness, will be developed for the same equivalent. If you can achieve a little, you can gain a little. How much you gain depends on how much effort you make, but it is impossible not to encounter any problems and just to have your 'gong-fu' developed progressively."

"It seems to me, you are wrong about people!" the monk contradicted, attempting levity with a wink. Upon hearing this, the storekeeper put both hands on his friend's shoulders and searched deeply in his eyes. "Yeah, perhaps you're right," he admitted, chuckling despite himself. But almost immediately he was back on the gravity. "But I warn you, beware outflows! All excess is vicious and will definitely be your downfall if you don't watch your step."

Xue Feng couldn't help laughing at his final insistence on airing this old dusty warning.

"And you, my big brother. What about you?" the monk joked in reply, "Stay out of loans and stop trying to credit people with warnings. . ."

The storekeeper shook his head. "You are too illuminated for your own good, brother. One day you will remember what I have said. Take care that it isn't only after it's too late."

"But I wonder," suddenly, without rhyme or reason, the storekeeper inquired, as though recollected, "upon attaining one's final realization, would one not become godlike in appearance? Wouldn't such illumination change one's whole life for the better?"

"Not much," Xue Feng replied. As one Zen poet said, 'His head is covered with ashes and his face smeared with mud,' implying that while inwardly there is a great transformation, outwardly one's life may continue unchanged. And a good job too!"

Next morning, while walking along the pathway that led him back home and passing by a nunnery, the monk started to discern the words of a song, which sounded faintly behind the nunnery's walls. The song's words flew like this:

"A young nun I am, twenty years of age;
My head is shaven since early girlhood.
All this is for my father who loves reading
The Buddhist sutras, and my mother—
She loves the Buddhist monks and abbots
In their orange robes and brown frocks
With heavy bronze buckle, staff in hand,
Clanking evenly while walking with.
Morning and night, morning and night,
I burn incense, and I pray without stopping.
For I was born a sickly child, full of ills,
So my parents decided to send me here,
Into this monastery for nuns hidden deeply
From the public eye in these cold mountains.
Amitabha! Amitabha! Unceasingly I pray.
Namas Amitabha! Namas Amitabha!
O how greatly tired I am of the humming
Of these drums and the tinkling of the bells;
O how greatly tired I am of the droning
Of the prayers and the crooning of the priors;
O how greatly tired I am of the chatter
And of the clatter and of the tittle-tattle
Of unintelligible charms, the clamor
And the clangor of interminable chants,
The mumbling and the murmuring
Of monotonous psalms. Panjnaparamita,
Mayura-sutra, Saddharamapundarika—
O how much I hate them all! While I utter:
"Amitabha," I sigh for my admirer;
While I chant para, my heart cries, "Oh, no!"
While I sing panjra, my heart palpitates,
It palpitates so hard! Let me take a little walk,
Let me take a little bit of air—I just choke. . .
All rare visitors here just laugh at me,
They're laughing at me for when beauty is past
And youth is lost: Who will marry an old crone?
When beauty is faded, and youth is jaded,
Who will marry an old shriveled cocoon?
Some of them, holding a dragon, they're cynical;
Some of them, riding a tiger, they look quizzical;
And some of them seem pitiful, for what
Will become of me when my beauty is gone?
These candles of the altar, they're not for my bridal;
These long incense-containers, they are not
For my bedchamber. And the straw prayer-cushions,
They cannot serve as a quilt or cover. O, Heaven!
O Lord on High! Whence comes this burning
And suffocating ardor? Whence comes this infernal
And fervent ardor? I will tear my nun's sackcloth!
I will bury all the Buddhist sutras; I will drown
The wooden fish and leave all the monastic code!

I'll leave the drums, I'll leave the bells
And the chants and the yells and all the interminable
And exasperating chatter! I will go downhill
And find me a young and handsome lover—
Let him scold me, beat me, let him kick me
Or ill-treat me! I don't care! I'll not become a buddha
Or a bodhisattva! I'll not mumble "mita, metta,
Panjra, para! Mita, metta, panjra, para!" I just cry. . ."

The monk could tell some strange emotion had seized him that he was struggling to control it. He held himself above the level of the wall so that he could peep over. He found to his delight that that was a nice-looking young nun, no more than twenty or so. He was instantly taken with her. She glared at the monk with an intensity that almost made him cower. She was sitting on a stone bench, so close to the wall that he could even see the dark-water glaze of her eyes, reflecting his own image back to him. He saw the eyes that watched him from within her heart -- she held and held that frightened gaze, sizzling him. And he could feel its heat. When in a while the blush passed off, her face became unnaturally pale, even livid. The monk could never have anticipated what happened next. An alarming change came over her as soon as he tried to speak with her; she stiffened as though frozen; then she blushed again as profoundly as a ripe peach. After she had refreshed herself and they had chatted briefly, he took her to a secluded spot to listen to her story with sympathetic understanding. She told him her personal story which ran like this. From the time Chun Qing (this name means Spring Cleaning, and general bodily maintenance) was very young, with the same dark, illicit craving with which an ordinary girl fantasizes about sex, when she looked forward to the day she would get married and initiate her sexual experience -- that most mysterious part of the human being. It was perhaps the source of her keenest wish to get married. With the repressions of family and social conventions, she did her best to cover up this vague but strong yearning, subconsciously youth dreamed of. Yet pre-marital love was a forbidden fruit, open courtship was impossible, and she knew from conversations that to love was to suffer. For that reason, she dared not let her thoughts dwell too fondly on the spring and the flowers and the butterflies, which were symbols of love in ancient poetry. She kept herself busy with her home duties and guarded her feelings as sacredly as a delicate flower preserves itself from premature contact with the bees and butterflies. She wished to wait until the time should come when love would be lawful and sanctified by marriage, and happy was she who escaped all entanglements of passion. Yet nature sometimes conquered in spite of all human restraints. For like all forbidden fruits, the keenness of sexual attraction was enhanced by its rarity. It was nature's law of compensation. Once a girl's heart was distracted, love stopped at nothing. That was actually the common belief back of the careful seclusion of women. If by casual chance she met one of the approved young men, even though it was only an exchange of glances, more than likely she succumbed, and had no more of the peace of mind of which she had been so proud. Then a period of secret, stolen courtship began. Even though an exposure would mean shame and even suicide, and in spite of the full consciousness that by so doing she was defying all codes of moral conduct and braving social censure, she would meet her young man. And love always found a way. In the mad, mutual attraction of sex, it was impossible to say who was wooing and who was being wooed. If you remember the old saying, which said, 'Happy the wooing that's not long doing,' that was the case. A girl had many ingenious ways of making her presence felt. One was accidentally showing one's face amidst reddish peach blossoms; another was going to the lantern festivals of January and June at night. Another was playing on the lute, a stringed instrument, and let the young man in the next house hear it. If both parties were attracted to each other, a secret meeting could always be arranged. Such meetings were extremely unhealthy; the young girl did not know how to protect herself, and love, which had been denied its gay flirtations, came back with revenge, as all old love stories portrayed, or wished to represent. She might come to expect a child. A real period of ardent courtship and love-making followed, overpowering and yet tender, precious because it was stolen, and generally too happy to last. In this situation, anything might happen. For the young maiden waiting in the secluded chamber, there was only sadness and longing. If the girl were a real and passionate lover, she became severely lovesick, with all light and gladness gone from her eyes, and her parents, alarmed at the situation, would then begin to make inquiries and save her life by arranging the desired marriage. But the trouble was with her man.

Shortly, after she had been married at the age of 17, her father, being unable to tolerate the foolish behavior of her husband, expelled this intolerable troublemaker from the household. In her eyes, however, her grumpy husband had certain virtues that dominated over his shortcomings but were hardly apparent to her father's attention. Being an obedient daughter, she did not say a word about them. However, that was the main reason of her keenest regret that she had lost her banished husband who, despite his abhorrent character, was her first 'guru' in the bedchamber art.

After spending several nights alone, she couldn't understand why she had tossed about in bed for hours without sleeping, and at last, it dawned on her: she was like a hard drinker who was suddenly deprived of his usual pleasure, without which he couldn't go. After all, she was now a married woman. Eventually, after six months of separation from her man, her mental and physical conditions became unbearable. Memories of those several months spent with her husband and flown so fast that she almost could not believe that all this was really with her, even further inflamed her imagination. A husband who didn't spend nights with his wife was nothing better than a dead husband, and she then started to believe that way. As a first entertainment after several weeks of solitude, she found his collection of erotic pictures and albums on the art of love and began to study them thoroughly, for hours, but instead of comforting her, they only more excited her untamable desire and indomitable imagination. To restrain herself, she tried to be absorbed in reading books from her girlhood -- some sort of exciting and enlightening writings, such as "The Stories of Noble and Famous Heroines" or "About the Filial Piety of Young Ladies," and the like. But very soon, they gave way to erotic books that her husband read her while in bed, before and after they indulged themselves in the pleasure of 'the wind and clouds playing.' At that time, they disgusted her, but now she treated them quite differently. She just couldn't tear herself away from the books. Her favorite ones were "The Stories of Women Obsessed with Sex," "Memoirs from the Embroidered Lodge," and "The Life Story of a Playboy." Those books were richly illustrated to make her not only wet but also compare the attributes of their heroes with those of her banished husband. Time and again she studied the visual images of the male's qualities thoroughly, following every action that they were engaged in during the never-ending bedroom scene. In all those descriptions they invariably had their 'incredible length' and were 'larger than the sea cucumber' and 'too thick to be grasped by a young lady's fingers.' Being in the state of erection, in strength and solidity, they were no less than an iron pillar and able to withstand the weight of a bushel of wheat and make at least a thousand thrusts without any repose. At first, she decided that all these things were used for exaggeration, to make the narrative more entertaining and amusing. However, when the weeks of despair of her situation had turned into months, she was ready to believe every word she read. That was the starting point when she began to compare her husband's manhood with that of the great Prince Wang and chief of the brigands by the nickname of Tiger-Dragon Jiang. As a result, she found out that her husband wasn't such a well-endowed man. As she could remember, his Jade Stalk was about only four inches long and two fingers thick; and he could produce a couple of hundreds of jerks only before reaching the state of Ultimate Extremity, coming out. If there were said of thousands and thousands of thrusts produced in succession by the heroic playboys, to whom she supposed to believe? And her answer to her own question had sense. She thought to herself: 'If there were millions of men living in the world, and she knew only one of them, her poor husband, how could she know if what was described in the books fit the truth or not? How could she know more about such things than the authors of those books? After all, it might be that abilities of the potent tool to withstand such pressure as a bushel of wheat and make a thousand jerks without a repose, while being at least twice as long as that of her husband's, were really in the order of things. And there was only one way to find out whether that could be true or not -- to expand her own experience in the field. Undoubtedly, her banished husband was like a dead husband, especially if to consider that her father did not show any desire to change his decision and allow him to return to the family. What should a young woman do in such a situation? To dispel the atmosphere of loneliness and despair that reigned in her bedroom, there could only be one solution; and even though her husband could hardly compare in abilities with those of the heroic playboys, he would definitely be welcome for the hottest reception if he had an opportunity to be back home. However, it was clear that his return to the family was out of the question. In her case, she started to be unfaithful to the family. Ultimately, her father found a solution, sending her to one of the nunneries in Tian-tai.

Yet despite his sense of foreboding, the monk's first reaction to Chun Qing's background was sympathetic. He felt a sort of kinship between them which somehow he'd intuited all along -- though in what it lay he was not sure he could say unless it was merely the fact that they both were the adepts of Tian-tai sect with its precepts and traditions; and in that sense necessarily open-minded. He caught her eye, smiling briefly at his own attempt at levity. Almost immediately, however, his face darkened into a frown, and he commenced his speech, saying pensively, "Following laws of etiquette that are not only Confucian but universal, I realize that my first obligation is to sympathize with you in your deplorable misfortune. On the other hand, I have to warn you of the destructive nature of any sort of overindulgence. In your case of a young lady, who had been seduced and given some knowledge about the way of achieving a pleasurable satisfaction, you should know that such kind of knowledge is not for good and all. Such kind of knowledge, like skills in any other fields of human activities, should be cherished and improved on a regular basis as a whole."

This was an alarming prospect, but he didn't balk at it. For there was another reason the monk felt he had to warn her. The disclosure of her background had quickened his protective instincts. On the other hand, with this discovery, the possibility that anything might come of their affair seemed effectively accelerated.

"I can stay here no more," she said, melting into scalding tears.

"My humble place is not far from here. Won't you come and have a look to see if you like it?"

Overjoyed, the nun agreed. When she was ready, the monk took her scrip from her and led the way.

Looking around the empty space of his cavern, she asked why he lived alone in such a roomy cave. He told her this was his casualty reception. "It suits me fine," she said then, "but if you truly pity me and let me live here, you must keep me a secret and not breathe a word to anyone."

The monk promised not to tell and kept her in the hiding corner of the cave for many days.

The monk opened his mouth to speak, but she interrupted and led him to the cave entrance which opened onto the garden.

"Listen," she said, putting her finger to his lips.

"As if from far away, the sound of music broke upon his consciousness. He held his breath and strained to hear. From the faraway came the strains of a mournful zither tune mixed with some sort of whistle. Someone was singing -- a female's voice, untrained, but as deeply moving as any he had ever heard. The song was vaguely familiar to him. It was a contemporary ballad called 'The Yellow River Upstream,' quite popular at the time. From its theme and its simplicity of style, however, one might easily have mistaken it for one of the songs from the Book of Odes, which were old even in Confucius's time. It told the story of a peasant woman whose husband had been conscripted and gone away. . . To fight and die; the die game:

"Over a bit of worthless,
Barren ground
Along with some distant border,
When your place was here.
For though you did not know it,
I am with child again. . . ."

The woman's voice went on to complain bitterly of the hardships of life without him. In a frenzy of spite, she taunted him with the offers of assistance other men, 'rich men, and strong young boys,' have made her. Then she broke into lamentation, ending thus:

"But I can never love another man,
Not even if I marry. For you left
This desolation in my flesh, this memory --
Your bright, young body --
And my heart refuses to be wise."

The music stopped. His eyes were full of tears, yet he wasn't unhappy. Instead, he felt like one waking refreshed after a long sleep. His curiosity as to the meaning of the scene had been mysteriously allayed.

This sensation lasted only a moment, however. Coming to himself, the monk gently shook off the nun's hand (she too stood as though enchanted) and came back into the cavern.

Though still under the music's spell, he could not make out for the life of him what he was doing in the bed in the middle of the afternoon, listening to sad songs as though there were no constraints upon his leisure except his own goodwill. Then he heard a whisper and realized he was not alone. For when the monk had fallen asleep, through his shallow dozing he hearkened to the noise of a hessian robe; he opened his eyes to see the young nun with a wistful look and a cold air, looking and smiling at him.

When he felt about the coming, first, he thought that that was his wet dream, but her mournful voice petitioned, "Please don't stop."

Changing his position slightly, he saw that the nun was lying beside him. It was she who had spoken. "We are here since noon," she whispered to his ear. His brain was in a buzz. He tried to comfort her a little bit and made him speak, but only shake his head when she asked him to continue with foreplay. The whistle-like music started again, and it seemed to ease his mind. What was it, he had no clue. He watched himself in dumb wonder as if he studied listlessly his own reflection in the deep pond hung above his bed. The stillness of the water was broken only by the surfacing of curious carps and goldfishes which floated up out of their murky world to gaze at him, as though afflicted with wonder, like his own. Their bubbles broke the surface as they lipped the same dumb 'pop-pops'. . .

Suddenly, he experienced a pang of sympathy so deep that his eyes welled up with tears.

"Pull yourself together and go on," the nun said sternly. Her admonition shamed him and roused him from his dreamy state. Casting a backward glance at her, he got up and went mutely to his part of the cavern. She followed his back with her expression of obvious disappointment and discontent. Her eyes were all unfocused and seemed to stare through him to something behind or beyond -- like an insane's. Then she just stuck up her nose and stalked off.

Staying alone in private, the monk consulted the oracle, the Book of Circular Changes, receiving a reading which he couldn't remember ever turning up before the 54th hexagram named 'Gui Mei,' or Marriage. This hexagram was built from the two basic trigrams, Lake and Thunder above it, suggesting to him incitement to some pleasurable but essentially frenzied and destructive act, as though saying, 'Take care in your pleasant satisfaction or you will be visited with punishment from Heaven in the form of the thunderbolt!' The Image of the figure stated unambiguously, saying: ' The superior man, accordingly, having regard to the far-distant end, tries to know all mischief that may be caused in the course of his moving ahead, to his destination, to be prepared in advance for all contingencies.' This interpretation was reinforced by the fact that the topmost divided line in its proper place said: 'The bride carries the bride's basket, but without any presents in it; and the bridegroom slaughters the sheep, but without blood flowing from it.' Then the line's judgment concluded, 'There will be no advantage in any aspect of this line subject's marrying off in the very end of Gui Mei's course. The absence of gifts in the bride's basket shows disrespect to her mother-in-law to be. Being without any support from the part of the not responded correlate below (the 3rd line, which supposed to represent nunhood), she has nothing to present her mother-in-law (correlation of the abbot) to receive her favor and blessings for marriage.'

As the monk had promised, not a single soul would have known of her staying in the cavern had he not paid a visit to the abbot. The abbot took one look at him and asked in alarm what had happened to him. "Nothing," was his reply.

"I see you are trapped in an aura of depravity and still you say 'nothing'?"

And again, the monk denied that anything was wrong. So, the abbot looked at him intently with these words: "Yet dare to deny! Death is at his threshold and still he refuses to rouse himself!"

"What a strange thing to say," the monk thought to himself and started to wonder about his new flame. No, she was clearly no fox-spirit, a poor girl like that who was compelled to become a nun. . . As though reading his thoughts, the abbot said, "Yes, she is a passionate creature; she can bring you pleasant satisfaction and even money, and help you through living by all sorts of cunning wiles. She can nurse you through sickness with more gentleness than an average nurse. What is stranger still, she will sometimes try to save a last bowl of rice for you and will wait patiently for you during your months or years of absence while you go to pilgrimage. She can, therefore, be chaste as well. The period of this cohabitation may last a few days or weeks, or it may extend to a generation until her fox-spirit becomes unmasked and her brush-tail stuck out to the view of the world."

Taking into consideration her background he had heard from her, Xue Feng pondered over the abbot's words, "For a young woman to please a man is a noble effort, but for her to please another woman in a nunnery is heroic, and many of them fail. Practically all tales of cruelty to women could be traced to an oppressor of the same sex. For love, which is a gushing and overwhelming feeling in nature, can become a small voice of the heart and mind. Nunhood may transform love, but it never stifles it. Love is there, only somehow receiving a different tenor and expression accidentally borrowed, as it were, from a different background. It peeps in at the hessian curtains, it fills the air of the nunnery's back garden, and it tugs at the maiden's heart."

So thinking, he arrived at his cavern -- there was deathly hush inside. Suspicious, he walked round to the far corner and, sneaking round to a stone, hidden behind it. Getting accustomed to the shade, he peered in and saw an ugly spirit with a hideous reddish face, a long brushtail, and sharp teeth; lay out on the mat before it was a piece of human-shaped skin on which it was artfully painting. Then, tossing the paintbrush aside, it lifted the skin and threw it over itself as if it were a piece of cloak and changed into a young fair maiden. The sight so appalled him that completely confused monk moved backward like a frightened horse and went looking for the abbot, who was by then nowhere to be found. Finally, he found him in his private joss house in the pose of deep meditation. The abbot was contemplating his horsetail fly whisk which was hanging on the wall. Bowing low on entering, the monk appeared before the abbot, begging for help.

"Use it without its usefulness," said the abbot, pointing at the fly whisk.

"You thus cut down both ends," remarked the monk, "how can I proceed to start just from the middle part of it?" Saying so, he held up the whisk without getting any permission for that.

"Use it without its usefulness!" the abbot exclaimed again.

Hearing this, the monk immediately restored it to its place.

Seeing this, the abbot said, "I'll get rid of it for you if you do as I say. That poor thing, just when it is found someone to take its place; I don't want to hurt that critter if I don't have to." So saying, the abbot handed Xue Feng his fly whisk and directed him to hang it over the cave's entrance. Before they parted, they agreed to meet again in the monastery's main hall for preaching.

The monk went directly to his cavern where he hung up the fly whisk and went straight to bed. At midnight, he heard a shuffling outside the cave but was too afraid to look out. Actually, the nun approached the cave's entrance, but then stopped short at the sight of the fly whisk. She stood there a long time, staring at it, shaking with rage, and then left. Shortly afterward, she returned, and this time hollered, "I'm not going to be scared away by that abbot's tricks; he cannot make me spit out the morsel I have already put in my mouth!" So crying out, she pulled down the whisk, tore it to pieces, broke into the cave, jumped onto the monk who was lying in his bed and violated him cruelly.

Next day, upon coming to senses, the monk went after the abbot. When the latter heard what had happened in the dead of night, he exploded: "So that is how the fox returns my kindness?! What the gall!" He immediately followed the monk's cave, but the nun had disappeared. The abbot looked about and sniffed the air. "Luckily, she's not gone far," he proclaimed. "She is in the south outhouse of the Mountain Lord Shrine right now," he concluded.

The monk looked at him in disbelief.

"Has anyone unusual stopped by recently?" the abbot asked.

"I have no clue. Let me go there and ask." The monk came back shortly and said, "Yes, an old woman came this morning asking for work, sweeping. The Shrine-keeper let her waiting at the outhouse; she's still there."

"Very good!" said the abbot and headed toward the Shrine's outhouse. Brandishing his iron staff with a couple of clanked rings on top, he halted in front of the Shrine. "Accursed fox-spirit," he shouted, "Return my fly whisk, now!"

Inside, the old woman turned white and tried to slip away, but the abbot was right at her heels. He struck her hard with his staff. As the woman dropped to the ground, the human skin ripped open and fell from her, revealing a wicked evil spirit lying flat on her back, snorting like a pig. The abbot smashed its head up in half. As he did so, her body turned into a whirl of black smoke, hovering above the ground. Then, the abbot took out a wine gourd, uncorked it, and placed it in the center of the courtyard, after that the smoke was sucked up with a loud slurp and disappeared inside the gourd. Then he had corked up his catch and stuffed it into his bag; everyone was staring at the piece of human skin complete with eyes and brows, hands and feet, while the monk proceeded to roll it up like a painting scroll, tucking it away as he bowed deeply twice and bid farewell. Later on, remembering this episode of his life, the following poetic lines were composed:

"White fly whisk of horsetail with the sandalwood handle --
Its pervasive fragrance can be smelled all day.
Gentle and soft, like a roll of smoke -- waving and twisting,
It fleets in the air like a rack of the clouds. Presented solemnly,
It suits to the summer season's rites and ceremonials;
Lifted up high, it brushes off all dust just at one sweep.
Time and again, in the abbot's isolated quarters,
It's used to point out the proper way to those who are lost."

Chapter 10: The Middle Path

Subsequently, many times the young novice by the nickname Foundling approached Xue Feng and begged him for his instructions regarding the secret methods of internal alchemy. At last, the monk suggested, "Before I can teach you anything you must say one word of Ultimate Truth."

The youngster thought for a moment. "Buddhahood!" he responded in a while.

Disappointed, the master dismissed him. "Come back when you can speak a word of Truth! . ." he grumbled out after the leaving novice. The latter thought and thought and decided on a better answer. The next day he returned to the master, knelt respectfully at his feet and whispered, "Compassion. The word you demand is Compassion."

But again the monk dismissed him. The kid struggled to find a more impressive answer, one that would surely be undeniable in its truth. Thinking he had seen it in the word 'Affection,' he returned to his master.

As he began to kneel, the master suddenly pinched his nose so hard that he started to yell out.

"Ouch!" the poor novice screamed out.

"Sit down," said the master. "You have finally uttered a truthful word." (This means a spontaneous response by definition that's not corrupted by second thought and influence of the Self.)

"So what if I really teach you to the Daoist method of internal alchemy?" the monk's question sounded mostly rhetorically. He continued, "There's suffering, and its cause is obvious. But will you be able to recognize that you were not suffering while on the method I'd teach you, only while off it? There is the possibility of cessation, and the whole experience is the Path, and no matter what happens it will illustrate the temporary nature of existence."

"What is the origin of suffering?" the novice asked.

But the master, without turning an eyelash, went on, saying, "Following the causal chain of existence, you first contemplate how the fundamental ignorance sets in motion the life cycle. Ignorance creates conditions for action, but action creates conditions for consciousness. From consciousness, you will contemplate name-and-form and on to the six sense faculties so far. Finally, you will see that your desire leads to grasping; because there is grasping there is existence, and when you exist you were born, then you have your desires, then become sick, and finally die. And, of course, there is much suffering between birth and death. Contemplating this process, you can arrive at a profound understanding of the state you find yourself in. As it goes in the Heart Sutra:

"Once realized that mind is not the mind,
You find yourself beyond any sicknesses
And remedy. When in confusion you have
To discard affairs, for the enlightened one
It makes no difference which ends to cast."

He added, "Ordinary people may think they understand the mind, but they grasp it only through analogy. It takes personal experience, in fact, to understand what is called Enlightenment. In truth, there is no mind, and there are no obstructions. Furthermore, you cannot have one without the other. If there is no mind, there will be no obstructions; and if there are no obstructions, there can be no mind."

"What causes sickness and death?" the novice questioned again.

"They are caused by existence, which is at least one feminine (Yin) and one masculine (Yang) entities put together. When we are talking about the practical course of internal alchemy, it can be adequately expressed in sexual intercourse produced knowledgeably on the subject. There are the following six signs of existence, which are: attendance, raising, absorption, inhalation, closing, and extension. The Attendance means that during copulation make sure that the heart is beyond all things, do not concentrate your attention on the actual current coitus; otherwise, your ejaculation can easily be produced. Remember, it is your body that involved in coitus, not your spirit. If you don't focus on coition then, even if your semen is spilling involuntarily out, at this you lose the dirty energy, saving the pure one within yourself. You must always direct the semen moving up; thus, even after a long time, you will not feel any fatigue and loss of your sperm.

"What does it mean 'Do not focus on coition? How is it possible?" the next question was asked. "I don't understand it," the novice confessed then. "You must know some kind of trick. Please, explain your method."

Clucking his tongue with disapproval, the master shook his head.

"My friend," he said, "you haven't yet caught on. It's precisely this -- excess of method -- that frustrates your ac. When you carry water in buckets, don't fill them up to the brink, leave them a little bit empty, and may yet force my foot to punish you from behind. Ha! Ha! Ha!" the monk burst his sides with laughter at his own joke.

"Take it easier, and don't overthink," he noticed at last. And then advised: "You should instead be like a centipede who simply responds to the situation with complete awareness. You have to abandon conscious guidance all the time. . . We are not good at doing a thing as long as we are taking ourselves through it. Your pace is neither natural nor satisfying if an inner voice is still going, 'Now left foot first, now right foot. . .' When you reach that level of capability, your inner voice is likely to detract from smooth, compelling performance. In a nutshell, account your thrusts, don't think of copulation itself!"

"And what has happened with the centipede?" the novice was really tuned in to what the master was saying.

"Once a walrus said to the centipede, 'I hop about on my belly but not very successful. How do you manage all those legs you have in so many?'

'Don't ask me such a stupid thing,' retorted the insect. 'I don't manage them at all. Didn't you ever see how people spit? When saliva is ejected, the big drops are the size of pearls to fly further; the small ones like a mist -- at random they fall in countless numbers just in front of one's feet. So, too, doesn't my natural mechanism move without my knowing how I do it?'"

"The symbol of reaching that level is that was hard then, now comes to look and feel both easy and natural. You may even lose the sense that it is you who are doing it. It seems as if the world is simply inviting you in, like the space between the bones. It is as if the Dao has shifted from being in you as a guide to being out there, pulling you effortlessly through. You often express this as a sense of entirety, the Oneness with your instrument, your dick. Absorption in activity is total so to complete that you lose awareness of your ego, your Self. You cannot be skillful while focused on what you gain from it. If you stop seeking for the gratification, the activity itself will be gratifying, and you will experience a kind of absorbing tranquility. With satisfaction 'strop your blade' and put it back in the scabbard," said the monk, "as if your puny brains were smart enough to outwit the steep incline of these rocky cliffs, you go through carrying your nearly filled buckets with water."

"All right," the novice sullenly rejoined, "if you're so smart, how do you do it? I mean 'in the bed?'"

"How do I do it?"

The master stared over the edge into the abyss. "I close my eyes and think of nothing. My mind is somewhere else; my jade stalk finds its way without me, even over the most sophisticated hindrances, through the most protected gates."

Upon saying so, he became uneasy under his friend's suspicious look.

"How can I tell you how I do it?!" the monk, at last, shouted defensively, looking around as though the answer might materialize from the air.

Then an idea seemed to strike him, and he began again, "Will you ever learn? Feel the force, brother! Let go of your conscious mind! This makes the outcome of skill transcendence radically independent of any learning phase. As it is said, 'One longs for three thousand; the three thousand longs for one.' Those who see the difference show their utter sincerity and courage, but those who see the likeness become unified, as one with all the myriad things around. And all this is created by your mind. Who truly knows how far is the difference between the size of a mustard seed and that of Mount Sumeru?" Saying so, the monk let out an ebullient and strange belly laugh. "How can I tell you how I do it?" he repeated time and again, "I can't even remember myself! Ha! Ha! Ha!" This is how a true Attendance could be depicted. Then he started to sing loudly his song, in which one of the alchemist secrets was disclosed in such an easy way:

"Between the kidneys, there's the spot called Mingmen,
Or the Gate of Fate, in which the spirit nests itself.
This acupoint is the source where the semen hides.
Do not allow your Jade Stalk to lose the power; for this,
Observe the state of the gate of life and death carefully --
The Gate of Fate (Mingmen), putting your tool in and out
Of her Chamber, you reach a breakthrough for both of you."

As for the Raising, it means that during copulation, the energy rises up; do not allow it to go down. When the energy falls down, the semen becomes ejaculated. Therefore, when coition is complete, take a sit down as if you're relieving nature, take half of your divine stalk out from her jade gates, inhale profoundly and cling to the woman's lips to absorb the saliva which has been accumulated under her tongue. Then take a deep exhalation and direct the energy into the middle elixir field in the lower part of the belly. Afterward, mentally lead the energy to your Divine Stalk. Upon doing this a few times (three, five or seven), the vital force of your reproductive organs will be strengthened a lot. As the secret song runs:

"When the semen is looking for a way out,
Not a single ban will be helpful to stop it.
But the fingers of the right hand must be able
To play a part of a great clamp.
Looking upwards, take your Jade Stalk
And pull it slightly backward; --
The whole body is like a trunk of a lofty tree,
On which a nimble monkey climbs up on top."

Absorption actually means making love leisurely, without worries and hurries. Cling to her mouth and absorb the saliva slowly, soaking up through your nose the energy which is coming out from her breath. When the excitement reaches its extreme point, quickly take in her saliva and swallow it. Don't breathe through the mouth to avoid the damage to your brains caused by the air entering through your mouth. The more you absorb her saliva, the stronger your Jade Stalk comes to be in the state of erection, and the longer your spiritual force will continue growing. As the saying goes:

"Entering her Jade Gates and kindling the fire,
Keep the purity of your desire; first of all,
Follow the formula: one deep thrust per nine short.
Don't astray from the method of 'slow and fast thrusts.'
To replenish your semen and strengthen the elixir pill."

Inhalation is all about soaking up with your jade stalk her spiritually increased vaginal discharge; that's all. Above, breathe-in thru your nose her spiritual energy evaporations; below, absorb with your jade stalk her vagina's fluids. Thus, your consciousness is present in her Jade Passage, while you breathe-in her energy at both levels; therefore, your strength does not go away from you. You draw her juices of life, swallowing them along with saliva. As a result, the skin of your face will be smooth and light, and the spiritual energy will grow up stronger. As is said:

"Absorb within yourself her infusion of the Flowering Pond (vagina);
When the passion rushes up, take your divine root out from her gate.
Suddenly, the source of life comes to be disclosed: do not interfere
With its activity, accept its power, absorbing in yourself to meet then
Ten thousand springs which are waiting for you every single moment."

The closing means that after being engaged in the intercourse, don't open your mouth and let the energy getting out. The mouth is the gate of the primal condition, it is firmly connected with the Gates of Fate (acupoint Mingmen located on the spine at the level between the kidneys). When your mouth is not closed tightly, there is a chance to lose your spirit and damage your qi-energy. It is straightforward to miss the semen; therefore, you should observe the implementation of all the six precepts thoroughly. Only by sealing all the nine openings, you can reveal the secret of saving the vital forces naturally (which means effortlessly). As is said:

"The semen feeds your Divine Root,
The qi-energy nourishes the Shen-spirit;
The primordial Yang does not go away,
Giving one a chance to reveal its essence.
A treasure is growing in the elixir field,
The value of which is much higher than
Many thousands of the golden coins.
I won't be ready to give it to other men,
Exchanging for all the worldly wealth."

Extension resembles action on the battlefield; when horsemen fight, their horses are at a gallop; when warriors do not fight, their horses get excited no more. Copulation of man and woman is like the battle of two clever generals: a woman can win without even being engaged on the battlefield, as long as the rest always conquers the motion. A male, it sometimes happens, upon seeing the opened Holy Gates of a female loses his spirit and suffers defeat even before entering the action. If a man, upon entering his Jade Stalk into her Holy Gates, does not count the number of producing thrusts he loses even easier. This happens only because he didn't learn properly. Once he studies the proper instructions thoroughly, he will be able to strengthen his vital power every day, even every hour, driving away his aging. This is the right way not to be afraid of copulations!"

Then, as though recalling the question, he asked himself once again, "What causes existence? First of all, existence is eternal notion due to a proper understanding of the balance between the Yin and Yang forces; and there's no fundamental ignorance, to begin with."

Suddenly the monk realized that there was something else that he wanted to explain. He tried to avoid putting him in a position of having to believe or disbelieve anything he said. This was in the Kalama Sutra and in no time it came to his mind. He recited:

"Do not believe in anything because
It is accepted by the masses of people,
Because it is written in books and scriptures,
Because it is spoken by teachers and elders,
Because it is handed down throughout ages."

Upon saying so, he concluded, "But if, after analysis, it is found to accord with reason and to result in the common good, then accept it and live up to it."

Although meditation is ordinarily the proper path leading to enlightenment, once the adept has arrived at the doorway of Samadhi, even a method of meditation is rendered useless. It is like using various means of transportation on a long journey. When you reach the final destination, you find a steep cliff standing right in front of you. It is so high you cannot see the top and so vast that its side cannot be found. At this time a man who has been to the other side of the cliff comes to tell you that on the other side spreads out the world of Samadhi -- when you scale it you will enter its realm. And yet, he says you not to depend on any means to fly over or penetrate through it, because it is infinity itself and there is no way to climb or bypass it.

When the monk became a Zen master, he advocated that ordinary mind is the way of Dao, too. Whether you are walking, standing, sitting, or lying down, everything is Samadhi practice. He taught that one should not intentionally fabricate some kind of exercise, nor get involved in what is right or wrong, grasping or rejecting. This was the practice of what he termed 'the ordinary mind.' This was the teaching that more than any other opened the door to Zen, and for the novice too. Of course, many other systems and doctrines were important to him, but what first got his attention was an invitation to come in and bring all his faculties with him to be not a follower but a participant of the cognitive process. Perhaps, it would appeal to any other as well. Someone begins with fundamental ignorance contemplating that once there is no ignorance, there will not be any deluded actions; once there are no deluded actions, there is no defilement of consciousness. One proceeds in this manner on to the six sense faculties, which give rise naturally to the stages of contact, desire, grasping, existence, birth, and death. Ultimately, there is also the cessation of birth and death; in fact, the true cessation is not the process of ending suffering, true cessation is a state of complete realization. It means having completely terminated emotional affliction and having fully realized the way of Dao. It is liberation from the causes and effects of suffering; it is a state where there are no more outflows. What does the term 'outflows' mean? Well, there are many kinds of outflows: anger is an outflow, and so is greed. To be stupid is also to have outflows. Having a temper, one has outflows; and if one is a glutton, one has another kind of outflow. In a word, anything that is not proper that you like out of habit is called 'outflows.' Outflows are the root of birth and death. Why can't you end Samsara, the cycle of birth and death? Just because of your outflows. To be without outflows is to be like a bottle that does not leak -- one has to be devoid of all bad habits and faults. Then you are not greedy for wealth or sex or fame or profit, you are not greedy for food or sleep. When you are not greedy for anything, you have penetrated to the state of no outflows. This state of mind that is our real home, the dwelling place that is not constructed out of dust and noise, it is our birthright.

"So what are outflows?" the novice wondered.

"In other words," the monk tried to be more understandable, "they're just men's bad habits and faults that they have amassed from of old, life after life. That is what I meant by 'outflows.' Outflows are insatiable. For instance, eating is an outflow," and the monk looked down at his own belly. Smiling to himself, he continued, "and wearing good clothes is an outflow. When you like to sleep that is an outflow. Any state that you go along with and end up getting afflicted with is an outflow. If you have thoughts of desire, then you will have a lot of outflows. Outflows are just all our various bad habits and faults."

"You say that eating is an outflow and that wearing clothes is an outflow; even sleeping is an outflow," Foundling reflected on, "then tell me, what is not an outflow? Eating is an outflow, but everybody has to eat. Nobody can go without eating. How can we eliminate that outflow? Nobody can go without wearing clothes, so, how can we get rid of that outflow? Nobody can go without sleep. How can we dispense with that outflow? If all those things are outflows, then how can anyone be without outflows?"

"You are right," the master nodded his head. "There is not anyone who doesn't need to eat, sleep, and wear clothes. Outflows mean over-indulgence in these things. As an example, if when you eat you just eat your fill, then that's all right. You shouldn't pay attention to whether the food is delicious or bad. The important thing is not to have a lot of false thinking about what you eat and then you won't have any outflows. This can be likened to a bowl of water in it. If there aren't any cracks in the bowl, then when you put water in it the water won't run out. It doesn't have any outflows. But if there are cracks, then the water is going to leak out. People's false thoughts are just like cracks in a bowl. If you don't have any false thinking, then you don't leave any cracks for outflows." Saying so, he recited his song in some didactic tone, saying:

"A decent man will never exceed his simple needs;
I'd like to suggest you be spare with stingy thoughts.
Otherwise, as getting old, you will not be at liberty,
And you will gradually be repulsed by other folks.
Even sent off to the top of some desolate peak,
Your desire for a lifetime in vain to be cast away.
When a sheep is fled, but you give up mending the fold,
Your disappointments till the end will not desist."

"If you have attained purity of the six sense organs, at encountering someone who is sexually attractive, no thought of desire will arise, you will not react physiologically or psychologically. There will be no temptation. This means purity of the six sense organs, and it is also freedom of desire. Most of the men, even at this monastery, are easily tempted. Some of the monks may be able to resist temptation, but they recognize that they feel tempted. A bodhisattva who has attained purity of the six sense organs feels no such temptation -- precepts are followed and kept pure."

"I can understand this all right," said the novice, "but what is the outflow of sleeping like?"

"When it is time to go to sleep, you lie there, but you can't go to sleep. Once you start false thinking, sleep runs off, and you don't know where to find it. You toss and turn, and still, you can't go to sleep. Would you call this an outflow or not? It is the outflow of sleep. And if you don't get enough sleep, then the next day you won't have enough energy and strength, because you used it all up false thinking all night. Not getting enough sleep is an outflow and getting too much sleep is also an outflow. If you get just the right amount of sleep, then there is no outflow. And so, tell me now, which isn't an outflow? Eating? Sleeping? Wearing good clothes? What were you opposing? Not only eating, wearing clothes, and sleeping are outflows, but whatever you like is an outflow. Your hot temper is also an outflow. Worry, hate, and desire are also outflows. All the seven emotions of happiness, anger, grief, fear, love, hate and desire are all outflows. But these outflows can be stopped. If you get to the place where you can flow and yet not flow, then you can be said to have no outflows."

"And what about you?" all of a sudden wondered Foundling. "Have you got such a place?"

"Yes, my good friend," the master's voice sounded unhesitating. "I've got the place, which is my own self, my true nature and which is called the Snow Peak of Mt. Nirvana."

Chapter 11: Predestination

Before going on, a word should be said about the ancient oracle entitled "Zhou Yi," also known as "The Book of Circular Changes." The Oracle is about the logic of changes, primarily in symbols, which when combined together formed entirety, Oneness, and to which can be assigned the principles already derived from the material known as the body text of "Yi Jing" with its Appendixes completed by Confucius (551-479 BCE). The readers familiar with the oracle have already known that it consists of sixty-four diagrams of six lines each with accompanying text, which forms some layers, like geological strata, each layer representing a different period of the changes in composition. With layer upon layer, its wisdom piles up on the handmade paper of its pages over time; it can be a regime for spiritual development. Equally well, therefore, along with high-ranking officials and rulers, peasants and laymen may also consult the oracle concerning the proper date for waging war or arranging a wedding or planting rice or sowing barley. More pointedly, gamblers can use it to predict the roll of dice, though in their case the odds are longer since the one but the main condition the oracle requires of its questioner the purity of heart. To those who are not in contact with the Dao, the Oracle does not return a clear answer, since it would be of no avail. Of course, this purity is not easily ascertained. However, a pirate or a gambler may possess it and a Daoist priest or Buddhist monk may not. Perhaps the best description of the "Circular Changes" was given by the Tian-tai Patriarch Zhi Yi who said that it was like a well, the bricks of which were laid by human workmen to brim the cold and transparent water of the Dao drawn up from the pure reservoir of Being, which had no bottom that men could sound. His definition captured the idea of a primitive force, the Absolute, ethically neutral in itself and indifferent to men, obeying no laws but its own -- always following the line of least resistance and seeking its own level -- but which, nevertheless, could be channeled towards a human end and used for good. This end, this goodness is wisdom, which a sage who studies the "Circular Changes" may hope to gain, drinking long and cool, satisfying draughts from the bucket which he draws up heavy, spilling over from the darkness of the human heart. By using the yarrow stalks, a man may read, as precisely as an alchemist measuring quantities of basic elements in some solution, the composition of one's fate. The way it works is based on the concept of the great primal opposition, familiar in the Tai-ji symbolic motif as the 'Wheel of Life,' in which the light and dark, Yin and Yang cleave together like two great beasts grappling in a perpetual dance, rather than mortal combat. All things arise from this ongoing intercourse between the opposites, which alternate cyclically, each regenerating from the disintegration of the other, and which it carries in its womb like a fatal embryo and nourishes at the expense of its own life. All the Daoist and Buddhist arts, one hundred pathways of meditation of which reduce to the study of the "Circular Changes," and this is the only principle that unifies the opposites within itself to recover the wholeness (Oneness) that had existed even before the universe splintered into multiplicity.

From the time the novice had appeared in the monastery a day never passed that he didn't send the abbot a dozen of fresh-cooked rice rissoles. He was so grateful for the job he had in the monastery's kitchen that took to cooking round rissoles daily as a gift to his generous patron. Each morning they appeared in a shallow wicker basket outside the abbot chamber's door, carefully wrapped in a palm leaf. For a long time, except the abbot, of course, no one knew how they got there, and who brought them. They appeared as if by magic. This became an inside joke among the inhabitants of Go-qing monastery. Yet, it was innocent enough; the novice delivered the offering personally. As for the abbot, each time upon receiving the rissoles, he used to give back one of them to the novice with the words, "And I present you with this one. I wish your family and your family's clan ever-increasing prosperity!"

This gesture caused the novice to wonder. "What does it mean?" he thought to himself, "I present the abbot my rissoles but every time, one of them he returns as though it was his gift for me. Incredible!" At last, he went to ask the abbot directly.

"It's very simple," the abbot explained. "You present me, I present you. What's that to you?"

Hearing this, the novice realized that the abbot merely exchanged roles with him to show the indifference to the idea of 'mine -- yours,' 'me -- others' in the enlightened mind. As a result, he decided to follow the teaching the abbot preached, becoming a full-fledged inhabitant of the Guo-qing monastery.

Later he confessed, "Though I started practicing I didn't have much experiences to talk about, such as seeing the 'true self-nature' or the like. Nevertheless, I was anxious to turn to esoteric teachings. I had been obsessed about the golden elixir pill manufactured from lead in precise accordance with the alchemic formulas and methods. In the meantime, whenever there was an opportunity, I visited temples, and I maintained my spiritual preparedness. Once I met a master from Wudang School who prophetically said to me: "You are a monkish material. Neither the position of a civil official nor that of a military officer suits you." It was that encounter that I first began to understand the inconceivable workings of karmic affinity. The master helped me know that it was not a coincidence that we had met. In that chance encounter with him led me to the right path. After entering the monastery I, however, didn't obtain full ordination. Then I spent some time in solitary retreat in the mountains, and which should last totally thirty-six days, but which was interrupted much earlier. Why didn't I take my monastic vows? It's not easy to explain in short. Partly, it is due to my inherent nature of a Daoist, which I'd never succeeded to curb. The initial few years of my staying in the monastery were significant to me: I spent most of my time practicing in retreat, reading scriptures, writing, and composing 'Gathas,' some short Zen verses. Poetry was especially important for me during those hard years of first practice. Even though I was staying in the mountains, the physical space was insufficient. My hut was only about one-third the size of the monastery's cell, but it seemed spacious to me due to many graphs of my verses I wrote on trunks and rocks all around my dwelling. Through reading scriptures and writing poems I've got my chance to meet with buddhas, bodhisattvas, immortals, and deities of all the times, and gradually my life started to be meaningful and solid. Due to an intensity of practice, I've got numerous experiences during those years; they occurred all the time and, therefore, became part of my life. When people asked me about my progress in practice, I answered that there was not much progress. Practice, experience, and progress simply became a way of my life. I started to be one with Dharma and, what's more, I learned to follow the ways of Dao. Though I didn't really spend much time writing in those days, I wrote very quickly and composed many verses. Others found it quite challenging to read scriptures or to compose poems when they were on solitary retreats because those activities interfered with their meditation. However, reading and writing did not bother me during my practice, not at all. From time to time, I guess, we all should flow upstream to feel alive and challenged. One day, on the way back to my hut I met an old man who was cooking gruel. He saw that I was tremendously tired, gave me a pillow and told me to rest. I lied down and fell into a long dream. I dreamed that I allegedly achieved the highest scores in my governmental examination. Afterward, I married a princess and became the prime minister at the imperial court. I kept my many concubines, and by the time I reached the hundredth year, my children were too numerous to count. I saw how I enjoyed my long life and even in old age, I did not want to die. But when the time came for me to die I could not avoid it and, like everyone must, I passed away. After my death, two demons led me down to the underworld because I had abused my bureaucratic power and embezzled court funds. I was punished by the judge of the dead and made to climb a mountain of knives, after which I was thrown into a cauldron of boiling oil. I felt tremendous pain and screamed. Just then the old man woke me up. Upon waking up, I found out that the gruel was done right at that moment.

"But why didn't you obtain your full ordination?" the monk asked.

Thinking a while, the novice said, "I've heard that after becoming a monk, one's perceptions about being a monk change over time. I had tried to imagine the life of a monk, but things became very different after I entered the monastery to become one. Before your ordination, you may think that you have learned enough about monkhood by talking to people, but different people have different mental states and hence experience monkhood differently. After you become a monk, you are constantly practicing, and your mental state matures over time. You will naturally have different thoughts, reflections, and perceptions about monkhood. I remember that before taking my first vow, I was directed to the fifth figure of the oracle named Xu, a symbol of waiting for an opportune time and abstinence from reckless activity, which denoted that with the faith and sincerity there would be a brilliant success. The reading literally said that he who has a sense of harmony will be a hearty welcome in each and every placement. Only he who dwells on correct firmness will reach good luck and fortunate end. It will result in crossing the great stream, which means the successful passing of all difficulties on the way by taking into account all aspects that the case stands. The previous diagram Meng (4) described what was undeveloped and young and, therefore, required to be nourished. Hence Meng was followed by Xu. Diagram Xu is descriptive of the way in which meal and drink come to be supplied. Xu means 'necessity,' as long as the food is necessary to support the spirit and the vital substance of 'the holy embryo.' It is made up of the upper trigram for Water positioned above the lower Heaven. The attribute of Water is the impending danger; Heaven means strength. Therefore, one shouldn't proceed further with a light heart but wait till the situation makes better. The fifth undivided line is the main in the hexagram and correlates with the ruler who overrides all the others. It is not so easy to surpass Water (clouds) that places above Heaven; however, it will be completed successfully if you have some patience to wait to strengthen in your mind and to believe in the welfare future. If so, the crossing of the great stream will be advantageous. Firm correctness, as one of the four main traits of Heaven, is the particular quality to be employed here to achieve a good fortune through waiting for an opportune time."

After a short pause he continued, "At the reference to 'danger' (correlation of Water), I pricked up my ears. I didn't know what it specifically meant, but it set a resonance within me. A chill of premonition passed down my spine, intensified by what I found in the judgment which stated: 'It will be advantageous to cross the great stream.' I knew very well that 'to cross the great stream' was a metaphorical usage and could refer to any determinative action, even at the moment which could demand great patience and precision of actions termed 'wu-wei.' But the real significance of the phrase lodged in my mind and an image from my dream the night before flashed in front of my eyes in an illuminative way. I saw myself waiting afar, as though in an attitude of deference, staring toward the horizon over the expanse of the great ocean, while the sun sank into it to be extinguished. Turning to the explication of the bottom line of my construing, which was a moving one, I read the judgement, which said: "He is raring to step into the big city (the temple), still staying and waiting in the suburb' -- he makes no movement to meet the difficulties of the coming event rashly. 'It will be well for him to take his time in maintaining his advance gradually, in which case there will be no calamity' -- with the full support of his responded mate in the fourth place he will not fail to pursue his regular course of welfare.' Though the repeated reference to danger alarmed me somewhat and even titillated me a little too, I was determined not to court it. I thought I would follow the oracle's advice and made no movement to encounter the difficulties of the situation rashly. It was in keeping with this resolve that later, the same afternoon, I attended the abbot's sermon on the subject of retreat, which was almost upon a group of novice-monks as the first one since coming of age. It had a particular significance for me since at the end of forty days of solitude and fasting I was about to receive final initiation into the order. That day I composed a poem which read like this:

"If all your previous life you were stupid and dull,
You couldn't be utterly enlightened by today.
If now you're poor, it's all of what you did before.
If in this life you still do not cultivate your soul,
In your next life, you will be in the same marsh.
When neither bank has a ferryboat nor bridge,
The rapid stream is hardly possible crossover."

"'Wreckage of sentient flotsam and pieces of driftwood floating on the ocean of this life destined for disintegration and remaking,' the abbot began his preaching, 'in such sinking we find the true image of our own pathways. But, even so, we have a meaning and are indispensable to life in the larger scope. It is our purpose to enrich the solution of Dharma and assure the future. Should the least grain of sand be lost, the world would end. . .'"

"A destiny, unmoored sensation came over me with this echo of the evening reading. The abbot's 'private pathway' recalled 'the path to the meritorious achievement' mentioned in diagram Xu. 'It is only when we dare to face things exactly as they are, without any sort of self-deception or illusion, that a light will develop out of events, by which the path to the meritorious achievement may be recognized. I was unsettling to think that this might be the same as the 'private pathway' of every single soul which converged upon the pathway the abbot spoke of. That night I dreamed again of the dangerous water; again I stood on the strip of beach peering away over the wide expanse of the ocean, listening to the melancholy rhythm of its waves. On the next day of my retreat I repeatedly consulted the oracle. To my surprise, it directed me back to the same diagram. The moving line raised one notch to the second place, determining: 'The second undivided line shows its subject waiting on the wet sand. He suffers the small injury of being spoken against, but there will be good fortune in the end.' This meant that despite his placement now closer to the dangerous water, he occupied his position at the center with a generous forbearance to bring things to a good outlet.

"Recurrence of the dream and mirroring of its imagery in the Oracle convinced me again in the fact that more was there at work than mere coincidence; I was witnessing something dark and mysterious unfolding in my life, like a withered ancient scroll, on which in weird archaic graphs was written a recondite judgement of inevitable fate. The thought that it was critical for me to penetrate the meaning of the dream took hold of me. I tried to cool myself as the Oracle suggested, but all through that day I was anxious. The more I tried to calm down through meditation the louder cicada chirruped within the temple of my heart.

"On the seventh day of my retreat in the chill mountains, there was no surprise forthcoming, no reprieve. With the morbid insistence of a wandering mendicant carrying his ghastly message, like a lantern through the thick forest, the illuminated text of the Oracle pointed me back to Xu, again, all as before. Only now the moving line had ascended yet another degree, explicating, 'The third undivided line shows its subject waiting in the riverside mud. He thereby invites the approach of injury.' This meant that calamity was close at hand, starting from the adjacent line of the upper trigram (Water) denoted danger. In other words, if he were to be extraordinarily reverent and careful, he wouldn't be worst. For on that day a part of me gave way from within, like planks of an old bridge I had walked across each day of my life, never dreaming it might be rot, that it was rotting even as I used it. The gave way plunged me back into the fetid sink of nature, the life mire, all the squalor and the beauty I had not partaken of and thought to have no part in. . . But from it I had arisen and now back to it after the respite, my peculiar destiny afforded me, my youth, that brief sojourn in the stainless asylum of the Dao, to the Yellow Spring of which I should return. I composed the following lines:

"Sailing a boat made of the rotten wood,
We reap the bitter fruits from the tree of peril.
Gone with the current, we flow into the open sea,
Where waves repeat themselves without respite.
We have brought provisions for one night only,
But to the opposite shore ten thousand miles ahead.
Where vexations come from? It is sad to admit,
But they go out from the bitterness of karma
You have accumulated in previous lives."

"The 'open sea' represented a large quantity and did not necessarily denote an actual body of water. It most likely could symbolize the powerful karma of mine, as vast as the boundless sea. The 'ten thousand miles' represented all the deeds I have done by my body, my mouth, and my mind. But I couldn't believe that anymore. The hatred had emerged full-blown and roped uneasily beside the love, racing with one another like two billows at the harbor mouth, competing in might for a single beach, catching for the flood tide to cross over. That night, despite my resolve to ban all worldly thoughts, my mind wandered to my lover I'd left in Xian-jing City. Yet I wanted to. I'd loved her too much to let her go away from my mind, loved her with love as strong and unquestioning as my love of the Dao, the pristine faith. Not even her revelation, which I could not choose but believe; I could change that, or diminish it. In fact, in a subtle treatment of light and shade, the play of shadow I had sketched in her features brought the highlights out, made the brightness brighter -- the Yin embracing, giving definition to completing Yang. And the Yin was not evil, no more, so that the night which ceaselessly followed a day in the ebb and flow of time, part of nature's cycle in the changing of the changeless universe. Perhaps she was as blameless as the night. . . Then I composed the following lines:

"Green waters run thru a thousand lumps in my throat;
Yellow clouds equal all the four corners of the world.
What a pity! In this life no more than a hundred years,
It grieves me deeply to contemplate Xian-jing City."

"I pulled up short on the brink of an abrupt precipice. It was a good move, but it didn't save me so far. The seed of doubt had been implanted, much earlier perhaps, pressed into the soft furrow of my fontanel as I lay prone in a narrow cave with my feet out. But when my crystal, Clay Pill, had been melted down was insignificant. Sometimes I think that from then on everything that happened to me was the pure necessity. After a sleepless night spent pacing back and forth in front of my shallow den and listening to the cicadas droning their fated prophecy on the other side of the darkness, I turned again to the oracle. But that time I had a sense of inevitability and awe, like a guilty man awaiting the sentence of the court -- a sentence which in the temple of his heart had been already known. It was the Xu hexagram again, declaring, 'The fourth divided line shows its subject waiting in the place of blood. Bleeding in a cavern, he can get out of the dark cave of the mortal danger only through voluntary self-regulation.' This meant that he accommodated himself to the circumstances of the time. In spite of his bleeding wound that he had got in the aftermath of his entering the dangerous water, due to his ability to hearken to the voice of reality and its requirements, he would find the way out. However, the situation seemed to be quite dangerous. First I thought I was of utmost gravity -- a matter of life and death. There was no going forward or backward; I was cut off as if trapped in a cavity. Actually, I was sitting in one. But then I suddenly realized that I might simply stand fast and let fate take its course. My fate was the pure nature of Yin: pitch dark and feminine. Though the divided line was weak and listless, its position under the even number four, which completely suited to the feminine nature of Yin, added some supplementary, if not to say productive forces. Somehow compensating the gravity of the situation, I was given hope for upcoming to light, as a tunnel boring back into the dark of prehistory, darkness unrelieved by any ray of morality. I decided to die to be reborn. That was a nightmare, my nightmare, my dream, and its beauty made me gasp for breath even as it threatened to consume me, consume the world, in one great and instantaneous inflammation. Yet I couldn't sit still, much less meditate. The world was throbbing, one vast hive of buzzing sound around me. My mind, rather than letting go and rather than becoming still and pure like the mirror unstained by any image, was growing increasingly restless. The reflection which arrogated that mirror's surface was not growing glow, but more vivid, as though composed of celestial light -- the whiteness of the sun focused through prisms, etching the image of my expectation. Because I couldn't meditate anymore, I resorted to the expedient of reciting one of my verses over and over again simply to keep my thoughts from following their unruly and precipitous descent. But the words repeatedly coursed through my mind like water over stones. Again and again, I found that I had drifted back to the statements of Oracle, like an arrow shooting through the universe unerringly toward the dim constellation of my fate that run a distance between the sun and the moon. I found myself moving from tigers that snatched up infants and devoured them to earthworks and fortifications, from tears stained the graves of the newly deceased to receiving property. Then I saw the whole family plunged into ruin and the new constructions to be; I talked to the rat, the symbol of great wisdom and swallow, the sign of caution. I soared in the area sometimes known as the celestial marketplace and suffered the torture of underworld. Then I quickly caught myself up and began to whisper earnestly, hoping the mantra might loosen me from the gravity of the situation, releasing me from the compulsion of this spell. But it was the mantra itself, which finally undid me: all in an instant, cleanly, efficiently, a part of me snapped, or was severed, as though my heart, my liver, some internal organs, snipped and discarded. I was awake and watched it went on composedly. I could point with precision to the moment it occurred. Only later, when I divined the change within myself, the lack, did I surmise the magnitude of what I'd gained. In no time I composed another verse:

"In former years I made once a journey to the vast sea,
For getting the Mani Pearl, I vowed in earnest to seek.
I went directly to the Dragon's Palace --
The place most deep and dense; at the Golden Gates
I broke off the lock to make His Majesty be worried a lot.
The Dragon-king, to guard his treasure, had hidden it
Inside his ear; his knights in many,
Brandished their sparking blades were on the alert --
There was no way to seize the treasure,
But when I, a poor pedlar, withdrew from inside the gate
To escape, all of a sudden, I became enlightened
That the pearl had been cherished right inside my mind."

"Once I completed this verse, I experienced a hallucinogenic clarity, in which the familiar features of the world I knew were changed forever, and the words of the vow turned to ashes on my lips. I suddenly remembered that I did not believe it, or at least was no longer sure. I doubted. And I knew then that I would never take the vow, full ordination. To do so falsely would be to invite damnation. Yet I was damned and lost in either case. The recognition which the oracle had spoken of had occurred. I recognized that my faith had been damaged, possibly irreparably, by the oracle's judgments and its intimations of another world, another order of experience, entirely outside my own, finally irreconcilable with it. That was what had gnawed at me, working its slow attrition on the shoring of my certainty through the days of my retreat. The seeming intransigence about that world, the world impossibly exotic, glittering, beautiful, malign, a place of magic, madness, power, pelf, desire, where all the certainties were turned upon their heads, where dishonor was not incompatible with the highest courage, and the way of self-interest led not to destruction but to giddy peaks of ecstasy and power. In a nutshell, that was the world of enormous challenges and boundless possibilities, where every dream came true. What was it about this vision that so fascinated and at the same time so appalled me? Was it that a part of me? Was this the new me by the nickname of Foundling? Partly a novice, partly a monk, partly an odd-job layman in the monastery's kitchen? Some volatile essence passed through my mind, longed with the homing instinct of a migratory fowl, to return to the Yellow Spring, that origin -- not monastery at all, but the great Dao itself. Just recently, this old novice despised this longing, considered it heretical, a betrayal of the faith. But was it really? Was this pun a monstrous hoax of nature, two heads on a single pair of shoulders, or did it reflect a real identity between the two? Were they finally one? On the truth of that proposition I was staking my future, and beyond that, the salvation of my immortal soul. But what if it weren't so? And how could it be! I was about to tie myself indissolubly, with the pain of hell, with a faith which I saw mocked by the smile of mischief on King Yama's lips, confidence shattered in a thousand fragments in the glittering, malignant, multifaceted reflection of all regarding Tian-tai, the Heavenly Terraces. . .

"It was over. There the road divided, and both forks led to perdition. Either I renounced my childlike faith and so lost all I'd ever had or known, or else I held it falsely and so damned myself forever. Images of my childhood flooded back to me like ledger after ledger of outstanding debts, and below each one, my name, the only security I'd been asked to pledge. With that I was startled, awake by the frenzied surf. At first, I could not be sure whether it came from without or had been produced by my own mind, a figment connected with the dream. Opening my eyes, I had a sensation of surfacing from a great ocean depth, coming from the darkness and the pressure out into the light where I could breathe, again. I sat up and looked around, partially refreshed by sleep, though far from sober. All was as it had been. There was a great buzzing stillness over the world, in which I reposed and listened. The surf I had heard or thought I'd heard, had vanished, so I was forced to conclude that it had been imaginary. Yet the intermittent rumbling of thunder, booming far away over the river and echoing cavernously against the canyon walls, was real enough as was the strident trill of the cicadas tuning up in the darkness. In the intervals between the throes of my despair, a deathlike peace stole over me. I was like a man calmly witnessing his own demise in the total combat at the end of the world. The great slow-rolling cloud unfolded before my eyes, petal by petal, like a vast white lotus blooming, silently, at the heart of space. 'Even in the midst of danger there are some intervals of peace,' the fifth undivided line of Xu predicted for the fifth time. It showed its subject waiting amidst the appliances of the feast, pointing out, 'In gratitude, he fairly shares his food and wine with all those who have helped him to rise. Despite the perilous nature of the upper figure (Water), he provides himself with his correct position of the ruler and the host of the entire situation right in the upper center, as the earnest of welfare.' The appliances of the feast and good fortune through being firm and correct were indicated by the position in the central and proper place. Again, I experienced the oppression of something and, at the same time, the hollow and weighty burden at the center of my being, which would rarely leave me after that, except in sleep, and, for a while, in wine drinking. I couldn't explain it to myself, but a change had come at that moment of hardship. I was no longer happy or unhappy. Even my whole being was affected. I ceased to pass at once into the state of quiet intensity I'd become accustomed to. Instead, I experienced a regression and was distracted by a certain trilled sound in the temple of my heart. When, as many kalpas ago as there are fine motes of dust, the Buddha named Sunlight, embodiment of the Crow, Moon, and Lamp appeared in the world; under that initial Buddha's shine I left the home-life, yet I was deeply committed to the worldly fame and liked to fraternize with people of great prosperity. For the whole of the next day, until the cave began to dim and I knew dusk had come, I lay on the cold stone, staring at the cliff, seeing nothing, neither moving nor thinking. Finally, I began to revive a little. I got up and took a dipper full of water, drinking some and using the rest to wash my face. I experienced a surge of hope. Though I could not take the vow in good faith now, in time, I might, in a year maybe, if I devoted myself each day to meditation, immersing myself completely in the flood of Dao. That was a setback, doubtless, but it did not have to be an insuperable one. Life might give me a second chance. That time I was inspired by the following lines:

"On the top of the age-old stone
The ancients left their graph-prints;
On the front of the bottomless cliff
Gapes a round spot of the dark hole.
When the full moon's disc shines,
It becomes transparent and bright;
Now, no need to seek anyone to ask
Where's the west, and where's east to go."

"And that night I dreamed the same dream again. Only this time there was a slight variation. As I stood listlessly surveying the grey expanse of the sea, I was seized by a premonition. Turning around, I looked back over the ground I'd covered and, for a disoriented moment, got the incongruous impression that some footsteps were following me, as though an invisible beast was on my trail and had been all along. It closed in crunching in the sand, and I backed terrified into the water. I felt its breathing onto my face. I was in up to my waist before I realized what was happening. Wheeling violently, I screamed as a gigantic wave crested over me and broke, sweeping me under. After a while, I rose mechanically and, taking down the cypress box in which I kept my yarrow stalks, opened it and took them out, move under my own momentum. I decided to consult the oracle for the sixth time. Since then two terrible watches (four hours) had passed, and truly I thought never to be bothered with the trilled sound in the temple of my heart again, the obsessive buzzing of the mundane world, from which I couldn't free my mind. Thus I was understandably distressed that early morning in the temple when the fatal tune, which I knew so well, struck up within me. Then for the final time, I tallied up my destiny. Occasionally, a pulse of heat lightning flashed across the sky, lighting up the outline of the mountains. And once, piercing the din of other sounds, the shrill and plaintive cry of a night bird broke across the cliffs. Its song was unfamiliar to me and, at the same time, resembled me vaguely something I had known, deeper than memory, almost like a cry for help, but after the damage had been done and was beyond redress. Like a voice ascending through the scale towards the highest note, its crisis and apotheosis, the moving line had risen upward through diagram Xu one step each time I divined. But then it could go no higher. It had come right to the edge of an abyss, delivering a judgment which said: 'The topmost divided line at its proper place shows its subject as one whose course has entered into the cave of deadlock for resting there. From now on, there is no waiting state at all. By riding on the subject of the hosting fifth undivided line, he has provoked the three unbidden guests (represented by three lines of the lower figure of Heaven) coming to him with their different intents to get the full picture. If he receives them correctly and with proper reverence, they will leave him alone before long and let him attain his good fortune upon the ending of his living course.' Riding on the ruling fifth line (this means a sort of disrespect to the strong hosting line), he had only provoked appearing of the unbidden guests, among whom the subject of the second line who was the responded mate of his upper correlate in the fifth place and who came with no good intention of revenge. However, his repentant conduct at the end of his course would protect him from severe damage due to his proper place on top of the whole situation and, due to the kind support of his correlate in the third place which was among the coming guests, too. This intimation showed that though the occupant was mostly out of the whole picture, there had been no great failure in what had been done if he could conduct properly. And if he was sincere when confronted with difficulties, he could wholeheartedly penetrate the meaning of the situation to get a way out. Once he gained personal mastery of a problem, it would come about naturally that the action he took would succeed. The waiting was over; the danger could no longer be prevented. The subject of the position fell into the pit and must yield to the inevitable. Everything seemed to have been in vain. But, precisely in this extremity, all things took an unexpected turn. Without a move on his part, there was outside intervention. There the mate of the topmost divided line was the subject of the third undivided line, which corresponded to it within the harmonized framework of the Yin-Yang forces. The subjects of the first two initial undivided lines all over followed on the third's heels, as a thread after its needle, and all together the three were ready to deliver their bills accordingly. But who were these three guests? I had to know. Was among them a madman who dared to risk his own life for the sake of the others? Or was there 'an untapped immortal,' a sage, a bodhisattva in the rough? Maybe a different creature, entirely unique, unprecedented -- an animal, which experience had not prepared it to identify itself. Maybe some kind of magic dragon-fish, or a giant mythical critter which slumbered away one hundred thousand years at the bottom of the sea. Maybe some tiger-mutant being still slimy with the pleural fluid of creation, quite difficult to have been classified, but which had breached into the traps, tearing them like gossamer, or a critter they had seen but couldn't capture. It had slipped back into the open sea and was last seen heading northeastward in the direction of Peng-lai, the Isle of Immortals, to hit the fan. By what accident, or chance, or according to what unknown law had they all arisen out of nature? Were there others like him -- an entire civilization, perhaps, made up of such men, worshipping their barbarous god the name of whom would never be uttered. . . Really, what did they call their fierce wormlike divinity? What name did they whisper in their subliminal prayers? . .

"This was a last resort, just as if I had been pierced by a poison arrow; as if in answer to this query the crucial pun recurred to me and in a brilliant mental burst all my questions. At that, all my doubts and fears resolved themselves into that single word, those syllables, itself an issue and its solution, all at once, a spell, which I repeated over and over to myself, feeling that somehow it was the key to everything, the key which opened up the grave secret of the Mind. For this one had to have this bold and persevering mind, like one warrior fighting off ten thousand enemies coming from every quarter, going straightforward without regressing and letting loose. That was it -- a single word, Deliverance. What was this mysterious entity? I had no idea. But it charmed me fatally; the word that was the Zen notion and, at the same time, the thought to eradicate many other thoughts. What was its relation to the flow of Dao? Where was the point of confluence, where that foaming stream flew back into the calm and abiding ocean of Dharma? Was it upstream or a downstream? For the back, I had to flow or otherwise? Everything came back. It had to.

"Shutting the oracle, I got up and, violating the protocol of the retreat session, left my seclusion. Having no idea what I meant to do or say, I went instinctively to the abbot's chamber. My sandals left moist prints on the slate stones as I crossed the inner courtyard towards the southern part of the monastery, where the abbot kept his quarters. I came by a plum tree planted, they said, by Guan Ding, a disciple of patriarch Zhi Yi, the founder of the whole Tian-tai tradition. The tree was twisted and knotted, yet full of pith and bearing. As they used to say: 'One plum for each monk every year.' As I stooped beneath its branches, I noticed with a feeling like chagrin that the blossoms had already been succeeded by the ovary. Mostly green and small, the seed-buds hung from the crusty branches like driblets of water along a blackened ditch edge after the rain. Scrutinizing this, the following lines leaped to my mind:

"The people are the basis of each country --
It's like a tree that is nourished by the soil
In which it roots. If the ground is fertile,
The tree grows in flourish; otherwise,
The tree withers and rots.
You should never bare the roots;
When the branches dry up, the seeds fall first.
To break a whole dam to get the fish
Means to reap just immediate benefits."

"The abbot was sitting on a prayer mat at the far end of his chamber, legs folded underneath him in the full-lotus posture, hands clenched into fists lying in his lap, knuckles upward. First I thought he hadn't noticed my entrance, but without opening his eyes, he said softly, 'Welcome, brother. I've been expecting your visit.'

Slowly his eyes opened. As his eyelids opened up, I saw eternity receded before him, extended section by section until it was gulped by itself. His squire pupils resembled the tiny spots of darkness, floating silently at the core of kaleidoscope, serene and still amid the feverish, ever-changing spectacle, like Truth. Gradually, the radiance of the other world began to leave his face. He was pale, his skin almost translucent, his breathing was barely perceptible; he looked at me with an impassive expression, which bore no trace of familiarity or emotion, unless far down, far and far down, there was a spark, a memory of pity.

"A-mi-tuo-fo," he murmured, measuring me in a glance; and at this word, the floodgates of his compassion burst open. Clasping my hands, I kept guiltily silence. 'Don't worry, brother,' he said first, but his voice quavered. Looking up, I noticed the corners of his mouth fell down. At this, I lost all hope.

"It's over, over," I groaned softly to myself, to no one else.

"The abbot sighed. 'Now you begin to understand the difficulties of grasping the Dharma. It is hard, my young brother, really hard. But over? What is over?'

"Grandmaster, I've betrayed you. I'm unworthy."

"How have you betrayed me?"

"Then I told him everything: about the footprints leading me night after night back to the edge of that gray-bluish sea, into which the sun was falling like a tear of blood; about my night flying, my fantasies. . . I told him of the oracle, its remorseless and uncanny repetition of the sign of danger, of the trilled sound within me, of my crippled meditation, and finally of my blasted faith. I told him of my doubt, my intuition of a fugitive, the different truth that the ways of Dao could not accommodate -- ten thousand things, equal and coeval of Dharma. The separate and inassimilable, the trail of crumbs, left behind me, leading back not to the monastery, but into some natural and hospitable terrain down the mountains.

"Ah," the abbot sighed. "So it has come to pass. The more spiritual you are, the more truthful the dream you experience. When an adept is bent on selfish behavior, if he is enslaved to his own ego, this will tilt the scales of power from the spirit to the body."

"Silence reigned again. We both fell silent, pondering; only the soft sound of my own sniffing could be heard in the abbot's chamber.

"Stop sniffing now," he said at last. "Your snot cannot paint over the route of your destiny. It is fate. Better to accept it." He shook his head. "Perhaps, it's for the best."

"How can you say so?" I protested. "I've betrayed you, shamed myself, and lost my faith, all in a stroke. And you ask why I say it's over?" I uttered bitterly.

'As for your debt to me,' the abbot replied, 'and to the others, anything you owed us you have long ago repaid. You gave freely of your joy, your innocent enthusiasm, your gentleness, your compassion, your incredible rice rissoles -- and these things were leavened to our hard bread. The other charges are more serious. But I can neither judge you nor exonerate. That I must leave to you. Justice or mercy, these you must mete out as your heart commands. But tell me, is it possible that monkhood has vanished so completely from your mind, that in a few moonlit nights you have discovered to be false what the monastery's lifestyle had taught was true for so long?'

"I didn't answer immediately, weighing his question. 'Deep down I still believe in the monastic vows,' I replied at last. 'But I've had a vision of another reality which I think I believe in, too. According to the vow, the world is One. If Dharma is only partial, it is false. If what I've seen is real, then the way of Dao must be an illusion.'"

'Now I begin to understand,' the abbot said. 'You have not rejected faith out-of-hand, but merely begun to doubt. Doubt is not incompatible with conviction, though it may seem so. It is the Yin substance, while faith is the Yang essence. Doubt is the darknet, with which we seine for faith. But both doubt and faith are only stages on the way back to the certainty which comes, not from faith, but from direct experience of the unity of nature and parity of the world, the truth that 'Reality is One, and the Dharma is Reality.' The fact is that what you have lost was never yours by right, young brother. Your faith was borrowed from the rest of us, as you were too young to pay the price yourself. But now the time has come. If you would have it back, then you must earn it.'

"Only teach me how!"

'The secret is locked within yourself. Seek it there. The clues are in your dreams and in the oracle, which is your guiding star no matter which world you choose to get to know. Remember where did the footprints lead -- always back to the same beach, the miry sand on which you was waiting, gazing away over the wide, spreading water. As you have divined, this is the 'great water' the oracle has said that you must cross. It occurs only when we dare to face things exactly as they are.' The abbot smiled and on that instant, taking a deep breath, I forced my heart to open to the terrifying initiative.

"What is the water in my dream?" I asked gingerly.

'You already said yourself, it is the sea.'

"But. . ."

'But is it a real sea, or a portent, foreboding of peril in yourself?' The abbot cut me off. And then he answered himself, 'The Buddha said, 'Those who follow the Dharma are like pieces of wood in waters of the stream: they are borne on the current, not touching either shore, not picked up by anyone, not intercepted by ghosts or spirits, not caught up in whirlpools, even never rot. I guarantee that these pieces of wood will certainly reach the sea. I guarantee that adherents who are not deluded by emotional desire, not bothered by myriad devious things, but who are vigorous in their practice on the unconditioned basis, will certainly attain final realization.' How come that the adherent of the Buddha's teachings resembles the great sea? The ocean is the connector. Every part is connected, and things can move freely within it: there is no obstruction. The ocean also has tremendous dynamic energy, and it has tremendous capacity. It can symbolize the Buddha's wisdom. The great Samadhi that the Buddha entered is called 'the Ocean of Samadhi.' It has the attributes of the ocean that we are talking about. The Buddha's wisdom is also like a perfect surface of the calm sea. The analogy of water and waves is used in the sutras to illustrate this point. Water is the normal state of existence. But when the wind blows, waves form. These waves are of the same substance as the sea water, but originally they did not exist. Water is the ever existing, waves are ignorance. Water can exist without waves, but waves must have water to exist.'

'Tell me again,' after a short pause the abbot asked me, 'you said the sun was setting there. . . Does this not tell you something?'

"I thought a moment. "West?"

"The master nodded, and again I felt the tingle of impending revelation in my spine.

"What about the beast, the footprints?"

'That!' the abbot exclaimed. 'I'm surprised it still hasn't occurred to you, brother.'

"You mean you know?"

"He shook his head sadly, 'Would that I could? But, as I've said before, there are some types of knowledge, the primal and final truth, that no man can ever give another. Ask yourself, 'Are there not regrets and aversions that time and again entailed in yourself by the daemonic beast?' This act of self-awareness, of course, one has to take oneself exclusively to remain a human being conscious, obtaining the true liberation through weakening the egoistic tone of the self.'

"What must I do?"

"The abbot searched deeply in my eyes. 'I think you know already.'

"I stared at him as at a prodigy. 'What do you mean?'

'You must leave the monastery for good.'

"A thunder of joyous, bell-clear laughter rose out of my heart. I felt the first pale tints of dawn began to break inside me, a promise of warmth and comfort daybreak after long shivering night.

'So, you see, brother, nothing is over. Rather I should say it just begins. Not yet having entered the gate, you, nevertheless, have discerned the ways of Dao. You have not failed or betrayed us. You've found your way and only your private pathway back to the source, the Yellow Spring.'

"I took a deep breath. 'I am resolved,' I said. 'There are only two things I regret.'

'What are these?'

"First, I have lost my opportunity for initiation into the rites of alchemy forever; second, I'm losing you, Grand Master, forever too, that we will never meet again."

'Never meet again,' he repeated, as though astonished. 'Is not our destination one and the same? Keep the appointment, and we will be reunited -- you may be sure of that! As for alchemy, ask me, and I will tell you that the truest alchemy occurs only in the firepot of the sage minds of some of us. Only in appealing to one's mind directly a devoted adept can see the self-nature, becoming a true man, a real buddha.'

"How come that it is so?" I asked.

'The positive is not correct, the negative is not correct either. The unity of the positive and the negative is not correct as well. What is to be done?' instead of reply, the abbot asked me.

"I couldn't find what to say. "You tell me, Master!" I dared to utter at last. Then the abbot said, 'Sometimes I ask this to raise its eyebrow and blink its eye; sometimes I don't ask this to raise its eyebrow and blink its eye. From time to time, it is this itself that raises its eyebrow and blinks its eye; but sometimes it is not this that does it. So, how are you going to realize what this is?'

"After hearing this, my mind became unclouded; the scales fell from my eyes. I expressed my thanks to the master, kowtowing four times in succession. When I was about leaving his chamber, I heard he asked me, 'Why do you pay me so many respects?'

"Because I can see now," I replied, "that when I first asked you this question, it looked as if a mosquito had bitten the iron ox.' Then I composed a verse, which read like this:

"When you come upon a demon or a ghost,
The first thing you must do is to be out of fear.
Be firm and quiet, don't pay it any heed.
If you call out its name, it will leave you,
Vanishing without a trail. But to burn incense
And pray for the vigor and strength
The Buddha can endow you with,
Or worship and seek some aid from masters
Is to be similar to a mosquito biting an iron ox --
There is no spot where it could sink its sting to bite!"

"My question to the abbot was no more than a pet phrase because I didn't know yet the meaning of what actually I asked about. Who could answer such a question? That was why the abbot replied with a contrary question that was too inexplicable for me to understand. The metaphor 'I ask this to raise its eyebrow and blink its eye' is equivalent to the positive, while 'I don't ask this. . .' correlates with the negative; and 'it is this itself. . . and it is not this' represents the unity of positive and negative mentioned by the abbot. 'This' meant 'self-nature'; 'a mosquito biting the iron ox' referred to my poor condition of 'gong-fu' during my conversation with the abbot. It was he who opened my eyes, making me realize the fact that inquiring him I had merely tried to enter the painted on the wall doors. How funny it was after all."

Chapter 12: Dreams

One day in the early autumn, when Foundling went to visit Xue Feng during his practicing alone in retreat on Mount Nirvana, on his way to the peak he kept on to hear the tiger's roars and harrowing cries of birds of prey all around the mountain. That made him be scared to death; he complied:

"The evening sun flames up the western hills;
Plants and trees light up with their magnificence.
Still, there are places here dim and hazy,
Where pines and creepers meet up and entwine.
And here are so many waylaying tigers;
When they see me their manes swiftly, stand on end.
In my hand -- not as much as one inch blade,
Yet I strive with myself not to be dreadfully intimidated."

When told Xue Feng noted, "I see you are frightened nearly out of your wits," he said, smiling. "Do you still have 'this'?"

Later on, while having a meal, the novice stole a chance to write the character for "Buddha" on the spot the monk was sitting. When intending to take his seat, he found the written on his mat the graph of 'Buddha,' he was dumbfounded for a while.

"Ha! Ha! Ha!" the novice broke out in laughter, "I see you still have 'this' as well?"

In the twilight of the day, when his consciousness became lapse, worn out after the long journey the novice fell into a dream, in which he was serving wine to his friend in a ritual vessel borrowed from the monastery. There was a satisfied justice in the correspondence, the vessel was undoubtedly authentic and appeared to recommend the sacrificial wine. At a little distance, sitting in silent dignity, the monk's tigress was waiting to receive her portion. As the novice pressed down the lid and poured the wine, the tigress looked up at him with a quizzical expression, drawing her head aside. Curious to ascertain the meaning of that glance, the novice looked down. From the spout of the vessel, not wine, but a thick stream of steaming and viscous blood was pouring. Recoiling with horror and revulsion, he almost dropped the vessel. But the animal, noting his distress, said something soothing to him in a human voice, which immediately clarified the situation and relieved the novice's terror -- something he could never afterward recall. Then the tigress bowed her massive head and began to lap the contents of the cup. Finishing, she held out the bowl to the novice, and he took it. There was no threat, no violence in her expression, nothing that compelled him against his will, only a mute, a request of solidarity, in which he intuited a commandment of self-abandon, some sort of fraternal pact between them; but in what its basis lay and when concluded, the novice could not have said. The only thing he could feel deeply at that moment in his belly was what Xue Feng meant by the term 'this.' What else was it but not 'the cicada in the temple of his heart?' Taking the thin sip between his lips, he swallowed. Screwing up his brow in concentration, he waited for the magic to transfigure him. Yet nothing happened. He sipped again from the very bottom of the accepted cup -- still nothing. He was beginning to wonder if the efficacy of the 'celestial wine' were purely mythical, or if perhaps he was impervious, or doing something wrong when his bowels became enveloped in a cloud of instant warmth and pleasantness. It was as though a magician had whirled his magic box, snapping it in the air. With a burst of intoxicatingly sweet and rainbow-colored smoke, a small ghostly outline materialized in front of him. It was a small, green, and muscular devilish critter with brass earrings and bracelets on his arms and a topknot on his bald head; his black eyes were glittering with mischief. Some new element in the novice's consciousness corresponded to his presence. The little demonic spirit had a dreadfully prepossessing aspect and did the damnedest tricks, appearing variously as a filthy beggar, or assuming the point of buddhas or bodhisattvas or monks or nuns or producing magical lights or sounds. The novice fell for him at once -- the pointed ears, long whisk-like beard, his cute, frisky manners. . .

"I am your servant," he said with a gallant bow and started there with a grandiose transformation of the world into a living organism, which breathed and glowed and seethed with the liquid magma beneath its skin, like the coursing of blood in human veins. But very soon the so much powerful demon's exertions tired him -- he grew wan and irritable and then he discovered that the phantom required constant stimulation, constant feeding, lest he became petulant and dull. At last, the creature lay down and began to shiver, staring at the novice with big, imploring eyes. More to appease the phantom than to please himself, the novice took another sip, which immediately revived him and brought him back to snuff; after that, the spirit swore with great sincerity and heat to serve the novice better ahead. He did this over and over again. Finally, he came to the inevitable waning of his vigor. With each new sip, the little servant's rein vigor became less and less complete, until the end, when he fell into torpor, shivering and convulsing at the point of death. Suddenly, the novice realized with a shudder that the complexion of the situation had changed -- reversed itself, to be exact; he now served the slowly vanished phantom. A surge of panic rose from his belly like a white-hot bubble and, bursting on his lips in one last parody of innocent pleasure, it became a flower, a huge-size pink lotus flower, which, with childish delight, he reached out smiling to snuff. Then the dream finally lapsed. Yet he couldn't dismiss it out of his mind.

The novice couldn't say why exactly, perhaps it was the violet fungus intoxication he tasted with the monk that night, but in the stillness and coolness amid the crying of birds and the roaring of tigers he was filled with an odd sense of imminence. He felt restless and curious. In an indefinite while, a hallucinogenic beauty lay over everything; he thought he was hanging low over the grass... Upon drinking cold water in unison with the pulse, his mind came to be saturated with it, winding drunk. He recited, trying to get over it:

"I sit here on top of this huge and uneven stone;
The mountain streams are cold, icy, and chilled.
For my quiet fun, I prefer the beautiful and delicate;
Hills and cliffs are covered by a mist of mirages.
Happy and serene -- I have a rest in this place;
The slant of the sun -- shadows of trees grow long.
As for me, I look into the ground of my mind,
And a lotus flower is coming out from within."

When asked, the monk interpreted this dream in this way, explaining: "That other-worldly Juggler did a lot of its tricks purposely to delude your mind. There is only one resort against the demon's tricks -- the way of practicing silent stillness. This means nothing to see, nothing to hear. Even myriad tricks must eventually be exhausted, but as to the method of stillness itself -- it is boundless and can be employed forever. But since you let the demon play with you, making you be partial to his 'charm' and involved in various transformations, it could probably have resulted in endless dodges of both of you to the point of fatal exhaustion. Only be adherence to nothingness could make it possible to overcome the demon, negating its skills."

He emphasized, saying, "Everything has its limit; even the largest and strongest things are not immortal. As for 'nothing,' it is unlimited because it is unformed, and owing to this fact, it can be used universally. It is just so with emptiness, that is in the pure mind and proves the most useful and meaningful among the true things. When we talk about the Yin and Yang opposite forces, the empty space between the two signified by 'and,' is what makes them stay together, arranging a certain harmonized proportion."

In fact, the method of practicing stillness in silence can produce something everlasting, in full accordance with Lao-zi's concept which states that 'the tangible is born within the intangible' to reflect dialectical movement along the way of Dao. How can 'intangible' (nothing) give birth to 'tangible' (something)? These two are incompatible, like fire and water, and, therefore, are unable to establish the proper relationship between each other. However, the logical rules tell us that 'something' is an essential attribute of objective existence, while 'nothing' is just the formal attribute of objective reality. These two attributes make Oneness and cannot be separated from each other, like the Yin and Yang's entities.

After a while, the novice perceived that he must have dozed again. When he awoke the second time, he felt the sun warm on his face. For some time he basked in this gentle light without opening his eyes, until a shadow crossed his face. Imagining a cloud had passed before the sun, he regretfully recognized an opportunity to repair his indolence and prepared to rise. Sighing, he opened his eyes and saw the tigress standing over him: her molten yellow eyes glowed with the light of the great fire like magma at the heart of the underworld, even more, alive than anything he had ever seen. Her massive muzzle resembled stoked furnaces that could turn a water buffalo instantly to ash. The novice gasped for breath, almost cried out, but managed to stifle the scream in his throat. Her moist nose was not ten inches from his own: her black nostrils dilated and contracted as she sniffed at him. He could tell it was afraid, excited; just as he was. All in an instant he recalled the strange intimacy which exists between the predator and her prey, the sense of hyper-reality that visited one only at the point of death. He understood it then, as the magnificent animal stood over him glaring down into his soul. Her gaze was unbearable as if you were staring straight into the disc of the noonday sun. The tigress was first to break eye contact. Raising her muzzle, she sniffed the wind, as though distracted by a disagreeable scent, something she feared and hated. In that meantime, the novice's mind raced desperately over the possibility of escape, but when she looked down again she began to pant, her eyes gone more profound than he could read, stern with ferocious justice, like the World Sacred Mother's own eyes.

She opened her red mouth, and a drop of saliva dripped from her tongue splashing in the middle of his forehead. He took a deep breath, closed his eyes, tried to relax and let her go inside his mind, opened full for death. Again, he tried to imagine how it would be, whether she would crush his chest beneath her paw or if he would feel her hot breath in his face, the slick interior of her mouth, blanketing his head as her jaws clamped tight around his skull crushing it. In the end, it wasn't the matter.

It is sometimes difficult to distinguish between dreaming and waking. Sleep is made up of short dreams, while life awake is merely a long dream. You may become aware that you're dreaming only of falling back into the dream once again. For whether the soul is locked in sleep or whether in waking hours the body moves, you are striving and struggling with the immediate circumstances. Some are easy-going and leisurely, some are deep and cunning, but some are secretive. Now you are frightened over petty fears, now disheartened and dismayed over some great terror. Now the mind flies forth like an arrow from a crossbow to be the arbiter of right and wrong, now it stays behind, as if sworn to an oath, to hold on to what it has secured. Then, as under autumn and winter's blight, comes gradual decay and submerges in its own occupations; it keeps on running its course, never to return. Finally, worn out and imprisoned, it is choked up like an old drain, and the failing mind shall not see the light again. But whether or not you ascertain what the true nature of this soul is, it matters but little to the soul itself. For once coming into this material shape it runs its course until it is exhausted to the fullest.

When the novice opened his eyes again, the tigress was trudging off, swaying her vigorous hips side to side. Going to the edge of the stream, she took a drink and lay down on her belly, looked back. To his astonishment, she was playing with him. Leaning sideways, she cropped in her mouth a beautiful red flower. As she chewed she glanced back at him, almost sheepishly, as though dropping hints about the fathomless meaning of the casual flower and expecting for his reflected smile. Then she got up and padded delicately through the mountain stream. Reaching the far side, she stopped and sniffed the air again, having completely forgotten his existence. Quickening her pace, she disappeared in the shadow of the bamboo grove.

Upon recovering from the spectacular vision, the novice retold the continuance of his 'no-dreamed dream' to the monk who reflected, "This is a message and a lesson for your lot. You should make every attempt to remember this dream and absorb the message being conveyed."

When asked, "What kind of vision the tigress was?" the monk replied: "It was the blend of blood and fluids -- the two had been changed in you to produce the pattern of the tigress. It comes into existence in the figure of Fire, which is strong from outside but weak within; it gets control of the real breath of the celestial wine. Upon reaching the heart, it transforms there and flows then round the palace of kidneys to refine the qi-essence and jing-substance until the spirit would be attained. This long-term process is called 'the production of white lead and vermilion mercury,' or 'the white tiger and green dragon yoga.' On the other hand, the water dragon is situated in the symbol of Water, which is soft and gentle from outside but very strong inwardly. It is the root of 'the Life Mandate,' the Sacred Mother of gods and spirits.

Looking into the novice's eyes, the monk revealed entire emptiness, a full failure of understanding. Trying to put it in more or less comprehensible way, he explained,

'Our practice as the Daoists does not coincide with the norms of culture in the proper sense of the word. The basis of our tradition is the principle of 'doing from within,' which means the erection of each thing to its internal limit, the self-loss of all images in the fullness of being, while traditional culture is based on the identification of the external images of the world. We are directed to the Secret Female, the Great Mother of the World, and her ideal femininity is mostly unattainable in the masculine implementation. There is no absolute need for physical closeness. The liberation of the spirit is not the overcoming of the instinct, but the freedom to accept instinct and, even more, its complete overcoming. There cannot be universal law and rules where life becomes itself a sort of pure creativity. It's enough to look at the bedchamber art of love to understand this truth. Verily, he who comprehends this art is worthy to be called a heavenly lover!

The monk continued, saying, "You can learn many things from your dream. On the one hand, it was a wonderful device to encourage you in your attempts to find out more about your own dreams. But, on the other hand, it may serve you as a warning of the possible dangers of attempting to get into other people's heads to understand their dreams. Since dreams are often the core of men's whole unconscious personality, to apply someone else's level at this point may uproot far more than you intended. It may tear out not only the roots of your own particular life but also the deeper roots that the monastery's community has implanted in all of us, roots that are also, by this time, deeply embedded in the unconscious. This may catapult you, as well as anybody else, into the entirely different world and, as your dream has demonstrated, it is not always as easy to get out of such a world as it is to get in, my friend, because so much of life is merely a farce. It is sometimes just as well to stand by and look at it and smile, better perhaps than to take part in it. Like a dreamer awakened, we see life, not with the romantic coloring of yesternight's dream but with a saner vision. We are more ready to give up the dubious, the glamorous and the unattainable, but at the same time to hold on to the few things that we know will give us happiness. We always go back to nature as an eternal source of beauty and of true and deep and lasting happiness. Deprived of progress and of attaining practical wisdom, we yet open our hearts and listen to cicadas or to falling autumn leaves or inhale the fragrance of chrysanthemums or the winter snowing, and over the top there shines the full moon's disc, and we are completely content for a while. There comes a time in our lives, as individuals when we are pervaded by the spirit of early autumn, in which green is mixed with gold and sadness is mixed with joy, and hope is mixed with reminiscence. There comes a time in our lives when the innocence of spring is a memory and the exuberance of summer a song whose echoes faintly remain in the air. When, as we look out on life, our problem is not how to grow but how to live truly; not how to strive and labor but how to enjoy the precious moments we have. We don't care how squandered our qi-energy, but we concern of conservation it in preparation for the coming winter. A sense of having arrived somewhere, of having settled, and found out what we want. A sense of having achieved something precious, little compared with its past exuberance, but still something, like autumn mountains -- shorn of their summer glory but retaining such of them as will endure."

As the saying goes, "Life is but a dream." Literally, according to the ancients, our physical world is an illusion, a temporary residence, and not actual reality. Our world of morning dew and evening sunset is just one of many dream worlds and dimensions that separate us from the ultimate truth. These other dimensions are accessible in a variety of ways, one of which is through the dreaming state. When the sun is set, and the stars spatter the heavens, a part of our ten souls (seven of which belong to Heaven and three to Earth) leaves our bodies. Even if we remain awake, some of the souls still depart. This is one of the reasons why we began to feel more tired and drained as the night unfolds. When the body is in slumber, the chains of physical existence become suddenly broken. The souls are now free to ascend to a high place in the spiritual atmosphere where they receive nourishment, power, and the occasional energy recharge. We need to be continuously recharged, and sexual intercourse, when done correctly, is an excellent remedy for that. Why we need for reloading? In a chaotic day, the limitations of time, space, and motion extract their toll on the body and spirit. It is well known that time, for example, continually keeps men under extreme pressure. Either we are playing catch-up, madly trying to meet deadlines as the clock races by, or we grow wildly impatient as time slows down to a crawl. Still, the time is out of men's control. Again, during our 'metaphysical tune-up,' the souls are in a realm beyond time and space: past, present, and future are unified into one. The panorama of a human lifespan is fully displayed from birth to death. Thus, in addition to getting a recharge, the souls often catch sight of events that are coming our way, both positive and negative. These glimpses are then filtered down to the body, where they take the form of dreams. In other words, one aspect of a dream consists of the events, experiences, and thoughts currently occupying our conscious minds. Interspersed into this mixture are visions of the souls that dwell in the subconscious. So, our dreams offer us the opportunity to understand our negative character traits. They can help us learn what it is we need to change to grow spiritually. Of course, we must know how to read and interpret the dream to discern this wisdom. On that account, the interpretation of a dream is actually more important than the dream itself. Hence, it behooves one to make every effort to find the right person to interpret one's dream. It should be someone who truly loves and cares for you, or it should be a spiritual person who possesses a love for all people because the interpretation will color the dream's influence in your life. Namely, the act of interpreting dramatically impacts and influences the dreams' expression in the physical world.

In scriptures and sutras, we also found that there are various ceremonial means to have a dream, such as performing a specific ritual: going to sleep in a sacred place, praying for a dream, or simply concentrating the mind on having a dream before going to sleep. Such dreams are referred to as 'the sought dreams,' those that occur when someone consciously seeks a dream, and they have been documented by many ancients. The devotee both sees the deity and is seen by the deity. When the verb 'to see' is also used for dreams (instead of the more usual 'to have') one begins to sense the power of the dream in that the dreamer not only sees the dream but can be seen by it. The progression from spontaneous dream to sought dream is a reasonable development. If one accepts the predictive value of dreams in general, then whether the dreams occur spontaneously or as a result of consciously setting out to have a dream, one still has received a prophecy.

As the legend goes, at the beginning of time nothing existed but a vast ocean and god Vishnu who slept on the coils of a giant snake. As he sleeps, he dreams, and a beautiful lotus grows out of his navel, from which arises the universe. God's dream is the basis of all that exists, including waking reality. Thus, by entering into the dreaming state, one can possibly come into direct relationship with God and His creative power.

A dream is the meeting of minds; an event in our waking consciousness is the coming together of sensible substances. Hence, our feelings by day and our dreams by night are the meetings of mind with mind and of substance with substance. It follows that if we can concentrate the mind in abstraction, our feelings and our dreams will vanish of themselves. The ritual to gain spiritual and worldly power and seeing a dream is a significant part of mental well-being. The ceremony lasts for a fortnight and invokes the increasing power of the waxing moon by beginning with a sacrificial consecration on the night of the new moon and ending on the night of the full moon. On the last night, the dreamer drinks a mixture of herbs, molasses, and curd. Then one cleans the cup and lies down behind the fire either on the skin or the bare ground, remaining silent and non-resistant. If he sees a woman in a dream, he should know that this rite has been successful.

There were many complicated ideas about female, death, and awakening in the monk's dreams. The goal of Buddhism is to achieve liberation front the endless cycle of being born and dying through ritual techniques and practices that utilize the human body. However, it appears that the female body, at least when used by men through actual or symbolic methods, is particularly useful in achieving this end. They ended, and they began without knowing either the beginning or the end. Unconsciously, they strolled beyond the mundane world and wandered in the realm of practicing 'wu-wei,' which actually was 'doing without further ado and regret.' Verily, that was the practice that the venerable Zen masters had not actually articulated, but that the novice-monks were capable of intuiting through their dreams.

The dream is sought for a prophecy of the ritual's success or failure, and it is a particularly intriguing example when compared to later Zen Buddhist dream practices that seek the approval of dream women, especially semi-divine women, before proceeding with an initiation. While men dream they do not know that they are dreaming. In their dreams, they may even try to interpret their dreams. Only when they have awakened, do they begin to see that they have dreamed. By and by comes the great awakening, and they will realize that it has all been a great dream.

We are in a dream too. And when someone says that we are in a dream, this is also a dream. This way of talking may be called paradoxical. If after ten thousand generations we could once meet a great sage who knew how to explain the paradox, it would be as though we met him just this morning or last night. Let us not proceed now. We had better let it alone.

The first set of Tian-tai School's instructions to obtain dreams was as follows: "On a seat of fine grass prepare a pillow of fragrant grasses and put on a wreath of omen peach-flowers. Recite mantras to consecrate tea made from cypress or pine cones and then use it to anoint the eyes. As one of his dream mantras the monk used to recite his own verse, which read as follows:

"From the time I have resided on Mount Nirvana,
I've already pierced through tens of thousands of years.
Believing in fate, I fled to the forests and springs,
And here I tarry, contemplating freedom of all cares.

Mount Nirvana—people do not reach;
White racks—always dim and dense.
Fine grasses I use for my sleeping mat;
The blue sky serves me as my blanket in all seasons.
Joyous life! I rest my head on a rock;
Heaven and Earth, I comply in full with turns of my lot."

One day the novice awoke from a frightening dream that predicted the monk's imminent desertion for dwelling on Mount Nirvana. He rushed to tell him the dream and asked what it could mean. It was a long dream, and the monk gave it an equally long and detailed interpretation. Several things were going on in this exchange, not the least of which was the master's affirming his access to the dreaming realm, both as dreamer and interpreter. The novice's dream accurately described the emotional consequences of the monk's desertion. He saw the whole earth shaken and himself naked with his hair, hands and feet cut off.

"Be joyful," the monk concluded. "Such dreams are not evil. Those who have previously practiced good works have such dreams. Miserable people have no such dreams. The omens are auspicious."

Another day the novice saw a dream, in which he wandered in the nearest mountains until he came to the monk who was in retreat. The master told him the following story: 'In the old days,' he said, 'I became Amitabha Buddha and lived alone in the Pure Land of the West. I studied magic and could enter someone else's body, examining all the internal organs. Once upon a time, I entered someone's head and then I saw a universe with the sun and oceans and mountains and gods and demons and other living beings. This universe was that man's dream, and I saw his dream. Inside his head, I saw his city and his wife and his servants and his son. Once darkness fell that man went to bed and slept, and I slept too. When his world was overwhelmed by a flood at doomsday, I also was swept away in flood, and though I managed to obtain a foothold on a rock, a great wave knocked me into the water again. When I saw that world destroyed at doomsday, I wept. I still saw in my own dream a whole universe for I had picked up his karmic memories along with his dream. I had become involved in that world, and I forgot my former life. I thought to myself, 'This is my father, my mother, my village, my house, my family. . .' Sometime later, I, as Amita Buddha, saw doomsday once again. This time, however, even while I was being burned up by the flames, I did not suffer, for I realized: 'This is just a dream.' Then I forgot about my own experiences. Time passed. Manjusri Bodhisattva came to my house and slept and ate, and as we were talking after dinner he asked me, 'Don't you know, Amita Buddha, that all of this is a dream? I am in your dream, and you are in someone else's dream, too. . .' Then I awakened and remembered my own nature; I remembered that I was a monk by the name of Xue Feng. And I said to him, 'I will go to that body of mine that belongs to the monk by the name of Xue Feng for I wanted to see my own body, as well as the body, which I had set out to explore.' But Manjusri replied, smiling, 'Where do you think those two bodies of yours are?' In fact, I could find nobody, nor could I get out of the head of the person I had entered and so I asked him, 'Well, where are they, these two bodies?' He said, 'While you were in the other person's body, a great fire arose that destroyed your body, as well as the body of the other person. Now you are a wandering hermit by the name of Xue Feng, not a monk named Xue Feng.' When Manjusri said this to me, I was amazed. Then he lay back on his bed in silence, and I did not let him go away; he stayed with me until he died.'

After hearing such a great dream-story, the novice said, 'If this is so, then you and me and Amita Buddha and Manjusri Bodhisattva, all of us are men in one another's dreams. . .' Then in the dream of the novice was that the monk continued to teach him and told him precisely what would happen to him in the future. But the novice left his master and went on to a new rebirth. Finally, he became Samantabhadra Bodhisattva and found release.

Upon wakening up, the novice retold his dream to Xue Feng in all details. The monk listened to the story attentively and said, "As I was listening to your dream I became confused and was tempted to draw charts to figure it all out. It is not clear, for instance, whether I had entered the waking world or the sleeping world of the man whose consciousness I penetrated, and whether that person was sleeping, waking, or, indeed, dead at the moment when I met with Manjusri. But as the narrative progresses, I realize that my confusion is neither my own mistake nor the mistake of your narration. I have realized that it is a device of your narrative constructed not by you, but by someone else to make you and me understand how impossible and how irrelevant it is to attempt to determine the precise level of consciousness at which all living beings are existing. Nobody can do it; and, actually, it doesn't matter. People can never know whether they have become trapped inside the minds of those whose consciousness they have come to share. Inside this dream, the hermit meets another sage who enlightens him and wakes him up. Yet, though he is explicitly commanded to wake up, he stays where he is inside the dream; the only difference is that now he knows that he is inside the dream. Now he becomes a sage again, but of a different sort of sagehood, he is a hermit-sage, inside a dreamer's dream. While he is in this state, he meets you and attempts to instruct you. But you miss the point of the sage's intention. If this is so, you have to experience everything by yourself, dying and being reborn, you can't learn something valuable yet merely by dreaming, as the sage does."

After hearing this, the novice stood up and stretched himself. From his position on top of Mount Nirvana, he looked down to see a flurry of lights moved over the ravine like a cloud of lightning bugs seen at a considerable distance in a high. His glance glided over the uncut mountain meadow through the silver haze of daybreak, as if diminishing torches carried by thousands and thousands of invisible hands. Facing the coming day, he recited to himself:

"Ten thousand clouds blend with a thousand rivers;
In their midst, a certain gentleman at his ease.
In the daytime he rambles in the green mountains;
At night he returns to sleep at the foot of a rock.
He has lightly passed thru the springs and autumns;
Silent and quiet, he has no mundane onerous ties.
Joyful indeed! On what does he count?
Calm and at peace, he flows like last autumn leave,
Giving itself in the power of the fateful stream."

Chapter 13: Magic Healing

The young official by the name of Li Qin Min came from one of the wealthiest families in the early Tang-period kingdom, a clan sired by worthies of the ancient Han dynasty (206 BCE–220 CE). They were such a class of people who arose like terrible predators out of old marsh of that primeval landscape, devouring their competitors until they had increased to such a size that they enjoyed an uninterrupted view of the horizon in the land between all the four seas. They were those who followed the way of brigandage promoted into the secret communities of princes, dukes, and marquises; those who were bent on stealing charity and duty together with the measures, scales, tallies, and seals of official regalia, landlord rewards, and uniform; those who were not deterred by fear of sharp instruments of punishment. They had continued to exercise direct control over their empire long after the others had been turned loose like sacred cattle to manure the green fields of charity. This doubled the profits of officials like Li Qin Min and a handful of others like him, making it impossible to get rid of them.

Culture, or cultivation of the right and beautiful, is the afterglow of pristine vigor. And beauty, though it alone may finally redeem and make life bearable in its starkest formulation, is no more than a gorgeous parasite upon life's body with a tall stature, strength, style, bravery, decisiveness, imposing presence, and so forth. When a man has all these to the degree that surpasses others, they will bring him trouble. This terrible truth must never be forgotten. The official, however, was in no danger of forgetting what he had not learned. He had long escaped this falling off. Being a well-educated Confucian doctrinaire, he was very proud of himself. His knowledge led him to make distinctions in his mind and lost himself in his world of doctrinairism. His numerous duties had erected a barrier to his original nature.

After obtaining the Dharma in Wu-tai, the monk went on traveling and preaching for some time in the capital. When he reached Yangzhou, he found that people there were preoccupied with the quest for rewards of heavenly blessings and unaware of how to seek the proper satisfaction in their lives. He taught them the meaning of discovering the self-nature and how their own natures were endowed with limitless meritorious qualities and blessed rewards. When the masses of people heard of Dharma, they stopped seeking blessings and turned away from the small to go towards the great, starting from their own bodies and going towards their souls upholding the sense of harmony.

Upon hearing of the celebrated Zen monk's preaching in Yangzhou, Li Qin Min become curious. He went to the capital to pay a visit to Xue Feng. Reaching the place, he confessed, "Recently, your obedient servant had a lot of governmental duties to do, and didn't have the chance to hear the preaching of the Venerable Master. May I ask for your valuable directions from whence should I start to turn away from the small and go towards attaining the complete enlightenment?"

At that, the monk was silent and remained motionless. The official didn't want to disturb him, so he waited. But in short, while he started to become impatient. Seeing this, the monk struck with his heavy staff the visitor's seat thrice.

"What's that for?" the official wondered.

"First of all, move with blessings," the monk whispered to the guest's ear, "and then I will teach you with wisdom."

Hearing this, the official said, "O Master! You have pointed me to the place from where I should start my search for enlightenment. Now I have achieved the realm which is endowed with the original self-nature," he declared.

That which the official asked about actually was 'gong-fu,' or cultivation of the body and mind. Striking silently on his seat, the monk indirectly said to him: "My meditation is wordless teaching for you. It is really testing of your patience and your resignation. The moment you succeed in passing my test, I will use the words of wisdom to rid you of your pride."

Very soon official Li was promoted senior judge at Tanqiu in Taizhou County. The day he was about to depart he had a terrible headache. He called a doctor, but that couldn't cure him, and it turned worse. Then someone reminded him of the master. The official immediately requested to rescue him from his sickness. After he told the monk his symptoms he was asked of his birth date: year, month, day, and watch (hour). The master calculated whether the relative influences of Yin and Yang were auspicious for the patient at that moment or not. Then he lighted sandalwood incense and while reciting oral secrets, computed for the month, day, and hour the direction of the Gate of Life, the course from which the spirits supposed to be summoned and blessings obtained for the afflicted official. Afterward, he cast the divination blocks: two crescent-shaped pieces of bamboo with one side rounded and one side flat. The flat sides down, Yin in the ascendancy, supposed to be a negative answer; the flat sides up, Yang in power, meant 'the gods and spirits are laughing.' One flat side and one round side up (the Yin and Yang substances in balance) meant an affirmative response, an indication that the proper spirits had been summoned there. Once an affirmative answer had been received, the talisman was burned, and a few of the ashes were mixed in a cup of boiled water. Some water was given the official as an exorcist cure. The monk said, "That which is designated as a matter of the syndrome is water accumulated within your head. It is the element of Water (correlated with kidneys) that ascended from the lower elixir field in the crotch alone the spine to the upper elixir center on top of your head. When the sexual energy reaches there, it must then be transported down to the middle elixir field in the lower part of the belly to transmute it into qi-essence, also known as the golden elixir pill. It is necessary to close the transmutation downstairs; otherwise, the excess amassment of the sexual energy represented by the kidneys' fluids in the upper center can cause a chronic headache."

When asked Xue Feng commented it in detail, saying, "The qi-essence of mind, in this context, is a quintessence made from the true breath of Metal (associated with lead, the lungs, and nose), and the true breath of Wood (mercury, the liver, and eyes). As long as the purest essence forms the ruler, its common manifestation forms high-ranking officials and officers, while its coarse fraction forms the ordinary people with their common mindset. As it is said in the Classics, 'The sage is governed by the mind, while ordinary people are governed by desires. The lord moves in the true breath, but the ordinary people move in the fake or evil breath.' The generated in the Grand Ultimate (Tai-ji) substance Yin has three names: Real Water, lead, and the earthly soul of the Tiger. Its color is white, and its nature is Metal. Therefore, it is called the Metal (Golden) Crow of the sun. The jade of stones, the water of Metal (as Metal gives birth to Water), and the blood of brain, once taken together, they are called the 'Sea of Blood,' which is located in the brains. Thereupon, the Real Water is in the very center of it. Originally, it comes into existence in the heart and then flows around the kidneys, transforming and producing jing-substance, which is commonly known as the sexual energy. If the spring of the divine potency flows to it, but the primordial qi-essence does not circulate properly, then the body's spirits are not in peace and produce disorder. This is known as 'a lack of Divine Water.' Therefore, the stagnant waters must be driven away and well refined."

Thus the phase elemental causes of the official's headache were first determined. The healer performed then a distinct meditation. He imagined the twelve earthly stems to be embodied in the joints of his left hand. Touching each of the twelve joints with the tip of his thumb, while holding his breath and envisioning the primordial breath caught in the elixir field, the locus of Tai-ji Mudra in the microcosm, he circulated through the corresponding organs. Facing the direction of north, which represented Water and black color, he started touching to seven joints corresponded to the seven stars of the Dipper -- the Pole Star constellation on his left hand, envisioning the power of Thunder, one by one entering into the corresponding organ. At the same time, he recited the mantra's spell that brought the power of stagnant water under his control. He ended the meditation by holding his breath and envisioning the potential of shaking Thunder as first entering the microcosmic center of the body, while circulating through each of the five central organs -- the spleen, liver, kidneys, lungs, and heart -- where it was stored and drawn upon until he made the final procedure. By quiet chanting of purificatory incantations, he summoned the spirits at his command, namely, the exorcist spirits of Pole Star, Ursa Major (that was the seven-star god who corresponded to the seven stars of the Dipper), His Excellency of the North, Representative of Water, and some others. He also summoned forth the five powers of the Thunder element stored in the five central organs by touching with the tips of all fingers of the left hand to the palm, making then a tight-fisted mudra and drawing the graph 'Thunder' with the tip of his tongue on the upper palate of his mouth. On a piece of the yellow paper (Imperial color) he drew a talisman and signed it with a special talismanic seal at the bottom. Next, he lighted an oil-burner at home altar and recited an exorcist mantra, which sounded as follows:

"I command the source of all pains in the body --
A headache -- with the use of this magic of mine,
Here before this altar,
May all stagnant waters, collected and shaken,
May they be cast back into underworld's depths.
Qiu-qiu Jie-jie,
You are sent back to your fathomless source!
Quickly, quickly, obey my orders!!"

Saying so, he burned incense at the altar and bowed formally four times. Then he recited the Water incantation, which based on the upper sound 'yu' matched with the kidneys and the cinnabar incantation with entering sound 'shang' corresponded to lungs. He also recited the incantation for writing the selected charm and finally the incantation to summon the spirits of the appropriate branches involved in the case. After this he painted the charm, repeating the Guanyin's chant rhythmically for healing. When he had finished, he wrote five characters, meaning "Induced to Come by the Imperial Order" on top of the paper and placed it on the altar. Having sprinkled three drops of water on the Summon the Spirits Charm, he took a mouthful of pure water and spat it on the writing charm he just held over the official's head. Upon uttering the healing spirit incantation, he clicked his teeth three times to mark a pause. Next, he bowed formally, picked up the charm and wrapped it in a white paper. He gave this to the official, who took it in his left hand corresponding to the Yang with instructions on how to burn it (this means how to send it back to the spirits) and what additional drugs to take, saying, "There are different sorts of miasmas in the area of Taizhou County. When you get there, please take good care of yourself."

In a very short while, when the headache faded, the delighted official asked the healer, "What was the cause of my indisposition? And what should be done to avoid it in the future?"

Xue Feng replied, "It's all about the kidneys' system, which is often seen in combination with dysfunctions of other organs. The kidneys have the unique function of housing man's corporeal substance or living power. Man is born with primary qi or congenital energy. He has so much primary qi-energy that can never be added to, but which can be topped up with the vital substance (jing) or nutrient energy coming from the spleen. This energy may also be considered as the motive force of the corporeal soul, due to which the body becomes animated. When one's essence is all gone, the body dies, and the corporeal soul dies with it releasing the ethereal soul. Man's essence is manifested in his semen; his sexual organs are considered as part of the kidneys' system. Overindulgence in sexual activity and masturbatory ejaculation are two ways that kidneys' energy may be depleted." Saying so, the monk was done treating and left.

Chapter 14: Preaching

Next day appreciated official decided to sacrifice massively in honor of the master and thus entertained him, inviting many others of the capital elite to feast. He asked Xue Feng to preach to a big gathering. At the end of the entertainment, the master was asked to mount the stage, to which he consented. After bowing twice reverently, in company with the other high-ranking officials, pious men and devout ladies, scholars, and officers, the official greeted the monk, saying, "Long since we all were told of your wonderful gift to cure through chanting and your chant were healing. Yesterday I felt it myself. To tell you the truth, it is really so deep that it is beyond my mind and mouth to express, while I have some doubts, which I hope you, Venerable Master, will clear up for me and the esteemed audience."

"Many people come to ask me for guidance. This makes me feel ashamed," the master confessed. "To understand the cause of the yesterday's treatment, we should know how the energetic mechanism of the human body works. As for the yesterday's particular case, which was mostly about the kidneys' operation, it should be said that excessive fear over a period of time could also deplete the kidneys' essential function. A severe fright and a particularly intense ejaculatory orgasm in a man would deplete the kidneys' essence almost instantaneously. Physical symptoms of the kidneys disharmony include weak or sore lower back, weak or sore knees, urinary dysfunction, darkness under the eyes, irregular or problematic menstrual flow, weak ejaculation, and seminal emission."

Despite these master's words of explanation, the official inquired, "To clear up my doubts, will you please tell us whether it is possible for the true devotees to attain enlightenment through sex?"

The monk modestly replied, "Each and every monk works so hard, splitting firewood, hoeing fields, carrying water, and grinding rice, and yet from morning to night not putting down the thought of practicing the ways of Dao to reach full realization. Such determination for Zen and Daoist teachings is touching me on my marrow. I deeply repent of my inadequacy on the way of Dharma and my lack of virtues. I am unable to instruct you and can use only a few saying from the ancients in response to your question, Sir," reflected Xue Feng, observing etiquette to the fullest. Then he started, saying, "There is no drive more powerful than the desire of man for woman. And there is no motive more compelling than man's need to please his woman. Every man wants to appear great in the eyes of a woman -- to be a hero. Every man wants to prove to his woman of choice, that he is worth every ounce of her love -- to be her fair warrior in shining armor. When closely scrutinized, all of a man's actions revolve around this desire and this driving motive. Remove this motive and this drive, and there will be nothing to fight for. That is the genesis of the power of women over men. No man is happy or complete without the modifying influence of the right woman. A man who does not recognize this important truth deprives himself of the power which has done more to help him achieve success than all other forces combined. When properly harnessed, the primordial power of sex and its creative essences that initiate all earthly existence can be used to achieve anything one wants. In the source of this vital power also lie the sources of good health, practical wisdom, and complete satisfaction in life. At the same time, sex can be the key to the men's degeneration. As a result, some extraordinary things concerning the mental and physical conditions of men or women can occur. Since the external sexual organs are easily seen and felt, sexual desire is easily aroused. There are so many literary examples of conversions of humans into seductive fox spirits and hungry ghosts, of young men who had been seduced out of their self-interest by powerful and conniving women who summon the most handsome men in the country to their boudoir. Some young men who had spent themselves for love, ejaculating load after a load of their sweet sexual albumen into the empty darkness, until their lovers' bodies were replete with it. Such stories are in many. A lot of mental and emotional energetics flow into sexual desire and its gratification, and mostly unconsciously. But the knowledge about the way of achieving a pleasurable satisfaction cannot be given for good and all. Such kind of knowledge, like skills in any other fields of daily activities, should be cherished and improved on a regular basis as a comprehensive whole. When properly indulged in, a sexual act produces such exquisite feelings of ecstasy and joy that can't be likened to any other, making the desire for physical, sexual contact quite intense and irresistible in most men and women. An intense desire, whether for sexual interaction or foreplay laurels, is creative potency seeking expression or outlet, and you have a choice of how and on what to invest it. The more intense the desire, the stronger the unseen forces propelling its actualization; however, like I said, this sort of knowledge requires a conscious approach of the practitioners. All your thoughts, desires, intentions, aspirations, associated feelings and emotions that have been generated in you are creative energetics, differing only in their coloration and final route of expression, brought about by the transforming action and power of your mind, and sexual desire is no exception. In other words, the self-same creative potency projecting as tumultuous sex drive or sexual energy can, by a mere switching of intent and focus, become intellectual energy, professional energy, income energy, spiritual energy, or whatever type of energy you need at any point in time. For men have every advantage over women outside marriage, while inside marriage women have every advantage over men, and they know it. The happiness of women does not depend on how many social advantages they enjoy, but on the quality of the men, they live with. When men are naturally reasonable and good-tempered and considerate, women do not suffer. Besides, women have always the weapon of sex, which they can use to great advantage. It is Mother Nature's guarantee for their equality. Somehow every man, from the emperor to butcher, baker, and woodcutter, has scolded his wife and been scolded by her because nature has ordained that man and woman should meet in their intimacies as equals. If nature is cruel, nature is fair. To the common women, as to the talented ones, she gives this comfort. For the joys of motherhood are enjoyed by the clever women and the common ones. The trouble is with a man. Man sins, and he must sin, but every time he sins there's a woman in it. Eros, who rules the world, rules family also. But this is only half the truth. The more apparent acceptance of sex applies to man and not to a woman, whose sexual life is often repressed. So nature has destined, and so let men and women live. Life is so precarious that when we know something truly satisfies us, we hold on to it tight, like a mother who hugs her baby close to her breast in a dark, stormy night. If we do not ache to reach the foot of the mountain while we are in the middle of the lake, and when we do not ache to be at the top of the hill while we are at its foot, that is the shortest path to be truly satisfied. If we use to drink what wine there is in the pot and enjoy what scenery there as before our eyes, we can enjoy to the fullest the beauty of everyday living. And that is the secret of satisfaction. As Lao-zi says, 'The less you possess, the easier you can be satisfied.'"

Someone from the learned audience asked, "What a man feels himself upon reaching the state of complete enlightenment, and how does it tell about his sex life?" After a short pause, the master said, "To be enlightened means to follow with the ways of Dao, not against them. To determine what Dao actually is, the great Master Confucius said, "The great Dao consists of at least one Yin (feminine) and one Yang (masculine)." That's why people are endowed by Heaven with love, affection, passion, and lust. Entering into love action, your Jade Stalk should be hard and full-sized so that it can fill in the entire space behind her Divine Gates and try to avoid ejaculation for the longest time. This is the way to bring a woman a great pleasure and, as a result, full satisfaction for both lovers. But if all of a sudden the semen rushes outwards, then, following the precepts, promptly interrupt the intercourse to avoid ejaculation and losing the semen. Do your best to make the energy nourish itself, reproducing some more energy when one partner nourishes another with essence and spirit through the close circle of them. He who is able to reach such a high level of intimacy can have effective relationships with a dozen women simultaneously.

Sexual intercourse provides an example of making an individual become one with the whole, the great Dao. Two individuals, physically interacting, take a passive and active role. Through this interaction, one experiences a sense of abandonment or chaos which is correlated to the second stage of one's 'gong-fu' or technical skill's development. This feeling takes over the body as a whole in a manner that the rhythm and pulses which were harmonized in the preliminary stage now become like a stream of music flowing through the whole being. Then, amidst this experience, there is a feeling of upheaval or orgasm, and the one is reborn, which is the third stage. At this point, the individuals have shifted from two separate entities to one single being, a holy embryo, to mark the fourth stage of spiritual development. Now, when the course started with the physical substance reaches the spiritual level of development, the whole diagram is completed. To those of inferior mentality, indeed, the matter of achieving complete enlightenment is far away, but as for the advanced men, we may say that it is quite near. Though the Dharma is uniform, men vary in their mentality so long as they differ from one another in their degree of awareness or ignorance; therefore, some understand the Law quicker than others."

"Like I said earlier," the master continued, "this transformational process is usually divided into some different stages. The amount of stages depends on the system of teaching. The first stage reduces to using the Post-birth or acquired vital substance to nourish the inherent or original one, the Pre-birth substance. The former is a sort of energy that is consumed from the environment through the air we breathe, the food we eat, and the subtle energy we absorb from the outer space. We use this vital substance to nourish our original strength. To build up and strengthen the original substance we must conserve it, because 'to save' means that we must cut down on our spending. Therefore, it is recommended that men should avoid ejaculating to conserve their sexual energy, sperm, while women need to regulate the menstrual cycle to conserve their substances. The microcosmic orbit and vital substance's cultivating techniques are taught at this level of progression. The second stage is known as 'transferring of the vital substance into the subtle essence,' deals with the qi-energy. When the substance is sufficient due to the proper nourishment, conservation and cultivation, we begin to transfer it into the subtle essence. You might ask, What for? Why the energy we have accumulated from our environment and transformed into the vital substance at the first stage we have somehow to transform back into qi-energy? The answer is simple. When you transform the jing-substance into qi-essence, it is refined throughout the process. The process itself is a perfect purifier so long as it works on a constant basis, which demands one's constancy. As a result, it is refined to the level where your body can easily digest stuff and store the energy for further application. It can be compared to the process when the liver transforms sugar into glucose when the body can use either store it or digest it. The liver removes excess glucose from your body's system; then it is stored until it is needed. Similarly, the middle elixir center can store extra qi-energy until it is needed. This stage of transforming of substance into essence, sometimes, is called 'the Water and Fire meditation.' It is expressed by hexagram Ji-Ji (63), a symbol of what is already completed successfully. In this hexagram, the Water element is on top of Fire. Water means the substance, sexual energy, while Fire means the flame under the cauldron, the true dan-tian or elixir field, in which the alchemical transmutation of accumulated energy into the golden elixir pill takes place. Conversely, when Fire is below Water, the latter is boiled and steamed. The Ji-Ji hexagram, Water above Fire, means steaming the sexual energy, which can be accumulated and properly transformed into a higher fraction, the subtle essence. Steam is light, so it moves from the lower dan-tian located in the crotch, just behind the scrotum, upward to the crown of the head, the upper elixir center. This process is an equivalent to the Indian Yoga's awakening termed 'kundalini,' which is merely a different name for the jing-substance. Daoism teaches us to bring the 'steam' down to the middle dan-tian located in the lower part of the belly, producing the effect of vaporing water that is condensed into clouds and come down as the fertile rain. When the rain comes down, we store it in the middle dan-tian. Dan-tian literally means 'elixir field,' or 'elixir center,' or 'the farm for concentrating the golden elixir pill.' Yes, the fertile rain we have harvested. What does it mean? -- No more no less but the Pill of Immortality called 'elixir' we have successfully cropped. That is where the name 'dan-tian' came out from. The special environment we create in the 'dan-tian' where the heavenly energy and the earthly energy interact and mix together to be called 'Reunion of Heaven and Earth.' The intercourse of Heaven and Earth gives birth to 'the holy embryo,' which is developed into what we call 'the spiritual body.' The Water and Fire Meditation is taught at this second stage along with the learning the way of opening the other eight miraculous meridians. The third stage is called 'transferring of the refined qi-essence into the Shen-spirit.' Once you have achieved the first two stages, you have an abundant amount of energy to nourish your holy embryo. This stage can be divided into three phases. The first one is to nourish this spiritual baby for nine months, just like a real pregnancy. You will feed it with the energy from the universal, the mix of the earthly and cosmic qi-energy. Since the vitality of your spiritual body, or the holy embryo, is strongly dependent on its nourishment during the pregnancy, you should be careful with what sort of energy you feed it with. Of course, you will want the best for your spiritual baby. After the nine months period, you will move the embryo to the upper dan-tian, giving birth to your spiritual body, also known as Niwan or Clay Pill, which is, actually, a solid crystal placed in the center of your brain. The second phase is to nurse the embryo for three years. During this three-year nursery, the baby should never leave the physical body for any long time, because it is still young and premature. At this phase, you can catch a glimpse of the fourth dimension or the immortal realm, but a distant traveling is not recommended yet. The third phase is the nine years of education. The spiritual body can now travel further and further each time, getting experience for its own benefit. During this nine-year period, you will teach it everything you know and help it to become completely independent. The fourth stage from our list of development is called 'the Spirit's Return to the Great Dao.' After nine years of exploring, the spiritual body can now travel freely anywhere it sees fit. It's time of returning to the Great Dao. You now can transcend space and time without any limitations so long as you've transformed yourself into a true immortal."

"Are there any regulations in the energy cultivating through meditation?" was another question from the audience amazed by what they had heard from the master.

Xue Feng said, "These days it would appear that many become monks and adherents of the teachings, and that would be wonderful, but, actually, most are attached to sound and form. By sound and form, I refer to the sensitive objects called 'dust' of the six sense organs and their respective consciousnesses. The six sense organs and consciousnesses are the eyes and seeing, the ears and hearing, the nose and smelling, the tongue and tasting, the body and feeling, the mind and thinking. The six specks of dust are forms, sounds, odors, flavors, objects, and symbols. Since men rely mostly on their ears and eyes to interact with others and the environment, many methods of concentration make use of these two senses, and their accompanying objects, sound, and form, to train the mind. Nothing is intrinsically wrong with the technical methods of practice, but problems can arise in your mind. In the course of meditation, you will undoubtedly hear sounds and see things. Some of these phenomena will be external, and some will come from within, but all should be regarded as an illusion. As the mind begins to move from scattering to clarity, it will often reach out to grasp things: the 'chirring of cicada' within you may sound like beautiful music. The main rule of practice is not to attach to phenomena, even if the sights and sounds of paradise fill your eyes and ears. This merely is an attachment to sound and form. But being attaching to sound and form, no matter how beautiful or expansive it may seem, is not for achieving enlightenment, and has nothing to do with liberation. Better it would be for the mind to be like a dead trunk of an old tree, or chilled ashes of a campfire next morning. These analogies describe a mind that is settled and undisturbed by sound and form. Such a mind, though not enlightened, is close to Zen, which is a sort of contemplation; still, it is not Zen as it is."

At the end of his short speech he emphasized, "As adherents of the course towards complete enlightenment, we can only contemplate the mind with obstructions. It is impossible for us to contemplate the mind without obstructions. There is no such thing. Any thought associated with a self, or any attachment, or any vexation is an obstruction. Our physical bodies are like the cities; our eyes, ears, nose, and tongue are the gates. There are five outer gates, while the internal one is ideation. The mind is the ground; the essence of the mind is the king who lives in the domain of the mind. While the essence of the mind is in, the king is in, and the body and mind exist interactively. When the essence of mind is out, there is no king and our body and mind decay. We should work for attaining enlightenment within the essence of mind, and we should not look for it apart from ourselves. He who is kept in ignorance of his essence of mind is an inferior being; he who is enlightened in his essence of mind is the true man, a buddha or enlightened."

Then he added, "No matter how distinguished one's social status is or how much wealth one possesses, be it the emperor, or a governmental officer, or someone of wealth, each and everyone dies in the end. Nothing in the world lasts forever. I recommend that you take up spiritual cultivation instead of accumulating multiplied riches. This is the ultimate way for everyone to see through all the suffering in life and counteract it."

Having heard what the master said that night, all those present there became to know the essence of mind very clearly. They made obeisance and exclaimed in one voice, "O Venerable Master!"

Li Qin Min stepped forward and knelt respectfully before the monk. The master reflected, saying, "Learned audience, those who wish to practice themselves spiritually may do so at home. It is quite unnecessary for them to stay in monasteries. Those who diligently train themselves at home may be likened to a native of the east who is kindhearted, while those who stay in monasteries but neglect their work differ not from a native of the west who is evil in heart. So far as the mind is pure, it is the pure land of one's own essence of mind. You can also practice meditation as a kind of private devotion, and you can in such practice, as well as in other aspects of self-cultivation, use steady or close meditative reflection -- the continued application of the mind. As long as you are not at this level, you need to cultivate yourself. First of all, stay on your method and disregard whatever is happening. Secondly, no matter what is happening to you, treat it as having nothing to do with you. You don't have to be completely enlightened to emulate this attitude. This should be your attitude while you meditate. Daily life is different; in daily life be mindful. Whatever you are doing, wherever your hands are, that is where your mind should be. This is a good practice. You may not become enlightened overnight, but you will be on a good path. That seems to me to be the only way of looking at the situation, by searching, not for the exotic but for the common human values by penetrating beneath the superficial quaintness of manners but looking for real courtesy; by seeing beneath the strange man's and lady's costumes but looking for real relationships. By looking for the campfire of pilgrims and monks laughter and the patter of their bare feet and the weeping of women during requiem service and the sorrows of men -- they are all alike. And only through the sorrows of men and the weeping of women can we truly understand all turns and curves of the Great Dao in our daily lives. The differences are only in the forms of social behavior. This is the basis of all sound endeavors to achieve enlightenment. A-mi-tuo-fo."

* * * * * *

Some time later, roaming about in the Tian-tai Mountains, the novice came accidentally across his elder friend and mentor's footprints where it crossed the level thoroughfare of his own destiny. He paused on his way, knelt down in the dust and touched the footstep, sniffed its odor on his hand. Then with his eye, he followed the track until it disappeared in the darkness of the bamboo grove where he dared not to enter, having neither time, nor inclination and, at last, the skill to follow the tigress's roar thundered in its depth.

〜

About the Author:

Alex Stone, a graduate of the Far-Eastern University in Sinology, lived and worked in mainland China for years as a translator/interpreter, a manager, and a martial arts' practitioner. A certified instructor of 'Chang-quan' (external-style boxing) and 'Taiji-quan' (internal-style boxing), he is a lecturer of Chinese culture and traditions at the Open University in Tel-Aviv. He also is the author of Lao-zi's "Dao-De Jing," Chan (Zen) masters' paradoxes, "The Illustrated Canon of Chen Family Taijiquan," a Chinese novel and some other editions, which are available in print and electronic publishing at most online retailers published in English, Spanish and Russian. What makes his books so appealing is profound analysis and authority with which various strains of the vigorous Chinese culture are woven into a clear and useful piece of guidance for a businessperson who conducts the affairs with Far-eastern counterparties and for a counselor who develops strategies that enable leaders to position their organizations effectively.

ENDNOTE

Discover other titles by Alex Stone at Amazon.com:

Zen 96 https://www.amazon.com/Zen-96-Stone-ebook/dp/B01MFA1F1M/ref=sr_1_fkmr0_1?s=digital-text&ie=UTF8&qid=1533682834&sr=1-1-fkmr0&keywords=alex+stone+zen+96

The Moon Pool https://www.amazon.com/Moon-Pool-Stone-ebook/dp/B01M8P99VC/ref=sr_1_1?s=digital-text&ie=UTF8&qid=1533682938&sr=1-1&keywords=alex+stone+the+moon+pool

Connect with Alex Stone Online:

AuthorsDen: http://www.authorsden.com/visit/author.asp?id=129491

Made in the USA
Middletown, DE
27 February 2021